High Impact

FREYA BARKER

High Impact

ISBN: 9781988733784

Cover Design: Freya Barker
Editing: Karen Hrdlicka
Proofing: Joanne Thompson
Cover Image: Golden Czermak — FuriousFotog
Cover Model: Skip Robinson

MANAGER FOR HART'S HORSE RESCUE, LUCY LENOIR, FINALLY FEELS SHE HAS A HANDLE ON LIFE AFTER HAVING WORKED HARD TO LEAVE HER OLD ONE BEHIND. SO HARD, THERE ARE TIMES SHE ALMOST FORGETS WHAT SHE ESCAPED. MEMORIES WHICH SUDDENLY COME FLOODING BACK WHEN SHE CATCHES A GLIMPSE OF A FAMILIAR HORSEMAN IN TOWN.

WHAT'S WORSE, HE'S IN THE COMPANY OF THE UNLIKELY COWBOY SHE'S ONLY JUST BEGINNING TO TRUST.

HIGH MOUNTAIN TRACKER, BO RIVERA, TRIES HARD NEVER TO REPEAT HIS MISTAKES. A HUGE ONE CHANGED THE COURSE OF HIS LIFE AND MADE HIM PARTICULARLY CAUTIOUS, ESPECIALLY AROUND WOMEN. SO MUCH SO, HE ALMOST PASSED UP ON THE BEST THING TO EVER WALK INTO HIS LIFE; THE COMPACT, BLONDE BALLBUSTER IN NEED OF A GENTLE HAND.

HOWEVER, THE MORE HE LEARNS ABOUT HER, THE MORE HE REALIZES A SOFT TOUCH ALONE WON'T KEEP HER DEMONS AT BAY. THOSE WILL NEED A FIRMER HAND...TO KEEP THE GUN STEADY.

One

LUCY

Look at those poor babies.

They can't be more than a week old but won't last much longer if I don't intervene. Their mother isn't looking any better.

I got the call earlier this afternoon and wish I'd been able to wait for a deputy to follow me, but potential cases of animal abuse aren't very high on their list of priorities. The woman who called insisted the situation was dire, and she's right.

"Hey! You!"

Oh shit.

A rough-looking, burly guy is coming around the corner of the dilapidated farmhouse, about fifty yards from where I'm crouched next to the pen. He has a shotgun in his hands and it's aimed at me.

"You've got two seconds to get off my property," he yells, looking pissed.

This kind of rescue work isn't without its occasional

1

challenges and dangers. It isn't the first time I've looked down the barrel of a gun held by some disgruntled farmer or rancher when they didn't appreciate my rescue of their abused animal. Still, it never fails to scare the crap out of me.

I don't like guns. I've never been comfortable around them, although I will say I won't hesitate to grab the shotgun we have by the front door at the rescue when facing anyone who threatens our safety or the safety of the animals. Too much has happened here over the past two years since we moved from Billings.

We, being Alexandra Hart and myself. I've worked for Alex for over eight years now. I joined her when Hart's Horse Rescue was on a much, much smaller property, just outside Billings, Montana. Then, two years ago, she purchased the property near Libby and I happily followed her here. Of course, since then, she's met and moved in with Jonas Harvey at the High Meadow Ranch, just down the road.

At the rescue we don't only provide a safe haven for the animals, but also rehabilitate injured and traumatized animals. Alex is something of a horse whisperer and has a special affinity with the animals I lack. Don't get me wrong, I'm good with the horses—all the animals—but they certainly don't respond to me the way they do to Alex.

Anyway, these days it's just me and the animals at the rescue, where I look after the day-to-day operations. Not a bad gig, not at all. I have a job I love; I have a roof over my head, and I live in what has to be one of the most beautiful places in the world.

Not that I've traveled much. I'm about the farthest away from where I grew up right now, although staring down a barrel is familiar.

According to Lester Franklin's neighbor, he leaves for work every day at the same time and doesn't return home until late afternoon. I'd parked on the neighbor's property and was supposed to wait for a sheriff's deputy to show, when I saw him drive off and came to investigate. I didn't want to miss the opportunity, so I went in without backup. Hindsight being twenty-twenty, that had not been my smartest move.

Today being the exception the rule, he obviously returned early and isn't happy finding me here.

I lift my hands up to show him I'm not armed.

"Your kid goats need to be supplement-fed or they're gonna die," I yell back.

"None 'a your goddamn business what I do with my goats. Yer trespassing!"

He racks his shotgun and repositions it against his shoulder, lining me up in his sights. The sound of it is a bit unnerving, but I know that's what he intends; to scare me off.

"Look, if you're happy to let them die, why not just give them to me to look after?"

The shotgun blast is loud as the dirt in front of me sprays up. I'm down on my face the next second. Guess he wasn't just trying to scare me. I vaguely notice a stinging burn on my shin but my eyes are locked on Lester Franklin, who appears to be cocking his gun, readying it for another shot.

"Hey! Lincoln County Sheriff's Department. Put that damn shotgun down!"

I turn my head slightly to where a fresh-faced sheriff's deputy is standing, legs spread wide and her hand on the butt of her service weapon. Sloane Eckhart. She's the niece of my friend Pippa's husband, Sully, and brand-new to the department. So new, I can still see the creases on her uniform shirt.

"I have every right to defend my property! She's an intruder."

"That's where you're wrong, Mr. Franklin," Sloane fires back right away. "She's at worst a trespasser and if you shoot at her you're the one who's gonna be going to jail! Now, I'm gonna ask you one more time; put the shotgun down!"

Despite my rather precarious position, I grin at the girl's attitude. Hell, she's probably early twenties, looks more like a child playing dress-up than an actual sheriff's deputy, but she's sure not easily intimidated.

"What are you gonna do about it?" Franklin challenges her.

Slow and easy, she slips her weapon in her hand, widens her stance, and aims straight at him.

"I outshot the entire department in an accuracy test two weeks ago," she says calmly. "Want to test me?"

For a few seconds, it looks like we might have a shootout when the guy pans his aim toward Sloane, but at the last moment lowers the barrel.

I get to my feet and notice my lower leg still burning. The front of my jeans on the left side is wet and stained dark. Wonderful.

"Were you hit?"

Sloane walks over, her eyes zoomed in on my leg.

"Just some rock spray hitting me, I think. Just a scratch."

I don't want her distracted, I want her to control Lester while I collect these poor goats.

"Right," she says, giving me a hard look before she walks to her cruiser, the driver's side door still open. "Gonna call some backup. Looks like we need Animal Control out here too."

While Sloane puts in her calls, I pull up the leg of my jeans as I try to keep an eye on Franklin, who continues to hover in front of his house. My leg is a mess. It's difficult to see anything, but I look to be bleeding from more than one source.

"Yikes," Sloane comments, walking up. "Maybe I should've called the EMTs as well. That doesn't look good."

❧

Bo

"Can you hand me the wrench?"

I dig through the toolbox and give James the requested tool.

We're out behind the ranch house, in the shed where the pump running the automated watering system is housed. The system provides water to the horses out in the fields closest to the house. There are only a few of the back meadows left to cart water to, but if we can't get this damn pump to work, we're gonna be back to hauling it everywhere.

It's a time suck and a general pain-in-the-ass job no one wants to do, which is why we're back here trying to fix it, even though neither James nor I are particularly talented in mechanics.

"Why don't I go ask Pippa to come have a look?" I suggest when James releases a few juicy curse words.

Pippa is married to Sully, another member of our team,

and she's a mechanic. They live in one of the cabins on the other side of the ranch house and just welcomed a new baby two weeks ago, so she's home.

"I'm sure she's got other things going on," James mutters.

"Are you kidding? If it was up to her, she would've strapped that baby to her body and already be back at the garage working."

It's true, I walked in on an argument about exactly that topic between her and Sully just yesterday. Pippa is itching to do something with her hands, while her husband feels she needs more time to recover.

He's just worried about her, being protective, and she's afraid to lose autonomy over her life with the new baby and relatively new husband. The fear-driven dynamics are clear to see from an observer's point of view, but I guess even a couple of weeks of sleepless nights, constant feedings, and endless diapers can make you lose perspective.

Pippa is a rock and I have no doubt she'll jump at the opportunity to get out of the house for a bit. Sully's back to work and manning the breeding barn with Fletch today, but there are many at the ranch who'd drop anything to keep an eye on that baby girl for a few minutes.

Poor kid was born into one of the strangest families I've ever known, with a whole bunch of uncles, aunts, an honorary grandfather, and a handful of cousins, of which only one aunt and one cousin are actually blood related. The ranch, High Meadow, is at the center of this haphazard family. Its owner, Jonas Harvey, was my commander in the armed forces. Jonas, Sully, Fletch, James, and I were part of a special ops tracking unit. Like me, Jonas came from a ranching background. When he aged out of the unit, he bought this place, pulling us in one by one as we each aged out.

High Meadow is a stud farm, but in recent years we've been developing our own breeding program as well. In addition to that, the ranch is also the base for High Mountain Trackers. We may all have been too old for Uncle Sam, but we're still able to put our skills to good use with HMT, which is a search and rescue—or recovery—unit on horseback. We get a variety of calls, anywhere from missing children to hunting down criminals, and often work together with local and state law enforcement.

The ranch is our home, even though I've never lived here like most of my brothers. I have my reasons for choosing an old apartment in town over one of the staff cabins on the ranch, although there've been many times I wished things were different. That's life though, you've just got to roll with it. I'm sure there'll come a day I can wake up to beautiful views and sweet mountain air instead of the parking lot at the rear of the restaurant next door, but that day isn't here yet.

There's no one at the cabin, but I find Pippa and the baby in the kitchen at the main house. Carmi is being burped by Alex, Jonas's woman, with his old man, Thomas, looking on. I bend down and give that little downy blond head a kiss.

"How's my little girl?"

"She sure don't look like yours," Thomas pipes up, unable to resist a tease.

There were too many years I would've taken that the wrong way, especially coming from an old, white, Southern boy, but I know he would've said the same thing to Fletch, who is white but dark-haired. This isn't about the color of my skin but the blond hair the baby inherited from her father.

"Hush, after her daddy, Bo gets dibs. He delivered her," Pippa reminds the old man with a grin.

I did. Two weeks ago, at the horse rescue.

It wasn't my first baby—before I joined the military I worked as a nurse in different departments—but it had been a few years, maybe even decades, since the last one. Luckily, the basic mechanics of childbirth stay the same and, other than the baby was coming fast, there were no complications.

"Hey, you got a minute?" I ask Pippa. "We can't get the motor on the water pump to—"

I don't even get a chance to finish my sentence before she jumps in.

"Yes. You don't mind, do you, Alex?"

Alex makes a face as she snuggles the baby closer. "Like you need to ask."

Pippa follows me outside where we almost bump into Sloane, Sully's niece, who moved here over the summer. She's a sheriff's deputy.

"I was looking for you" she addresses Pippa. "Where's the baby?"

"Kitchen." Pippa cocks her thumb over her shoulder. "I swear," she continues when Sloane rushes up the porch steps. "I've ceased to exist since she was born. Don't get me wrong, I love my baby beyond measure, but it's a little unsettling when I'm being treated like an extension of that little human instead of my own person."

I hear her. Fuck, I'm guilty of it too, heading straight for Carmi without even a hello for her mother.

Throwing my arm around her shoulder, I give her a little squeeze.

"Good thing we have a busted water pump to remind us you're not just good at making babies," I tease.

"Haha," she grumbles, elbowing me in the gut.

"Oh, Bo?" I hear Sloane call.

"Yeah, what's up?" I ask, turning around.

She's hanging over the porch railing.

"You may wanna swing by Lucy's, when you have a minute."

As always when I hear her name, my attention is piqued.

"Why?"

"She had a run-in with a rancher north of town. She didn't want me calling EMTs, but I think she got hit with some buckshot."

I don't realize I'm already moving until I hear Pippa yell out behind me.

"Go!"

Two

"Open the damn door, Lucy."

Like hell.

I'm not sure how he found out but I wasn't really surprised to see Bo's truck tearing up my drive, spraying gravel as he slammed on the brakes out front. Not much stays hidden for long in this community; if one person knows something, pretty soon everyone else does too. That's why there are some things I keep to myself.

I'd been out on the porch, trying to pick the buckshot from my shin and I knew right away he must've heard I'd gotten hurt. The man tests my nerves, always hovering around when he thinks I need him and I have to fight the temptation to lean into the help he offers.

I don't need anyone; I make sure of that. Life is much safer that way.

Bo doesn't seem to clue in though, and follows me inside, his big boots stomping on my clean floor. I manage to duck into the bathroom, but I know that won't hold him back for long. I'm determined, but that man is tenacious.

"Go away, Bo. I've got it covered."

"Open the door," he repeats, rattling the doorknob. "You're shot. Let me have a look."

Relentless.

"It's just buckshot. I can take care of it."

I hear a bump on the door, I'm guessing Bo's forehead since his rumbling voice suddenly sounds a lot softer, almost pleading.

"Come on, Luce, you're being stubborn. Do you really want to risk an infection? Let me have a quick peek and I'll be out of your hair."

If only it were that simple. The man doesn't even realize what a massive temptation he is. I bet those big arms of his could make me feel safe—protected—but I made that mistake once before and it did not turn out well for me.

Still, he's right; I'm being stubborn. Last thing I want is to run the risk of an infection, which requires a visit to the clinic. Something I want to avoid at all costs. Bo was a medic, and a good one from what I've been able to see.

Two weeks ago, my friend Pippa went into labor in my barn and Bo was the closest help I could find. I've assisted in a foaling or two but draw the line at childbirth. Way out of my wheelhouse. Bo was good; confident, reassuring, and surprisingly gentle for a man his size.

I would never have called him if it hadn't been an emergency. I've worked too hard to avoid him since I moved here. For one thing, he's a giant flirt to everything with a set of boobs and a vagina. I swear the man thinks he's God's gift to women. Been there, done that, and I got the shirt but I'm not even wearing it.

More than that, something about the intense way he can

look at me is unnerving. Like he can see into my deepest, darkest corners. Places I don't like to visit or share with someone else. That life is gone. Done. Last thing I need is someone like Bo Rivera poking and prying, stirring up the dust.

"Taking the hinges out in T minus five," he threatens. "Four...three..."

"Fine," I snap, unlocking the door and backing away. "Knock yourself out."

His wide shoulders push inside the door and I instantly feel crowded, despite the disarming grin he throws me.

"You know you wound my fragile ego when you look at me like you just stepped in a fresh cow patty."

I can't stop the grin pulling at my lips. Fragile, my foot.

"Your ego is the size of Texas and bulletproof," I point out, bending my head so he doesn't catch me smiling.

"Glad you like it."

I don't even bother correcting him, it would only encourage him. Instead, I sit down on the edge of the tub and pull up my pant leg.

He makes a hissing sound between his teeth. "Where's your first aid kit?"

"Vanity."

I watch as he tosses his hat in the hallway, ducks down under the sink, and pulls out the red bag with the white cross. We have well-outfitted kits, both in the barn and the house. Too many things can and will go wrong on a working farm, both kits have seen some use. He pulls out what he needs, sets it up on the closed toilet seat, and struggles to don a pair of latex gloves that look at least a size too small.

Then he crouches in front of me, bending down to have a closer look at my leg, and giving me a view of the top of his shiny bald head. Even in this position, the man manages to crowd me. Although Bo isn't the tallest guy I know, he is definitely the broadest. At five foot two it doesn't take much to make me feel small, but with Bo not just the physical discrepancy is responsible for that. There is something about this man that makes me feel vulnerable.

"Sure you don't want to go to the hospital?" he asks, looking at me with those soulful dark eyes.

"Positive."

He shakes his head as he squirts some alcohol on a piece of gauze and starts cleaning the wounds. I hiss at the burn.

"Your choice, but I've gotta take this buckshot out and all you have is a numbing cream. It's gonna hurt like a sono-fabitch."

I'm already aware of that after my attempts to accomplish that task myself. Grinding my teeth, I grip the side of the bathtub and turn my eyes to the ceiling.

It doesn't stop the hearty, "Motherfucker," bursting from my lips when I feel him dig around with a pair of hemostat forceps.

"That's one," Bo comments dryly.

Sweat is dripping from my forehead and my jaw hurts from grinding so much by the time he pats my knee, seven round pellets of buckshot later.

"The worst is over," he assures me in his low, rumbly voice. "Just gonna wrap this up."

I blow out a relieved breath and try to release the tension I've been holding in my body. If I didn't have animals waiting to be looked after, I'd be going down for a nap. I'm exhausted.

When Bo pulls himself to his feet, holding on to the vanity, his knee joints audibly creak.

"Sounds painful," I comment as I tug my pant leg back down. "You should try taking glucosamine."

"Is that a jab at my advanced age?"

I glance up and catch one dark eyebrow pulled high on his rugged face. I don't think anyone could consider Bo a classically handsome man—his face is too rough for that—but his infectious smile and dark, liquid eyes make for a striking appearance. One I find myself attracted to.

"Your age?" I echo confusedly.

Funny, I never really thought about him in terms of his age, but now I take in the gray in his whiskers and the deep lines on his forehead. With the kind of rugged face he has, it's hard to pin down a number. Since I know he aged out of special forces, I guess he could be anywhere from forty into his fifties.

"Never mind. Thought you were poking fun at me."

He tries to wave me off and starts returning the supplies to the medical kit, but now I'm intrigued.

"I wasn't, but to satisfy my curiosity; how old are you?"

His back is toward me but I notice him shake his head.

"Let's just say I have over a decade on you," he grudgingly shares.

"So around fifty?"

His head whips around so fast I startle back.

"Fuck no. Not even close. I'm forty-four," he sets me straight, clearly insulted.

I hold up my hands defensively. "Don't bite my head off. You're the one who suggested you were that much older than me."

Now it's his turn to look confused. "How the hell old are you?"

It's on my tongue to remind him it's not polite to ask, but then I remember I asked first.

"I'll be thirty-eight next month."

His face registers surprise but quickly morphs into anger.

"You've gotta be shitting me," he grumbles. "You barely look old enough to drink."

≈

Bo

Thirty-fucking-eight years old.
I could kick my own ass.

In hindsight it doesn't surprise me. Everything about the woman suggests a hardness and a level of maturity that doesn't quite jibe with her youthful appearance. A smarter man might've asked around instead of judging the book by the cover, but I was too focused on her looks. Of course, it didn't help the woman was as uncommunicative and closed-mouthed about her past as my buddy Fletch, who doesn't like sharing much either.

I'd pegged the tiny, fresh-faced blonde as late twenties at most, making me feel like some dirty old man for not being able to keep my eyes to myself whenever I was around her.

Oh, I flirted with her like I do every other woman, but that's what people expect of me. I didn't want to make the impact Lucy has on me too obvious to anyone who knows me by ignoring her. Instead, I try to minimize any encounters, although at times I have trouble resisting the protective urge I feel toward her, which is why I raced out the door earlier.

Thinking she was that much younger than me really messed with my head. Knowing I spent the better part of the past year avoiding her under that wrong assumption is worse. Of course, being the hard-nosed woman she is, it took her less than two seconds to kick me out of her house after I aimed my misguided frustration at her.

It was bad enough just moments before this revelation, I was chastising myself. Touching the soft skin of her calf had been enough to have the sweat break out on my brow. I normally pride myself on my restraint and strong will, but any efforts to keep my dick under control were futile. Heck, I still feel the effects backing my truck away from her porch.

This changes everything. At least it does for me. I don't care how reluctant and hard-assed she makes herself out to be, I notice how her breath hitches and her pulse beats in her slim neck every time I get close. That, and the way she broke out in goosebumps the moment my fingers brushed her skin earlier, makes me think she's more interested than she's willing to let on.

I can work with that. She may be stubborn, but she has no idea how relentless I can be when I'm invested.

Despite getting kicked out of the house, I drive off feeling pretty damn good about myself.

Bring it on, Lucy Lenoir. Bring it on.

"Beauregard James Rivera, you will mind your momma!"

Lord, spare me stubborn, pint-sized women.

I look over at my mother, who is glaring at me from the large recliner she's almost lost in. Eighty-one and her shrunken body is still full of piss and vinegar. What she lacks in height and mass she makes up for in strength and grit, making many a grown man think twice about crossing her.

My pops was in charge of the ranch, but my momma was queen. The hands knew and so did Pops.

It's the only reason she and Pops managed to hang on to the ranch in Idaho for so long. Momma's sheer grit and tenacity, even though black people running a small cattle ranch wasn't widely accepted, or made easy. Odds were stacked against my mother from the moment Pops died of a massive coronary. The bankers didn't care it'd been Momma's drive that had always kept that ranch going and pulled financing immediately. The neighboring rancher, Daniels, had been quick on the draw and snatched up the ranch he'd been coveting for years before Pops was cold in his grave.

I'll never forgive myself for not being there. Our unit was buried deep in the jungles of Colombia at the time, and word of my father's passing didn't reach me until we landed back Stateside three months later. Unfortunately, it was too late, my father was buried, the ranch was already gone, and Momma had moved in with my aunt in Boise.

When I aged out of the unit and Jonas offered me a job here at High Meadow, I set about getting my mother to join me here. She'd been lonely since Auntie Imani died a few months prior and was happy to move closer to me. I found her a place in a senior living facility in Libby, only two blocks from where I live. She can live independently as long as she wants in the small one-bedroom unit and has emergency buttons all over her little apartment if she needs help from the main building. If and when it becomes too difficult for her to manage on her own, she can opt to move into 'the big house,' which is your standard seniors' home.

It's one of the reasons I prefer living in town. I want to be close in case something happens, like now.

I was just dropping off a few things I got for her at the

grocery store when I found her lying on the floor right by the front door. She'd apparently lost her balance when she was bending over to pick something up off the floor, her cane unused by her chair. Stubborn woman has an alarm button around her neck, but didn't want to use it because she could tell nothing was broken and she knew I was stopping by anyway.

Now she won't let me take her to the clinic to get checked out, despite the goose egg on her forehead from hitting the hall table. I rub my hands over my head and try to hang on to my last thread of patience.

Hand to heart, I love that woman but she tests me.

"I'm trying to mind my momma but she makes it very difficult," I return with a scowl. "I want the doctor to have a look."

"And have him tell me I gotta move to the big house? Hell to the no, you can just forget about that."

She folds her spindly arms stubbornly over her chest and sticks her chin in the air.

"He's not gonna say that. Besides, would that be so bad?"

Wrong thing to say.

"Out!"

I never get the chance to clarify my words because she's rising from her chair, waving her cane in my direction.

For the second time in one day, my rescue efforts are rewarded with a boot to my ass. Guess I'm not much of a knight in shining armor.

Three

Lucy

"This one is in pretty rough shape."

Doc Evans gets to his feet, wiping the straw from his knees. I open the door to the stall to let him out.

These past couple of days, I've done my best with the goats I rescued from Lester Franklin's farm, but one of the kids is failing. I've had to separate momma goat who started rejecting the little ones. Not an uncommon scenario when the young aren't thriving. She's doing much better on her own, eating everything I put in front of her and I have no doubt she'll recover quickly.

But it's the two little ones I'm worried about. I'm trying to bottle feed with the formula but the runt of the two isn't taking the nipple.

"What do you suggest I do?"

"I can place a feeding tube, but you'll have to keep a close eye on him. For the next three days, syringe feed him smaller quantities more frequently—four ounces every three hours—and if he responds well, we can reassess."

I agree and give him a hand as he slides a tube down the little guy's esophagus. The tiny goat doesn't struggle much at all, he's too weak. Doc tucks his tools of the trade in the old leather satchel he carries around, washes his hands in the small tack room, and heads out of the barn.

"Walk me to the truck? I have a couple of syringes and a few samples of high nutrient supplement in the back seat."

After he's gone, I go inside to set up a space for the baby goats. I don't want to split them up, and having them both in the house is the easiest way for me to keep up with their feeding schedules. I do need to make sure the dogs can't get at them. Both Scout and Chief are good with the other animals, but especially Scout might be a little too rambunctious for the babies.

I end up prepping the floor of my bathroom with a horse blanket, a layer of newspaper, and some old towels. It'll do for now and I can always use the other bathroom to shower. No one is using it anyway.

"What on earth is that?" Alex says, walking toward me when I carry the runt out of the barn wrapped in a burlap sack.

"One of the baby goats isn't doing too well, so I'm temporarily moving them into the house."

I'd already spoken with Alex about rescuing the goats from Lester Franklin's place. Not that I need her approval for anything—she's happy to let me run the rescue part of the farm while she focuses on rehabilitating horses—but she is still the person signing my paycheck, so I keep her informed out of respect.

"Want me to grab the other one?"

"If you wouldn't mind."

She follows me into the house, and under the curious

scrutiny of the dogs we get the goats installed in the bathroom.

"You'll be a zombie by tomorrow tackling all these offset feedings by yourself. If you want, I can bunk here tonight and help you out?"

I bark out a laugh. "As if that possessive, pigheaded rancher of yours would let you out of his sight, even for a night."

Alex's man, Jonas Harvey, isn't really that bad, but I'm determined never to let him live down behaving like a misogynistic asshole the first time we met him. The truth is, he's redeemed himself since then, even to a harsh critic like myself. Hard to hang on to my poor first impression of him when he's since treated my best friend like sunlight shines from her ass.

"Oh, I don't know," she responds with a smirk full of innuendo. "I might be able to make it worth his while. I've got my ways."

Dramatically slapping my hands over my ears, I shake my head. "TMI."

Alex opens her eyes wide with feigned innocence. "What? I haven't even said anything."

I glare back in silent warning and change the subject.

"No need for you to stay. I'll be fine."

I walk over to the coffee machine to find the pot cold and pour out the dregs. I probably drink too much coffee, but that doesn't stop me from craving another cup.

"Got time for coffee?" I ask Alex.

"Always," she says, pulling out a chair at the kitchen table and sitting down.

I go about putting on another pot as I ask her what brought her here in the first place. She doesn't often drop in unannounced. She does most of her work at High Meadow now. It's more convenient to treat the horses there. She generally shoots me a message to let me know she's heading this way. Besides, it's not like we don't talk almost daily.

"Checking in with you. Seeing how things are going."

The way she stares out the sliding doors and avoids making eye contact tells me there's more to the story than that.

"Things are fine...but you already knew that because I talked to you yesterday."

"I'm your friend, am I not allowed to worry about you?" she asks, going the passive-aggressive route as she finally turns her eyes to me.

It only confirms she has an agenda and I fold my arms over my chest as I stare her down. Eventually she relents, throwing her hands up.

"Fine," she snaps. "Bo's been weird."

What the hell?

"Okay..."

"I know he came to visit earlier this week when he heard you'd been shot."

"Barged in here is more like it," I correct her.

"I bet." She stifles a grin. "Anyway, you never mentioned it and he's been weird ever since."

"Weird, how?"

"Different. He smiles a lot."

"He always does. He's a smooth operator, the smile is a tool of the trade," I point out.

But Alex shakes her head. "Not like that. These past few days he smiles when he doesn't know anyone's looking. He smiles when he gets out of his truck in the morning, when he pours himself a coffee in the ranch kitchen, or when I catch him walking to the barn. He seems perpetually happy, it's like someone threw a switch."

She looks at me with an eyebrow raised and I clue in what she's suggesting.

"You think I had anything to do with that?" I bark out a laugh. "Sorry to disappoint you, but I highly doubt me kicking his ass out after he insulted me would have done the trick."

"You kicked him out?" she asks incredulously.

"He insulted me," I explain a tad defensively as I turn to pour us coffee.

The truth is, I've replayed that scene over and over in my head since I told him to get out and have come to the conclusion I may have overreacted. Not that I'd ever admit that to him. He's the reason my mind gets scrambled and I feel off balance in the first place.

"Insulted you, how?" she asks behind me.

"He told me I basically looked like a teenager," I grumble, paraphrasing a little as I struggle to hold on to my snit.

I may have already decided being accused of looking younger than your age is not necessarily a bad thing, but the fact he seemed angry at the realization still irks me.

"Ahhh, now it makes sense," Alex declares.

Unfortunately, I'm still clueless. I set our cups down on the table and take a seat across from her.

"Pray enlighten me."

She lifts her head and beams a bright smile my way.

"I've wondered why he hasn't made a move when he's clearly been smitten with you this whole time. Guess he thought he was too old for you."

First of all, only Alex would use the term smitten, and secondly...*what*?

~

Bo

"Hey, watch it, asshole."

I have to duck to avoid the branch Fletch just let go up ahead. He's leading the way up the trail along the river where we're supposed to round up a couple of the older colts, who managed to find their way out of one of the back meadows.

It's been a while since I've had Blue out on a casual ride. Most of the time I'm so focused on work, I don't really take the time to enjoy simply being outdoors. It's a nice day; just a few clouds in the sky and the air is crisp and cool.

My Blue is a nine-year-old, blue roan quarter draft. Calm demeanor, steady on his feet, powerful, and with a stamina perfect for the kind of demands our work puts on the team's mounts. For the breed's large size, these horses are surprisingly agile and can cling to a mountainside as easily as they can trudge through miles of dense forest.

A ride like this, on a clear day, over a well-used trail, and at a casual pace is a nice break for him as well. He's alert, his ears occasionally scanning, but his body lacks the tension it usually carries when on the job.

It's not the first time these young escape artists have gotten out. They rarely go far and tend to wander back on their own, but Jonas is eager for some of the yearlings to be brought back to the stable. It shouldn't take us too long to round them up.

Apparently, a renowned horse trainer is flying in from

Kentucky later this week to have a look. His stable is researching the idea of developing an experimental, multidisciplinary training program that would be suitable for younger horses, between one and two years old. Darrin Ludwig wants to handpick a selection of yearlings of varying breeds and crossbreeds to work with. If Ludwig's program gains interest, it could mean some recognition for High Meadow's breeding program as well. Jonas is always looking at ways to diversify and increase business for the ranch.

Personally, I don't really have a head for business. Don't get me wrong, I enjoy my job here and I love working with animals, but I feel most alive when the High Mountain Trackers team is out in the wilderness on somebody's trail. Tracking is my jam, and if I'm able to put my medical training to use, even better.

"There they are," Fletch calls over his shoulder as he points ahead.

I ease up beside Fletch's horse, King, who snorts and tries to bump Blue out of the way. A grumpy bastard like his owner, King likes to be on point. Blue doesn't give a rat's ass where he is in line, but he's also not a pushover and nips at the other horse's shoulder in warning.

Up ahead I see one of the missing colts munching on a tall patch of grass on the riverbank. His head comes up when he notices our approach. For a moment, it looks like he might take off again, but then he whinnies softly and starts making his way up the trail. Behind him the other yearling comes into view and the two start trotting towards us.

"Beavis and Butthead," I mumble.

The colts are named High Meadow and Karma, but if you ask me my choices fit them better.

Fletch bursts out laughing, a sound I don't hear too often.

"Don't let Alex hear you. She's the one who named Missy's colt and is a little attached."

"I know. Which is why I'm surprised Jonas plans to offer the colt to Ludwig. I'd have thought she'd have a thing or two to say about that," I suggest.

"I imagine she did, but that ain't my monkey."

The colts are easy to round up and—having had their little adventure—easily fall in line with Fletch in the lead, and me bringing up the rear to make sure they don't get any ideas. By the time we get them back to the meadow, Dan and Sully are putting the last touches on the fence repairs.

"What's up with you?" Sully asks beside me when we make our way back to the ranch. "You've been grinning like an idiot all day. Win the lottery or something?"

"Ha! Wouldn't that be something?"

Feels a little like I won the lottery but I'm not about to share that. It's been a few days since I found out Lucy's real age and, in hindsight, I realize I've been an idiot. Blinded by my own hang-ups about an age difference that wasn't there. I'd been down that road once before with near detrimental results and was determined to avoid a repeat.

Turns out my restraint all this time was wasted. Of course, now I'm chomping at the bit to get in there, but I know enough about Lucy to realize that would backfire on me in a big way. So, I forced myself to let it rest for a few days before making a move. My plan is to stop by her place on my way home and see if I can coax her into sharing a meal with me.

Small steps, otherwise I wouldn't be surprised to see her bolt for the mountains. Much like the careful steps she takes to win over her rescue horses. I know the woman has a history—it's written all over her prickly demeanor—and I realize I'll have to dig it up bit by bit to find the soft underneath.

Man, I'd like a chance to make up for the time I've wasted, but first I'll have to win her trust.

Starting today.

Four

LUCY

I nod at Samantha for encouragement as I unclip the lead rope.

Ladybug keeps on moving as I step back toward the center of the ring. She's one of two of our rescue horses—the other is Hope—I've trained to work with clients like Samantha. Women, who for some reason, have had their self-confidence eroded. Some through abusive situations, some as a result of major life changes or physical challenges, but all women who need to start believing in their own strength and capabilities again.

Samantha was referred to my equine therapy program through my contact at the Lincoln County Family Crisis Center. She recently left a marriage of twenty-some years, over the course of which she had been reduced to a shell of her former self through the constant belittling and verbal abuse her husband rained on her. She told me herself it had been at the urging of her youngest daughter, who'd just left for college, to get out of the marriage.

As most abusive husbands, the asshole had not been very receptive to her leaving. He couldn't leave her alone and dogged her every step, even harassing the friend she ended up staying with until she had no choice but to take out a temporary order of protection against him.

That was the latest, and Samantha arrived here earlier feeling she'd failed once again, exactly the way her shit of an ex conditioned her to feel. Which is why I'm having her ride Ladybug all on her own, despite her misgivings.

The woman is in desperate need of a small victory— some hint of control—and I'm hoping this might give her a taste of what she is capable of. Never mind a cannon could go off and Ladybug wouldn't miss a stride, but Samantha doesn't necessarily know that. She holds her fate in her hands; I want her to know she can trust herself to handle it.

"You've got this, Sam. I trust you."

Her eyes seem big in her gaunt face but her lips narrow determinedly as she nods sharply. Then she casts her look ahead. Good, that's where it needs to be.

"Straighten your back. Shoulders down, head high." I watch her check her posture. "That's it. Nice. Now, whenever you're ready, nudge Ladybug into a trot. All you have to do is grab on to the horn, gently press your heels to her flanks, and click your tongue. She doesn't need much encouragement."

It takes her a few minutes to work up the courage but she finally takes hold of the horn and, although she slumps back in the saddle again, she urges the horse into a gentle trot. One of the reasons I love Ladybug for this work is her easy, almost lazy gait. It makes for less bouncing in the saddle, which can be a challenge for those not yet accustomed to the trot.

"That's awesome. You're doing great. Try to relax into

the horse's movement instead of tightening up. It'll make it so much easier. Remember to drop your shoulders, unclench your butt cheeks, and relax your hips."

It takes a few turns around the ring but she's already improving.

"Much better!" I call out.

She glows when she looks at me, a smile spreading on her face, but then her eyes dart over my shoulder and I literally can see the blood drain from her face. Next, I hear the crunch of tires on the driveway and swing around.

A black Dodge Ram rolls to a stop right beside the ring and a man gets out. I can't see much of his face, which is partially obscured by the brim of his hat, but he's packing a bit of weight and moves with determination. For a moment I think maybe Lester Franklin chased me down and is here to cause trouble about the goats, but I quickly realize the truck is too new and the man too clean-looking to be the farmer.

I shake off the involuntary shiver running down my spine.

A quick glance behind me shows Sam has brought Ladybug to a halt. Even the horse is on high alert, her ears sharply forward and her eyes focused on the man now at the fence. The woman is frozen in the saddle.

"Get off the fucking horse," he barks at Samantha.

Oh dear.

I reach a hand in my pocket, searching for my phone, but come up empty. Shit, I must've left it sitting on the ledge of Ladybug's stall where I put it when we were saddling her.

Dammit.

Straightening my spine and conjuring up as much

authority as I can muster, I force myself to move toward the man.

"Excuse me, can I help you?" I call out, drawing his attention to me.

He throws me a passing glance and continues to ignore me as he zooms back in on Samantha.

This is not good. I'd feel a bit better if the dogs were out here, but Samantha is nervous around them so I locked them in the house. I'm regretting it now and I'm cursing myself for not having my phone on me.

"Get your fucking ass down from there, Samantha!" he yells, loud enough for Ladybug to let out a startled snort.

"That's enough," I state in a firm voice, loud enough for him to hear.

I wrap my fingers tightly around the lead still in my hand as I step right into his field of vision. There's not enough of me to block Samantha from his view, but I at least make for a distraction. The leather in my hand is not much of a weapon, although the metal snap at the end of it could do a bit of damage if need be.

"Who the fuck are you?" The narrowed eyes he fixes on me seem slightly unfocused.

Great, he looks like he's been drinking.

"This is my property and I need you to leave."

He points over my shoulder at Samantha. "And that there is my property and I want it back."

"You can't be here, Dwight," she calls from behind me. "The judge says you can't be within two hundred feet from me."

"Fuck the judge!"

Then he starts walking toward the gate. Yeah, this is not going to be pretty.

"Samantha?" I yell over my shoulder, trying to desensitize the situation. "Would you mind taking Ladybug back to the stable for me?"

If I can get her out of sight, maybe he'll be easier to reason with.

"I fucking mind," he bellows, reaching for the latch on the gate.

Behind me I hear movement, and I can only hope Sam is doing what I asked as her ex steps inside the ring.

Instead of retreating as every instinct screams at me to do, I take a step toward him instead. One thing which always stuck with me from the hardcore self-defense course I took years ago is that offense is your best defense. I move both my arms to my sides, raising them slightly, both to make myself appear a bit bigger but also to show him the leather lead in my hand. I purposely let the metal clip swing back and forth.

Most bullies are cowards at heart, which is why they like picking on those smaller or perceived weaker than them. He doesn't want to get hurt any more than anyone else does, plus it throws him off I'm confronting him instead of cowering from him. He stops in his tracks, taking in my makeshift weapon before slowly scanning me top to bottom.

Then a sly grin spreads over his face.

Uh-oh.

Bo

There's a car I don't know parked beside Lucy's pickup when I come up her driveway.

Up ahead, an unfamiliar black truck is parked by the fence. Something about the way it's angled a bit haphazardly makes me uneasy and I pull up right behind it.

My good mood fades instantly when I catch sight of some big guy wearing a tan Stetson approach Lucy, who looks to have taken on a defensive stance in the corral.

I kick open my door, get out to stand on my running board, and bellow, "Hey!"

I catch Lucy's eyes darting my way, but I keep my focus on the guy whose body language leaves little to the imagination. I wait until he's fully turned in my direction before I step down and start moving toward them. Brushing by the guy I stop in front of Lucy, my back toward him.

"Everything all right here?"

Lucy's blue eyes show both concern and relief as she lifts them up to me.

"Dwight here was just leaving. Weren't you, Dwight?" she says in a firm voice, clearly intended for whoever the guy is.

I step to Lucy's side and turn around, slipping a casual arm around her narrow shoulders. I feel her bristle at my touch but to her credit, she stays put. It's clear Dwight is not happy with this turn of events. His eyes flit back and forth between the barn and us. Slight movement inside the barn alerts me someone is in there hiding. Given the work Lucy does alongside the rescue, it doesn't take much to guess the kind of scenario I walked in on.

"Anything you need, Dwight?"

He opens his mouth to answer me before thinking better of it. Probably a smart move. I have no patience for asswipes like him. Then he takes a single step back, throws a dirty look at Lucy, followed by a lingering one in the direction of the barn, before turning on his heel to march back to his truck.

With a dramatic revving of the engine and gravel flying in every direction, he pulls his pickup around and floors it down the driveway.

No sooner has he disappeared in a cloud of dust when Lucy shrugs out from under my arm. I can see the incident rattled her because for a moment her eyes are unguarded, showing fear instead of the customary defiance.

"I'm so sorry!"

A pretty, dark-haired, pleasantly plump woman rushes out of the barn toward us. I'm guessing the moron who just tore out of here is an ex.

Lucy turns toward her and the look on her face changes from concern to one of confidence and compassion.

"You have nothing to be sorry about," she reassures her, grabbing the woman's hands.

"I have no idea how he knew I would be here."

"He may have followed you," I suggest carefully.

Her eyes dart to me and immediately lower to the toes of my boots.

Jesus. The asshole must've done a real number on her.

"He's not supposed to come anywhere near Samantha," Lucy explains, clueing me in to the woman's name. "Not within two hundred feet."

"Good for you, Samantha," I praise the woman while pulling my phone from my pocket.

"What are you doing?" she asks suspiciously when I pull up a familiar number from my contact list.

"What one of you should've done right away when he showed up—call the cops," I snap, suddenly annoyed.

Women get fucking killed by crazy-ass exes all the time

because they're afraid to rock the boat. At least Samantha had the courage to go get a protective order, but what good is it if you do nothing to enforce it?

And don't get me started on Lucy, she definitely should know better or she has no business being in this line of work, dammit.

"It's just going to make him angrier," the woman sputters, having apparently found her spine.

"I have news for you," I address Samantha firmly. "Whatever line you think that would've crossed; he's already crossed it. Don't think he can get much more pissed. Besides, why serve him with an order of protection if you don't intend to hold him to it?"

"All right, that's enough," Lucy intervenes with a flat hand pressed against my chest. Her touch does weird things to me. Some of the anger dissipates as I meet her calm eyes. "I forgot my phone in the barn or I would've called them myself."

I take her words as encouragement to make the call. There's only one way to stop guys like this Dwight-character and that is to make them face the consequences.

My conversation with Reggie Williams—a detective for the Libby PD—was short and sweet and he showed up less than ten minutes later to take a report.

He and I initially met through our mothers, who live in neighboring units in the senior living apartment building, and then bumped into each other working on a case. Occasionally we go out for a bite and a beer at the Pastime Lounge, play a game of pool or darts, and talk shop.

Not a ton of black folk in Montana, let alone here in Libby. Doesn't really bother me too much, but I'm not gonna lie: from time to time it's nice to be around someone you share a heritage and skin color with.

I love my team—they're my brothers in every sense of the word and I'd lay down my life for them as they would for me—but there are some things that would be hard for them to understand because they haven't lived in my black skin. Not their fault, or mine, that's just a fact. Still, sometimes it's good to talk with someone who does get that part of you.

"Not sure I can do much more than pull him in for a stern warning, this is the first reported breach of the order," Reggie says when I walk him to his cruiser after he takes everyone's statements. "Maybe the judge can increase the range of the protective order, although I doubt that'll make much of a difference. I'll see what I can do, talk to my chief, maybe we can lean on him for a bit with a heavy presence. Frequent drive-bys at his house and place of employment. See if we can't scare him off."

He opens the door and leans an arm on the top as he glances over at the older sedan. Samantha is already behind the wheel and Lucy is bending down, talking to her through the window.

"Nice girl. She attached?"

"Back off," I snap, a little more forcefully than necessary.

"So that's her?" he asks, looking at me with one eyebrow up.

"What do you mean, *her*?"

He flashes a grin. "Gimme a break, you know what I mean; you're lookin' at her like you could have her for breakfast, lunch, and dinner. I've never seen you look at any of the chicks who sidle up to you at the Pastime like that, and to top it off, you bite off my head at an innocent question."

"That wasn't innocent and those women at the lounge are only interested in one thing."

"Right," he confirms. "And I seem to recall you weren't too averse to indulging one or two of them."

"That was a long time ago and don't remind me," I mumble before adding firmly. "Don't you have somewhere to be? Reports to fill out? Criminals to catch?"

"Relax..."

He chuckles as he gets behind the wheel. He shuts the door and sticks his head out the window.

"Your secret's safe with me. I won't tell your momma."

Then he pulls away and I can hear him laughing as he heads down the driveway.

Five

"I can't, I'm busy."

I turn and head up the porch steps, hoping Bo will take my refusal and leave, but somehow, I sincerely doubt that.

"Everyone's gotta eat," he persists, clomping his big boots up the steps behind me.

"Right, but I can't leave here."

I push open the front door and barely manage to squeeze to the side as the dogs come barreling outside. Poor things have been cooped up since Samantha got here around three. It's almost seven now. They don't even stop to greet Bo and find their respective spots to relieve themselves.

"Why not?"

I ignore his question when I hear a faint bleating coming from inside the house. Oh my God, I forgot all about the goats. The poor kids must be starving by now. I rush inside and head toward the hallway to the left where I left them barricaded in my bathroom.

The babies are now two weeks old. Midnight—the

stronger, black one—seems to be thriving, and I've been seeing a bit of improvement in Mocha, the runt I'm still feeding through a tube. But when I open the bathroom door, I immediately catch sight of the little guy, curled up in a tight ball in the corner by the tub, while his brother is screaming his hungry head off.

"Hang on, buddy. Let me check your brother first," I mumble as I go down on my knees and reach for Mocha's small, dark-brown body.

"Where do you think you're going?" I hear Bo's deep voice rumble behind me.

Great. He followed me inside, taking away the option to shut the door on him. I presume he's talking to Midnight, who is a bit of an escape artist.

A soft whimper coming from Mocha has me breathe out a sigh of relief and I quickly pick him up and grab one of the pre-filled syringes from the cooler in the bathtub. Sitting with my back against the side of the tub, I cradle the little goat in my lap while I quickly connect the syringe to the tube and slowly squeeze the plunger.

Only then do I look up to find Bo's almost black eyes fixed on me. He's holding Midnight in one of his shovel-sized hands and is absently stroking the goat with the other.

Dammit.

For some women it's men with babies, but my kryptonite are men with puppies, kittens, and apparently, we can add baby goats to that list.

"You're nursing baby goats," he comments.

"Very observant of you."

I wince at the snide words flying out of my mouth unchecked. My shield of bristles has become second nature over the years, and I'm afraid I've become irrevocably bitter and unpleasant. The upside, of course, is that no one bothers or dares to look any closer. Except a select few who don't really buy into the persona I put out there.

Bo, who is currently staring right through me, is one of them.

"I assume this little guy needs feeding too?" he finally asks.

"There's a bottle in the cooler," I reluctantly share.

When he moves into the bathroom, his bulk instantly fills the small room. He bends down, his body hovering over me as he reaches into the tub behind me. Then—to my surprise—he slides down beside me, his shoulder pressing against mine in the narrow space, and deftly plops the bottle in Midnight's impatient mouth.

For a few minutes all we hear is the sound of Midnight's eager drinking.

"How often do they eat?"

"This one every two hours, still. Mocha has some catching up to do." Then I jerk my chin at the goat he's holding. "That's Midnight. He feeds every three hours."

A soft whistle escapes Bo's lips.

"Sounds like a lot of work."

I shrug my shoulders, trying to brush it off. "It's just temporary."

"When do you sleep?" He wants to know.

That's the million-dollar question. The truth is, not much, but that's nothing new. Not that I'm about to share that.

"When I can. It's not that bad and like I said; it's temporary."

He hums low in his throat and raises an eyebrow, but doesn't push.

"All right, pizza it is," he announces.

I open my mouth to object but snap it shut again. It's

been a long day and it'll be an even longer night. The man's just offering pizza for crying out loud, surely, I can handle that.

"Roasted red pepper, hot Italian sausage, spinach, prosciutto, pesto, and hot pepper flakes. Mama Gina's, they deliver."

I sneak a peek at Bo when I hear his soft, responding chuckle.

"Yes, ma'am. I'll put in the order soon's I have my hands free," he mumbles, the corner of his mouth drawn up in a grin.

~

"Of course you do."

Bo drops the slice of pizza back on his plate, pretending to be shocked at my comment.

We've been discussing favorite TV series over dinner. Turns out we both like *Ozark*, *Bloodline*, or *Breaking Bad*, but while I get a kick out of Olifant's quirky character in *Justified*, Bo is more drawn to shows like *Jack Ryan*.

We're onto reality shows now which has spawned this last disagreement as we defend the merits of *Alone* versus *Life Below Zero*

"Only because it *is* better," he insists.

"How do you figure? Both are wilderness survival shows. What makes *Alone* so superior?" I want to know.

"They're stranded out there with a handful of items with the clothes on their back and have to rely completely on themselves. In your show they have tools, can get supplies in, and aren't even alone half the time."

"Yeah, but *Alone* is a game and lasts a couple of months at most. Besides, the participants can tap out at any time.

Life Below Zero is exactly that: Life. There's no tapping out, there's no big money on the other end of it, there is just survival."

He slowly shakes his head but his eyes are crinkling as he looks at me. Knowing I scored a point, I grin and shove almost my entire slice in my mouth at once.

Bo is about to say something when he's interrupted by a muted ringtone and picks up his phone instead.

"Yeah."

His eyes drift out the window as he listens to whomever is speaking on the other side, until he suddenly surges to his feet, shoving his chair back.

"She okay?"

The pained look on his face has my throat constrict and I drop my pizza on my plate, standing as well.

"When?"

Bo is already moving to the door, grabbing his hat from the coatrack. I'm following close behind. It's obvious something has happened, but I don't know what or to who. I just know it's not good.

"On my way."

He shoves the phone in his pocket and is already out on the porch when I manage to grab him by the arm. His head whips around and his eyes look angry when they land on mine.

"What's happening?" I ask carefully.

Instantly his eyes soften as they scan my face.

"My mother. They think she may have had a stroke. They're moving her to Cabinet Peaks Medical Center. I'm sorry, I've gotta go."

"Yeah. No, yeah, of course. Go."

I give him a little shove down the porch steps and watch as he gets behind the wheel of his truck, folding my arms around myself. He backs away from the house, looks up at me for a brief moment and tips his hat, and then tears down the driveway toward the road.

When I don't see him anymore, I go inside, close the door, and lean my back against it.

Bo has a mother and, apparently, she lives in town. Who knew?

∽

Bo

"I'm fine."

I close my eyes to keep her from seeing me roll them. It's just gonna piss her off more and she's riled up enough as it is.

"Did we not just spend the better part of the night in the hospital?"

"The doctor said nothing was broken," she persists stubbornly.

"This time," I remind her.

The ER doctor also mentioned that he suspected her bouts of imbalance may be the result of something call a TIA—or transient ischemic attack, which is basically a mini-stroke—and that at her age it was quite common, but Momma waved him off when he'd wanted to refer her to a neurologist in Kalispell.

"Damn Tonya for hitting the alarm. All she had to do was help me up."

She had been watching *Jeopardy* with Mrs. Williams

from next door when she got up too fast to grab a snack, got dizzy, and went down.

"Momma, the woman's got about ten years on you, can barely walk, and depends on a tank for oxygen," I scold her. "And do I have to point out you were lucky she was there or you might've still been lying there? That's my point, Momma. You have an alarm around your neck, but you don't want to use it. If you want to refuse treatment or a referral to a specialist, that's up to you, but don't ask me to sit by while your stubbornness could cause your unnecessarily slow and torturous death. Either promise you'll use the damn button or let me arrange for regular checkups from the main house."

As much as I want to shake my mother from time to time, she is of sound mind—albeit headstrong as a mule—and I have no choice but to respect her wishes. However, she'd better respect mine too, and I don't mind a little emotional blackmail to get my point across.

"And one last thing; I am spending what little is left of this night on your couch. For my own peace of mind," I add when she treats me to a mutinous glare.

With a last harrumph, she turns on her heel and hobbles into her bedroom, slamming the door shut behind her.

God, give me strength.

"Burns?"

Sully looks up from his computer where he has his browser open on the DMV website.

"Yes, Dwight Burns," I confirm.

I picked up the guy's last name when Reggie was interviewing the asshole's ex-wife at the rescue yesterday. The call about Momma derailed me for the past thirty-six hours or so, but I had every intention to look into him. Doesn't sit well with me he showed up and threatened Lucy on her own turf.

I'm sure Reggie is doing what he can, but he's got to go by the book. I don't have that problem, especially when it involves someone I care about, but I wasn't going to compromise his job by asking him for information on Burns.

"Got him," Sully confirms. "Pipe Creek Road. Looks like he's right across from the church."

I lean down and peek over his shoulder. The address is just outside town limits on the other side of the river. Not much out there except for the church, which is a fairly new addition. Shouldn't be too many people around on a weekday after work hours. I may drive by tonight after I check on my mother.

"Want me to poke around a bit?" Sully asks when I straighten up.

"Yeah."

Wouldn't hurt to know who I'm dealing with.

"How deep?"

"If you hit something, dig it up."

Who knows when a bit of leverage might come in handy.

I clap him on the shoulder and head back out to the corral where a small group consisting of Jonas, James, Doc Evans, and Darrin Ludwig are checking out the two colts Fletch and I rounded up a couple of days ago.

"*Asshole.*"

I whip my head to the side to find Alex leaning against the back of Doc Evans's pickup, her arms crossed over her chest and a scowl on her face. I quickly recognize the death stare is aimed at Jonas and I assume so was the comment.

"For a sec there I thought you meant me," I admit, leaning my rump against the bumper beside her, matching her pose.

"I might still, if you're only gonna tell me it's what's best for the ranch."

I know she has an attachment to the colt she named High Meadow, just like she has a soft spot for Missy—the mare who foaled him—and his sire, Phantom. The stallion actually brought Alex here to the ranch...and to Jonas.

"Then I won't," I'm quick to respond, before adding. "I'll stick to pointing out it might be better for the colt. He's not even two and already he's bored easily. He escapes because he needs to be challenged and there isn't much we can offer here to stimulate him, and you know it. He'd be happier than a pig in shit enrolled in this guy's training program."

She makes a disgruntled sound before turning her angry eyes on me.

"I don't like you very much."

I bite my lip to keep from chuckling at her petulant tone.

"Only because you know I'm right."

That invites a snort as she glances back at the corral.

"You really think he'd be happier?"

"You're the expert here, what do you think?"

Her mumbled, "*Dammit*," is enough of an admission.

I nudge her with my elbow.

"Think of it this way; if Ludwig takes him and this collaboration takes off, we should be getting regular updates on how he's doing."

She pokes me back with hers.

"All right, that's more common sense than I can handle in a day."

I look up at the sound of an engine and catch sight of Lucy's pickup pulling up to the main house.

"Oh shit, I forgot," Alex mumbles without explanation, as she pushes herself off the truck gate and jogs over.

Lucy has her hands full at the rescue and doesn't show her face that often, so I'm curious to know what brought her here. I also want a chance to apologize for blowing out of there two nights ago with only a short text explaining the situation after I got Momma home.

Alex is already dropping the gate on Lucy's truck and hauling out a large bag of dog food.

"Here..." I bump her out of the way. "Let me get that for you." I toss the bag over my shoulder. "You know I coulda picked you up some dog food in town," I mutter, a bit annoyed. "No need to bother Lucy with that."

Seems a bit crazy to me to have Lucy—who has enough work on her hands—run errands when there are plenty of available bodies here on the ranch.

"No need to get all growly on her," Lucy jumps in as she appears around the side of the truck. "My boys don't like that brand, but Max does so I offered to drop it off."

Max belongs to Jonas, a Bernese mountain dog who never ventures far from his owner.

"Besides," she continues, waving a pair of familiar sunglasses. "I was coming here anyway to return these to you. You left them the other day."

I take them with my free hand and tuck them in the front of my shirt, feeling a bit put in my place.

"Thanks, I hadn't even missed them yet," I admit. "I was going to drop—"

"Anyway," Lucy interrupts as she turns to Alex,

dismissing me. "I should be heading back. I have a client coming at two."

I take two steps to the edge of the porch to unload the bag of kibble but when I turn back to finish my lame excuse for an apology, she's already behind the wheel of the truck. I resist the temptation to intercept her when she backs up, deciding I'd rather make a stop at the rescue and do my groveling in private instead of with an audience.

"Gotta do better than that, my friend," Alex comments with a grin before she turns toward the barn.

I start back to the corral, where I find Darrin Ludwig staring after Lucy's disappearing taillights.

"Weird," he says when he notices me. "I could've sworn..."

"You know Lucy?"

My question comes out a little sharper than I intended. Something that does not go unnoticed by the trainer, who briefly narrows his eyes on me. Then he shakes his head and grins.

"Nah, don't know any Lucy. I was just reminded of someone who's been gone for a long time now."

Six

LUCY

Scout alerts on something up ahead. A ridge of hair stands up, running from the base of his skull to halfway to his tail. One front paw is raised and his whole body is leaning forward. Chief stops right behind him.

"Stay. Good boys," I mumble, easing my horse, Ellie, a few steps ahead.

There it is.

Maybe a hundred yards from us, the head of a black bear pops up from a patch of huckleberry bushes at the edge of the creek ahead. There can't be much left on those, the season's about over, but this close to winter every single berry counts.

The bear appears frozen, looking in our direction, and I hold still, waiting to see what he'll do next. After a minute or so he loses interest and returns his attention to whatever food he can find.

For the most part, I live in harmony with the wildlife, but I won't hesitate to defend myself or one of my animals.

I'm not a fan of guns, but I'm also not a fool and always carry a rifle in the scabbard strapped to my saddle. Especially when I'm alone out here.

I whistle softly and turn Ellie back down the mountain, trusting the dogs to follow suit.

The breeze is crisp and the tip of my nose is frosty, but the fresh air has done me a world of good. The lack of sleep is really starting to get to me and after my last session, I could've rolled straight into bed. Instead, I decided to take Ellie and the boys out for a bit of exercise. There hasn't been much time for that since I brought home those goats.

I feel refreshed and as we make our way back to the farm, I do a mental check of the fridge contents to see what I can scrounge up for dinner. Slim pickings, since I've also not been to the grocery store in over a week, but I'm sure I can do something with the leftover veggies. I have some stock in the pantry, a few cans of beans, so everything-but-the-kitchen-sink soup sounds doable. Pretty sure I have half a loaf of bread in the freezer and a few slices of cheese left, so I can even do a grilled cheese sandwich on the side. Perfect for this weather.

By the time I have Ellie rubbed dry in her stall and walk out of the barn, light snow is starting to fall.

I'm not sure if I'm ready for what will be my third Montana winter. They can be harsh, and long, and since Alex moved to High Meadow, they can be damned lonely too. I'm annoyed when right away Bo's warm smile comes to mind. I've got to stop letting myself get tempted like that. Especially when I'm tired and worn out, and resistance is low.

As I put a foot on the steps to the porch, I hear a vehicle coming up the driveway.

You have got to be shitting me.

Annoyed, I continue inside where I know the kids are waiting, but leave the door open behind me. I'm already attaching the syringe to Mocha's feeding tube when Bo appears in the doorway.

"Didn't get a chance to thank you for dropping off my glasses, or apologize for not getting in touch since I stormed out of here."

"Thanks," I respond curtly. "Although there's nothing to apologize for."

I focus on Mocha's big brown eyes so I don't have to look into Bo's. Lord knows what he'd be able to read in mine. I always seem to feel more exposed around him.

"But there is," he insists, reaching down to pick up Midnight, who is bleating up a storm. "He need feeding?"

"Yeah, it's in the—"

"Cooler, I know," Bo interrupts as he reaches over me to grab a bottle.

Then he sits beside me, the small goat wedged between his strong legs as he feeds him.

"How is your mom doing?" I feel compelled to ask.

"She'll be okay, stubborn as a mule though. She can't keep her balance but won't use her alert and doesn't want any help, which means I have to stop by before work and after to make sure she hasn't fallen again and hurt herself. She's a pain in my ass."

He sounds disgruntled and annoyed, but it's also clear from his mini rant he loves his mother. I'm a little jealous.

"But you'll check in a few times a day anyway," I conclude.

His head is bent down but he twists his neck to glance at me sideways, grunting confirmation.

"Yeah. She's all I got. You got folks left, Lucy?"

Not the first time I've been asked a question like that

but instead of my standard answer I was an only child and my parents died a long time ago, I find myself hesitating. Since it feels like Bo shared something private with me— it's funny I've never heard anyone mentioning Bo's mother before—I find myself tempted to reciprocate with honesty.

"None that I know of." When he looks at me questioningly, I add, "Raised by my grandmother and she died when I was a teenager. I'm not even sure who my parents were."

Hard to tell, since in the holler where I grew up a lot of people were related, one way or another, by blood or otherwise. For all I know, Grandma wasn't really a relative but I didn't care, she gave me all the love she could muster and a safe—albeit humble—home. That all changed after she died, but I stop myself from disappearing down that rabbit hole.

"I'm sorry."

I indulge myself for a second and allow the warmth of his compassion to wrap around me before decidedly shrugging it off.

"Long time ago."

My dismissal hangs in the air for only a few moments when Bo breaks the silence.

"Storm coming in," he rumbles.

"I noticed."

"Should snow most of the night. Could be up to a foot in higher elevations. Maybe six to eight inches here."

Fuck. That means I need to bring the animals in from the west meadow. They have no cover there. The field behind the barn has a good-sized roofed enclosure the horses can shelter in. Better get that done right away before the last of my energy is gone.

"Shoulda checked the weather forecast better," I observe

as I quickly finish feeding Mocha and get to my feet. "I've gotta get my animals in."

Then I step out of the bathroom.

"Wait!" he calls after me. "Need a minute to finish with this guy and I'll give you a hand."

I close my eyes and rest my head against the wall in the hallway. Unfamiliar tears sting behind my eyelids. I'm too tired to even object to the offer of help.

"Okay," I force from my closed-up throat.

Then I use the time to feed the dogs and get a hold of myself while I wait for him to finish feeding Midnight.

It takes us half an hour to round up Ladybug, Hope and her colt, Floyd, and our donkey, Daisy, on foot. The latter—Daisy—is not about to give up the last raspberries of the season from the cluster of bushes along the tree line. I finally manage to lure her with another sweet treat in the form of an apple and sigh a breath of relief when I shut the stall door behind me.

Bo, who is tossing some fresh hay in the stalls, grins at me.

"She's a handful."

"You have no idea."

I'm barely able to cover an inadvertent yawn that almost dislodges my jaw.

"You're tired," he observes as he brushes some twigs of hay from his chest.

Apparently too tired to notice I'm staring. My eyes snap up to his face when I hear his chuckle.

"I should get out of your hair and let you get some rest."

My whole body wants to say no—it feels so nice to share a little of the burden—but my head is still in charge.

"Sure."

The snow is really starting to come down by the time we

walk back to the farmhouse. I wait while Bo cleans off the windshield of his truck. Then he turns to me, his eyes piercing from under his hat.

"Luce..."

I'm afraid he's going to say something about what I shared earlier so I quickly cut him off.

"I appreciate your help, Bo. Again," I add. "Drive sa—"

My mouth is still forming the word when his hand shoots out and catches me by the back of my neck. One little tug and I'm suddenly inches from his face and covered from the snow by the wide brim of his hat.

"Hush, Lucy," he mumbles an instant before his lush mouth closes over mine.

≈

Bo

That wasn't the plan.

In the rearview mirror, I see her standing where I left her. Her lips still parted, her cheeks flushed, with frosted eyelashes framing those round, blue, shocked eyes as she stares after me.

That first taste of her is going to stick with me for a long time and it took every ounce of self-control to keep the kiss short and sweet. Mostly because I didn't want to give her time to react. Pretty sure given half the chance she'd have ripped me a new one or kneed me in the chicken tenders.

Guess I could've informed her of my intentions, but why waste time when the opportunity to show her was staring me in the face.

Nah, let her simmer on it for a while. If her experience was anything like mine, she'll be thinking of that kiss plenty.

Momma is on her feet when I get to her apartment, thankfully.

"Saved you some dinner," she announces, shuffling from her chair toward the small kitchen when I walk in.

I know there's no arguing with her when she has her mind set on feeding me so I follow her.

"You cooked." I notice the pans on the stove and it's pissing me off. "I thought we'd agreed you'd stick to food from the main house or ordering something in."

She snorts as she piles mashed potatoes and fried chicken on a plate. "Waste of money," she declares, shoving the plate at me. "They don't season the food from the house and I like my own fried chicken best."

The thought of her cooking with hot oil sends a shiver down my spine. She could've caused a fire. Hell, she could've burned down the whole damn building.

"Ma, no. What if you'd fallen, lost consciousness?"

"But I didn't."

She plants her fists on her hips and jerks her chin high. She still has to look up at me a ways, and I could probably knock her over with my pinky finger, but she still manages to pull off that same fierce look that had me quivering in my boots when I was a boy. Mind you, in those days she often held a wooden spoon, or even a rolling pin, and wasn't afraid to use either on me to get her point across.

Truth is, I probably deserved it. I was a little shit.

"But you could've, and I get you wanna prove you can still manage by yourself, but is it worth risking the lives of your neighbors? That's not like you, Momma."

Her body gives a little jerk at my words and I feel bad

putting it to her like that, but I have to break through that stubborn layer.

I give her a moment to process and take my plate inside to the small table by the window and grab a seat. At some point I hear her shuffling in and sitting down in her comfy chair.

"It's good. No chicken better than this, Momma. And next time you feel like cooking, all you gotta do is make sure there's an extra set of eyes, just in case."

"Like Tonya's?" she scoffs, but I recognize it as a last attempt to save face when she echoes my words to her from earlier in the week. "The woman moves slower than I do and she's on oxygen."

I twist my entire upper body in her direction and look at her sternly.

"But at least she knows how to use the alarm."

~

"I'm calling the police."

He wipes at his nose, only succeeding in spreading the blood running down.

One swing and he went down on his ass on the doorstep.

"Look, I'm sorry, I must've tripped. But I have Detective Williams' number programmed in my phone, I can call him for you," I bluff.

Asshole opened the door with an attitude, and I figured it was better to make sure I had his full attention. I think that was successful.

"You can't just come onto my property and attack me," he whines.

"You mean like you showed up at the rescue uninvited and threatened my woman?"

"I never laid a hand on her," he sputters.

"And we both know that's only because I showed up when I did."

I crouch down in front of him so I'm at eye level.

"Here's what I know; you've been socking away substantial amounts of money in an offshore bank account in Panama for the past five years. Deposited in cash. I don't know where it came from, but I'm pretty sure it would pique the interest of the IRS. Maybe even law enforcement."

What can I say? Sully is good. He found out the guy had frequent charges originating from Panama to his business credit card. Burns is a contractor and I'm pretty sure the guy has been doing jobs off the books, taking the cash, and stashing it in Panama. My guess is for a tax-free retirement or something.

His eyes dart around as his brain is looking for an escape. There is none, but I'll let him come to that conclusion by himself. I know he's reached it when his shoulders slump.

"What do you want from me?"

"You really need me to explain?" I grab him by the collar and pull him close. "You are scum—a fucking coward—and if I ever find out you threatened or touched your ex, my woman, or any other female again, I will ruin your reputation, destroy your company, and then I will take great pleasure in taking you apart piece by piece before I end you."

From the way he crab-walks backward the moment I let him go, I'm guessing he's taking me seriously. First smart thing he's done.

I straighten up, turn on my heel, and march back to my truck.

When I finally get home, it's already late and I have to get up at the crack of dawn again tomorrow. But my head is clear when it hits the pillow and I drift off into an untroubled sleep.

Seven

Bo

"Haven't seen you around much."

I spot Jonas's father, Thomas, sitting in the shade on the porch of the big house when I walk up the steps.

"I've been around," I tell him as I approach him and lean a hip against the railing.

"You tear out of here at the end of the day. You've got some hot young number you're hiding from us?"

The old geezer wiggles his eyebrows and I wince.

"Not exactly," I set him straight. "She's eighty-one and the only thing hot about her is her temper." At his confused expression, I feel compelled to clarify, "It's my mother. I've been checking in on her."

"You know, I meant to ask you about that. How come your mother lives in town and you never bring her out here?"

Seems like a simple question but I don't really have a simple answer.

"You know I grew up on a cattle ranch, right?" I wait for

Thomas's nod of confirmation. "My mother lost that ranch they'd worked so hard to keep going all those years, just months after my father died. By the time I got the news of his passing and rushed home, the ranch was already gone and Momma vowed never to set foot on another one again."

"Let me guess; you were young, didn't want to get tied down on the ranch, and went to chase adventure?"

That's not all of it but he's in the ballpark.

"Something like that."

"My Jonas was the same way." The old man chortles, his eyes almost disappearing in all the laugh lines on his face. "Didn't want a thing to do with ranching, and look at him now."

"Right."

I see the irony. Last place I thought I'd end up working was a ranch and yet, here I am. I just don't see what that has to do with my mother, but before I have a chance to steer the conversation back to her, the old man makes another observation.

"The fact you weren't there working shoulder to shoulder with your dad when he passed weighs on you."

"Sure it does."

As I'm sure it would with anyone.

Thomas leans forward, his elbows resting on his knees as he regards me seriously.

"Wanna know what I think?" he asks, but I'm pretty sure he doesn't need an answer. "I think you keeping your mom away from the ranch is not really for her sake, it's for yours."

"How do you figure?"

I fight to keep the annoyance out of my voice. Of course it's for Momma's sake.

"I think you're less worried about painful memories it

might bring to the surface for her, than you are of the feelings of guilt it might stir up for you," he pushes on, his eyes sharp and unwavering.

"Bullshit," I snap, uncomfortable his armchair psychoanalysis hits so close to the mark.

Guilt. The result of a series of questionable decisions made over twenty years ago that follow me to this day.

Thomas tilts his head to one side. "Is it?"

Like hell I'll give the smug old coot the satisfaction. Instead, I push away from the railing and tip my hat.

"Later, Thomas."

∾

Lucy

I catch myself checking the time again.

It's already seven thirty.

Stop it.

He's not coming, it's too late. Just because he's been dropping in almost daily after work—except for those two days over the weekend when the team was called in on a search, but he messaged to let me know—doesn't mean I should start counting on it.

It's ridiculous anyway; I'm playing with fire and I know it. Every time I see his taillights disappear, I'm resolved to put a stop to these visits, but then the next day comes and I find myself waiting for his truck to pull up.

I don't even know why he comes here. He never stays long, just long enough to give me a hand feeding the goats or anything else that needs doing, but each time he manages to steal a quick kiss. Sometimes no more than a peck on the top of my head, or a press of his lips to my cheek, but all of them high impact.

And I let it happen.

Oh, I pretend to be surprised and tell myself he's catching me off guard, but the truth is I'm getting used to it —to him. Worse, I've started to look forward to those seemingly innocent kisses.

Which is why—to my great annoyance—my eyes keep drifting to the clock hanging over the fridge. To distract myself I go out on the back porch to look in on the goats.

This past week it became clear the bathroom was too cramped for them—Midnight had started chewing the shower curtain and the baseboards—so I built them a temporary enclosure on the back porch. A bit of chicken wire stapled to the railing and the floor leaves them room to play, and the old feed drum on its side in the corner filled with straw makes for a warm shelter.

Not much left of that first foot of snow we got last week. It still warms up during the day, but the nights are getting colder. Winter is around the corner.

This morning Doc Evans came by to check on them. He was pleasantly surprised to see the little one strong enough to take a bottle and was happy with both their weight gain. He removed Mocha's feeding tube and suggested I start introducing both of them to dry food alongside the formula. It'll still be another month or two before it's time to wean them, but starting them on pellets early should make that transition easier.

"Finished already?"

The small food bowl is empty, but Mocha is still munching on a few spilled pellets. Midnight is standing with his front hooves up against the chicken wire, his focus on something out there, his little ears swiveling back and forth. When I sit down on the porch, he turns his attention to me, bouncing toward me, ready to pounce. At some point his smaller brother joins in to play, a little hesitant at first but quickly gaining confidence.

Then I hear the dogs alerting at the front of the house and I untangle myself from the goats, trying not to get my hopes up. As I make my way through the house to the front, the barking turns more frantic. That certainly doesn't sound like Bo, the dogs are used to him showing up by now. The moment I have the door open, Chief pushes outside, tearing down the porch steps and into the dusk with Scout close on his heels.

There is no sign of Bo's truck so I reach for the rifle hanging over the coatrack, the flashlight on a hook by the door, shove my feet in my boots, and follow the dogs outside. The two are heading toward the barn, and I start running when I hear the sound of hooves hitting barn boards.

The different scenarios swirl through my head as I make my way over. I don't smell any smoke, so fire is out, but it's possible a predator got into the barn. It would explain the dogs' fierce reaction and why they don't stop their stride as they scoot around the building. They're probably chasing off whatever spooked the animals.

When I come in and flick on the lights, Bella, the momma goat, has her front hooves up against the stall door and is peeking over, bleating anxiously. Ladybug and Ellie are the only horses left in the barn. The others I put with the rest of the herd in the back field. It's Ellie who seems most spooked, snorting and pawing at the floor of her stall, occasionally kicking against her enclosure.

"Easy, girl," I coo as I approach her.

Since the barn door stood open when I got here, I'm guessing it was that black bear I've seen roaming on the ridge out back scouring for food. They're smart animals and have been known to open doors, even car doors.

It's not often we get predators this close, but it's not unheard of. The bears are preparing for hibernation, trying to fatten up, but it hasn't been the best berry season this year. Supply is short, which may be why it was drawn to the smell of the feed. The lid is propped open on the bin holding the dry pellets, which supports my guess that's what they were after.

It takes me a couple of minutes to get Ellie calmed down. Then I check on Ladybug, who is munching on the fresh hay I left them earlier. This horse is truly unflappable, which is why she's perfect for the kind of work I trained her for. By the time I look in on Bella, the momma goat, the dogs wander into the barn.

"You chase him off? Good boys."

I reach down to pet them, pulling my hand back when I encounter something wet on Chief's head.

"Let me see, buddy," I mutter to him as I crouch down and notice the long fur by his ears is sticky and dark with blood. "Ouch. He got you good, didn't he?"

Could've been the swipe of a bear's claw he narrowly escaped. The dog has a decent gash on his head. I'm going to want to have a closer look at it inside. If he needs stitches, I'll have to take him into the emergency clinic in town, which is the last thing I want to do because it means a long wait when I have animals here to tend to.

And now I also have a rogue bear to worry about. Now he's discovered an easy food source in his desperation, he's bound to be back. I'm going to have to be vigilant and contact the game warden's office to give them a heads-up. I should let Fletch and Nella know, and warn the guys at High Meadow as well. They're my two closest neighbors.

"Let's go inside, guys," I tell the dogs, leading the way to the house.

Under the bright light in my bathroom, I'm able to examine Chief's wound better and clean it out. It's a bit ragged, but luckily it doesn't look too deep. I can probably close it up with some WoundSeal from my emergency kit.

"You're such a good boy," I praise.

There's the slightest tremble in his muscles—I'm sure the cleaning hurt him—but he hasn't moved, enduring my prying and prodding patiently.

After I've patched him up as best I can, I feed both dogs and the goats, before I put water on for tea and start making my phone calls. It's after hours, so the game warden's office is closed but I leave a message they'll get in the morning. Next, I get hold of my neighbors, giving both Nella and Jonas a heads-up about a possible bear roaming for food. By the time I sit down with a quick peanut butter and jelly sandwich and a cup of tea, it's already close to nine.

Then the dogs take up their barking again, but this time their tails are wagging as they wait by the front door. The beam from headlights hits the living room wall as a vehicle pulls up to the house. I know who it is even before I hear the heavy boots coming up the porch steps. I'm annoyed at the surge of excitement buzzing in my blood.

I jump to my feet at the sharp knock.

"Are you all right?" Bo asks, his eyes scanning me top to toe when I open the door.

∾

Bo

She looks to be in one piece.

We'd been saying our goodbyes when Jonas took Lucy's call. While Momma was bantering in the hallway with Thomas, like she'd done all through dinner, Jonas filled me in.

After Thomas called me out earlier, I drove straight to my mother's place and asked her if she wanted to come to High Meadow for dinner. You'd think she won the goddamn lottery, she smiled so big. That old son of a bitch was right; it wasn't Momma who was averse to coming to the ranch.

The woman put on lipstick, for crying out loud. I'd hate to think how long she'd had it for—pretty sure it passed its expiration date years ago—but when she applied some with a shaky hand, I didn't have the heart to point out she'd missed her lips in some spots. Instead, I shot Jonas a quick text telling him there'd be two more for dinner, there's always enough food for a battalion.

I left Momma waiting in the vehicle. All I told her was that I needed to check in on a friend. The meaningful look she sent me warned me she'd have her questions ready for me when I get back to the truck.

"I'm fine. What are you even doing here? I wasn't expecting you."

Maybe so, but she looked almost relieved when she opened the door.

I feel a bit guilty for not shooting her a text to check in, like I've done any night I haven't been able to stop by here. I'd been so wrapped up in what the old man threw at my feet, I wasn't thinking straight. When Jonas mentioned

Lucy had some trouble with a bear, I hustled Momma into the truck and floored it over here.

Pretty sure my abrupt departure was noted, word will spread, and I'll end up getting flack from the guys. I guess it was inevitable, after years of taking great pleasure in needling my brothers about their love life, they'd eventually find cause for payback. I have to admit I probably deserve it.

Lucy's still waiting for my answer, but I feel a strong urge to kiss her first. All too aware of my mother's hawk eyes registering every detail of this encounter from the passenger seat of my truck, I back Lucy into the house with a hand on her hip. Then I close the door behind me, slide my hand under her hair and around the back of her neck, and tug her to me for a hard, relieved kiss on her shocked lips.

"Jonas said you had a run-in with a bear," I finally respond as I reluctantly let go of her surprised mouth.

"Not exactly," she says, looking down at the dogs who are circling her legs. "These guys did. Chief was hurt."

I look at the shepherd and notice the wound on his head. Crouching down in front of him I grab him by the scruff and pull him a little closer so I can have a better look.

"You cleaned it."

"Yeah. It wasn't that deep so I used that wound glue."

I glance up at her. "You did a good job." I run my hands along the dog's sides. "Is he hurt anywhere else?"

"No, he was lucky. Damn bear got into the barn and the feed box. Freaked the horses. The dogs alerted and chased him off."

"Call the game warden?"

Lucy cocks a hip and plants her fist in her side, a scowl on her face.

"I'm not an idiot. Of course I did," she clips. "I'm not a

rookie, Bo. Nor am I new to roaming wildlife. I even took the shotgun with me."

Her tone is slightly sarcastic, guessing that whether or not she brought protection when she went to explore would've been the next thing I'd have asked.

I'm about to give into the temptation to kiss the stubborn pout off her lips when the dogs start growling low in their throats. I'm immediately on alert but before I can react, a knock sounds at the door.

"Beauregard James Rivera! Open this door. You leave your momma in the cold truck? What the heck is wrong with you?"

Fuck.

With my hand on the knob, I turn my head to look at Lucy, who has a sardonic look on her face.

"Prepare yourself," I warn her. "That woman is a lot."

Then I pull open the door.

Completely dismissing me, Momma's eyes shoot to the woman beside me. Doesn't surprise me, my mother probably got a glimpse of her when Lucy first opened the door and nosiness got her out of the truck and onto the porch.

"Well, aren't you a little thing?" my five-foot-nothing mother tells Lucy, ignoring me and the dogs, who sense she's harmless and look for some attention instead.

"Hi, umm, you must be Mrs. Rivera," Lucy says a little uneasily, offering her hand.

Momma looks at it like it's a bug. I scrape my throat in a warning my mother luckily responds to by taking Lucy's offer.

Instead of responding to Lucy, Momma holds on to her hand as she turns to me. Before she even opens her mouth, I know she's going to make me regret not taking the time to drop her at home first.

"Again? You sure about this, Son? Remember what happened last time?"

"That's enough, Ma."

But when I look at Lucy, I can see confusion and surprised concern staring back at me.

Fuck.

Eight

LUCY

I can't stop thinking about last night's unexpected encounter with Bo's mother.

It was kind of weird and a little unsettling. She didn't exactly give off warm vibes, and when I tried to be polite and invited her in, she all but grabbed her son and beelined it off my porch.

What did she mean, *"Remember what happened last time?"* Last time? I'm pretty sure I've never met her before. Or do I remind her of someone else?

But what really threw me about the strange encounter was Bo's reaction. He couldn't have looked more guilty if he'd had the word tattooed on his forehead. Guilty about what?

He escorted his mom to the truck and came back to the base of the porch steps, barely looking at me as he tried to order me around. Like hell I'm going to lock my doors, call for help as I cower inside, and wait for him to come to the rescue next time I hear something outside. What if something was harming my animals? Not going to happen, which is what I would've told him if he'd waited around long enough. Instead, he marched off without even glancing my way, got behind the wheel, and drove off.

His first message came through fifteen minutes later, which I ignored before turning my ringer off and flipping my phone facedown. I was too annoyed to deal with him.

I still am now, after a restless night spent tossing and turning, but I know the pounding on my door won't let up until I talk to him.

"What?" I snap, yanking the door open to find Bo on my doorstep, his hat in one hand and the other rubbing his shiny, black head.

After rolling around all night, I'm sure I don't make a pretty picture, but I don't frankly care. His dark eyes scan me from the rat's nest on my head down to the fringed cuffs of my flannel PJ pants brushing the top of my bare feet. Then he fixes an inscrutable look on my face.

"You're not answering your phone," he grumbles, grabbing my hips with both hands and moving me to the side as he walks into my house.

"How observant of you," I sneer, following him into my kitchen where he picks up my cell, which was still on the counter where I left it last night.

He turns the display toward me. Eight new messages and four missed calls. All from Bo.

A little niggle of guilt makes its way into my thoughts.

"Dropped my mother at her apartment and was on my way back here when Jonas called. A twelve-year old girl missing. The first message was to let you know." He points at the screen. "The next ones were to keep you updated when I realized you might otherwise be worried." He snorts derisively as if the thought alone is ridiculous. "The four phone calls followed after, when I started to worry about you not responding."

He tosses my phone back on the counter, his face an impassive mask as he looks at me. "I see my concern was wasted."

The cold tone is unfamiliar coming from him and cuts through my thick protective layer like butter to the tender flesh underneath.

Then he walks toward the door and leaves me standing in the middle of the kitchen, my heart aching, and my throat painfully tight. I catch him going down the steps.

"Wait! Did you find her?"

He stops, his head dropping forward, accentuating the wide expanse of his shoulders. He looks burdened and I have to strain to hear his response.

"Three hours ago."

"Was she..." I can't make myself finish the sentence.

"Alive," he says, and I'm about to breathe a sigh of relief when he adds, "for what it's worth after what was done to her."

I'm instantly bombarded with mental images that send shock waves through my system. *Oh no*...only twelve years old. I fight off the sudden nausea and focus on Bo's back. No wonder he looks and sounds defeated. My sleepless night and early morning snit are instantly forgotten as I hurt for the little girl, as well as the man in front of me.

"Please, Bo," I plead, stepping out on the cold porch in my bare feet. I feel horrible. "Come in. Let me put on a pot of coffee."

He turns toward me, his face barely visible in the faint light of dawn. I have no idea what he's thinking so I repeat, "Please."

I'm shivering with cold and am about to give up when he finally moves to face me fully.

"Get inside before you freeze to death."

I resist the knee-jerk reaction to argue with him and head indoors, which is what I was about to do anyway. Relieved, I hear his heavy boots follow me. I keep my back to him as I head straight for the coffee maker, putting on a large pot. Then I duck into the fridge to pull out eggs, ham, and some leftover roasted vegetables. The makings of a hearty omelet.

It's not until I have the butter sizzling in a frying pan and the coffee maker signals a full pot with a gurgle, I glance at him. Bo is sitting at the table, absentmindedly scratching Chief's head, his wary eyes following me around the kitchen.

"Toast?"

It takes him a moment to respond. "Sure."

I pull my bread from the freezer, pop two pieces in the toaster, and pour the coffee. Taking one mug over to Bo, I set it on the table in front of him but when I try to walk away, he snags my wrist in his large hand.

"Thank you," he mumbles.

"No problem." I gently twist my arm loose. "Let me get the omelet going."

I've never seen Bo like this before; down and dark. It's a side of him I don't recognize and I wonder if I should be worried.

"She threw herself off a cliff to escape her attackers," he says when I crack the eggs in a bowl.

It takes everything I have not to stop what I'm doing for fear he'll stop talking.

"They left her for dead."

"More than one," I can't help whisper in disbelief.

"Two," he confirms. "She managed to tell us that much before she passed out. We found her not far from the suspension bridge over the Kootenai Falls."

"Is she going to be okay?"

I look over to catch him shrug his shoulders.

"Physically...probably."

I have my answer in what he leaves out and my mind starts spinning. By the time I sit down across from him with my breakfast, I know I want to do something for her if I can.

"I want to help her."

He puts his fork down and scrutinizes me through narrowed eyes.

"What makes you think you can?"

I swallow hard, forcing the next words from my mouth.

"I've been where she is."

~

Bo

It takes a couple of moments for her words to register.

Then the penny drops and I surge to my feet. The scrape of my chair on the wooden floor is loud, startling the dogs who bark in reaction. Lucy shoots straight in her chair, wrapping her arms around herself protectively.

Still, she juts her chin out, a picture of strength and defiance.

"Sit down, Bo," she snaps at me. "It's ancient history. Don't make me regret I brought it up which, by the way, I only did to show I wasn't making an empty offer. I know what I'm talking about."

I lean my hands on the table and drop my head.

"Jesus, Luce," I mutter, reining in the anger burning through my veins. "Fucking hell."

Suddenly Lucy's face is superimposed on the image of that girl burned into my retinas. Her small body bloody and broken. *Christ.* I curb the urge to rage at the injustice.

"I'm fine. Like I said, old news."

I lift my head and meet her steady, blue eyes. "Not to me," I point out and watch as her expression softens.

"Trust me, it's best left in the past. Sit down and eat your omelet, Bo. You need to eat."

It's her calm tone that cools the hot blood raging through my veins and has me sink back down on my chair. What was a delicious omelet moments ago now tastes like sawdust, but I force myself to eat it for Lucy's sake.

I drop my fork on the empty plate, plant my elbows on the table, and fold my hands under my chin as I watch Lucy finish her breakfast.

"I'll pass your offer on to Sheriff Ewing," I finally say. "He knows the family."

The poor kid's gonna need all the help she can get to overcome the trauma she was subjected to. I'm never going to forget the way she clung onto me when I lifted her into the rescue basket.

"Appreciate it."

She gets to her feet and gathers the empty dishes, carrying them to the sink. I follow her with my eyes. Her ratty and shapeless outfit surprisingly enticing with the promise of those soft curves underneath. Lucy may be small in stature but she packs a punch. A core of steel, comfortably padded in all the right places, all of which has been the source of fantasies for longer than I care to admit.

I shake my head and squeeze the bridge of my nose

between my fingers, suddenly feeling like a pervert lusting after her, in light of what I just found out. I'm tired, feel conflicted, and no longer sure what I'm doing here.

Even last night I was so sure what the right path was, until one misguided comment from my mother shook the solid ground I thought I had under my feet. She and I had a heart-to-heart after I whisked her out of here, but the damage was already done. Then the team got called out before I had a chance to do any damage control and, to top it off, Lucy wasn't answering my calls.

By the time I showed up on Lucy's doorstep this morning, I'd already been spinning and that hasn't improved since.

"You should go home and get some rest," the subject of my thoughts suggests.

Probably not a bad idea. The likelihood of me making any good decisions at this point are slim to none. Safer to keep it for another day when I have my wits about me.

I hum my agreement and make my way to the door, feeling her follow close behind. The moment I have it open, the dogs scoot around my legs to get outside, almost tripping me as I step onto the porch.

"Thanks for breakfast."

There's a lot more I should be saying as I look down at her face—maybe an apology for showing up on her doorstep angry to start with, or disappearing after Momma spouted off—but I'm afraid I'll only bungle it, doing more damage than good.

"No problem," she mumbles, looking a little forlorn standing in the door opening.

I get the impression there's more she wants to say but when nothing's forthcoming I walk down the steps.

"Bo?"

I whip around. "Yeah?"

She seems startled and gives her head a little shake.

"It'll wait. Drive safely."

Before I can say anything in response she disappears inside, closing the door behind her.

"Apparently she lied about her age."

My hands clench into fists in my pockets.

"That's no fucking excuse," I snap.

Jonas raises an eyebrow at my outburst. "Didn't say it was, just passing on what Ewing reported. The good news is, she should make a full recovery and the two sons of bitches who did this to her were picked up and will face some serious jail time."

Not sure how much of a comfort that will be to Amelia Mills, but I guess it's better than having them still out there.

"Fair enough," I concede. "Thanks for letting me know."

"No problem," he says with a nod. "Staying for dinner?"

"Nah. Got a few things to take care of."

I leave him in his office and make my way out to my truck.

It's been three days since we found the girl at the bottom of a cliff, the experience still fresh in my mind. I thought knowing what happened would help put events into some context, but it doesn't.

The fact she misrepresented her age online—her profile claimed her to be sixteen instead of twelve—in no way takes away from the depravity of the twenty-one and twenty-four-year-old fuckers who thought it was okay to lure a minor to a remote spot and wouldn't take her no for an answer.

86

It fucking burns a hole in my gut.

It's also been three days since I've seen Lucy and that doesn't sit well with me either. With every day that passes that particular bridge becomes harder to cross. I know it's on me to clear up a few things—even if I wanted to, my mother is not about to let me forget, she's called me every day to remind me—but it would require talking about a part of my life I prefer to leave in the past where it belongs.

It's a can Momma inadvertently opened in her concern for me. Misplaced, as she realizes after I chewed her out, but it's too late to take it back. Which means I owe Lucy an explanation I'm afraid might blow whatever chance I may have had with her.

I'm afraid I've delayed the inevitable long enough and when my headlights hit the sign for Hart's Horse Rescue, I put my foot on the brake.

Nine

LUCY

"Easy, girl..."

I watch Doc Evans run a hand along Ladybug's trembling flank.

She was fine earlier today when I fetched her from the front field where she spent the past couple of days with Ellie, Hope and her colt, as well as Daisy. I didn't notice anything wrong when my client was riding her. She seemed fine when I fed her earlier. It made sense to keep her in the stable overnight since Samantha would be here for her session in the morning.

I'd gone in the house to check on the stew I threw in the Crockpot this morning and give the goats their bottle. I was almost out of formula and went back to the barn to grab some more when I noticed something was wrong with the mare. Her head hung low, tilted to one side, her eyes looked wild and her entire body was shaking. Fecal matter was literally dripping down her rear legs and her breathing was labored.

"Take my keys," the vet says, tossing them over with his free hand. "I need you to hook up your trailer to my truck and back it as close to the barn doors as you can."

"Poisoned?" I want to confirm my suspicions.

"Looks like. She's in bad shape. I need to get her to the clinic as fast as possible."

I don't waste any more time asking questions and run to get Doc's truck.

Poison.

It could be anything. There are plenty of toxic plants that could make a horse sick but we check the pastures frequently, and normally the horses are careful what they eat. Of course, they could accidentally ingest something, but there are only a few things that would cause the severity of symptoms Ladybug is displaying.

Shit. What about the other animals?

Even as I back the truck up to the horse trailer, my eyes search the shadows in the darkening field. First, we need to get Ladybug taken care of, then I can check on the others. I should probably call Alex but I have my hands full trying to hook the trailer to Doc's hitch.

I finally manage to get the trailer's coupler over the ball mount, lock the lever, attach the safety chain, and hook up the electrical. Then I slip behind the wheel and back the trailer up to the barn doors.

Headlights come up the driveway as I drop the ramp on the trailer. Maybe Doc called for help.

"Grab me a horse blanket," he calls out, and I snatch one from the tack room. "We're gonna fold it, wrap it behind her rear and grab a firm hold on either side. We can use it for leverage."

No sooner do we have the blanket in place when Bo comes jogging in.

"What's wrong?"

"Good. We're gonna need the muscle. Take Lucy's place," Doc says, ignoring the question.

Bo doesn't hesitate and bumps me out of the way. Forced to stand back, I'm suddenly hit with the realization I might well lose Ladybug. The poor horse is barely able to stay on her feet as the men physically heave her up the ramp and into the trailer.

"Lucy, call the clinic and let Bruce know I'm on my way."

"I'll come," I tell him.

"No. I need you to move the other animals out of that pasture until we know for sure what she ingested. Bo can help."

Before I can object, he gets behind the wheel and slams the door shut. Bo is already locking the ramp in place.

"Got flashlights?"

"Tack room. I've gotta give Alex a call."

I grab a couple of leads off the hook by the barn door and dial Alex's number. She answers just as Bo comes out of the tack room and lights our way, as we start walking toward the pasture while I get Alex up to date.

"I'll head over to the clinic but will send one of the guys over to give you a hand," she offers right away.

"That's okay, Bo is already here. He's helping me move the other animals inside so I can keep an eye on them."

"Good. Call if you have an update, I'll do the same."

I see Daisy first, or rather, she sees us and comes trotting up. She brays in greeting, nudging me with her soft nose. I clip one of the leads to her halter and hand the other to Bo. He walks up to Hope who is standing by the fence, shielding her foal. So far no one looks ill. I can't see Ellie but when I whistle through my teeth she appears on the far side of the field, her head high and ears sharp.

"Hey, girl," I call out. "Time to come in."

Bo starts walking Hope toward the barn, Floyd, her colt, trotting beside her. I turn to follow them leading Daisy. I'm not worried about putting a lead on Ellie, she'll trail behind us.

In the barn, I tuck Daisy into her stall when I hear Bo bark out a firm, "No."

When I swing around, I see him rushing after Ellie, who decided to wander into Ladybug's stall. He grabs her halter and leads her toward her own stall, locking her inside. Then he catches sight of my raised eyebrow as he's latching Ladybug's door.

"Until we know for sure what made your other horse sick, it's best to keep this stall closed off."

I nod, it makes sense, although I can't imagine anything in here that could make Ladybug sick. The horses were stabled a few days ago without any issues, and Bella, the goat, has been in the barn the whole time. She looks perfectly healthy to me.

Still, I won't be able to rest until Doc Evans figures out what is wrong with her, and in the meantime, I'm holding vigil right here in the barn.

May as well make myself comfortable, so I head over to the stack of hay bales next to the tack room when I notice the box of formula I came in here for in the first place.

"Shit! The babies..."

"Sorry?"

"The babies, the goats, I was about to feed them when I noticed there was something wrong with Ladybug. That was almost two hours ago. They must be starving!"

"Are they in the house?"

"Yeah, on the back porch."

I'm torn, it's going to take me a while to feed the kids and I really want to stay close to my horses. Bo seems to sense my struggle and makes a suggestion.

"Why don't I go get them. We'll just feed them here."

Bo

"Whoa, buddy."

I struggle to hold on to Midnight's squirmy body as he attacks the bottle with fervor. Across from me, Lucy is facing a similar battle with the other little one. Her eyes find my grin and one side of her mouth pulls up in a shared moment of amusement.

By the time I entered the barn with the two pitifully bleating baby goats tucked under my arms and a couple of empty bottles tucked in my pockets, Lucy had already made a makeshift pen with hay bales placed in a circle on the barn floor, with a couple of blankets tossed in the middle.

Sitting on the floor with my back against one of the bales and my legs stretched out in front of me is far from comfortable, but I'm not moving. Not going to leave Lucy by herself, and I'll sit here all night if I have to.

Lucy's horse, Ellie, pokes her head over the half-door to her stall, lifting her snout in the air and whinnying softly.

"You have to wait," Lucy tells her. "We'll get you something to eat as soon as we're done with the babies."

We. I like the sound of that.

Hell, I enjoy listening to her talk to the animals any

time, there's an easiness about her when she interacts with them. In contrast to when she's dealing with people, then she's guarded and bristly.

"What?"

I wipe the grin off my face and shake my head. "Nothing."

Not the time or place for the flirty banter I'd like to engage in with her.

Midnight is done with his bottle first, so I let him go and get to my feet, wincing at the creaking sound my knees make.

"One scoop?" I ask, lifting the lid on the feed bin.

"Yeah." But when I dip the wooden scoop in the bin she calls out, "Wait!"

Then she scrambles to her feet, putting the startled baby goat down, and rushes to my side. She shoves her hand inside the feed bin and scoops out some of the pellets.

"I need more light."

The overhead light we flipped on earlier illuminates the center aisle in the barn, but leaves this corner by the tack room in the shade. I drop the scoop and head for the hook by the barn doors where I hung the flashlight when we came in.

Flicking on the light, I shine it over her shoulder on the food she's rolling in her palm. I don't see anything particularly unusual about it.

"What are you thinking?"

Her eyes flick up at my face.

"I gave Ladybug a scoop earlier when I stabled her." She refocuses on the pellets in her hand, rubbing her thumb over their surface. "Remember the bear earlier in the week? I assumed it was anyway, when I found the lid of the bin up. It made sense, I'd seen a bear roaming around, the animals

94

were freaked out, and it sounded like the dogs were chasing something toward the creek in the back. Now I wonder..."

"You think someone was in here," I guess, doing my damnedest to control the sudden surge of rage.

Someone was in Lucy's barn, messing with her animals, her livelihood.

Who? That sniveling coward I paid a visit to the other day? Dwight Burns? I'd been so sure I got my message across last week. Fuck, the man was about to piss his pants when I left him. Is it possible he's stupid enough to go after Lucy's business? Maybe I should pay him another visit.

Dammit, I hate to think what might've happened had she caught whoever was in here.

"See this?" She drops the pellets back in the bin and rubs a powdery residue between her fingers. "This is too fine to be from broken up feed."

She lifts her hand to her face and sniffs. Her nose instantly scrunches up. Then she offers it for me to smell. I wince as a slightly acrid scent—reminiscent of cat piss—burns the inside of my nose.

"What the hell is that?"

"Not sure, but I'm giving Doc Evans a call."

I listen as she asks the vet how Ladybug is doing. From the expression on her face, I'm guessing not much has improved in the horse's condition. She goes on to describe what she found in the feed bin.

"Yew?" Her head swings around to face me, brows arching high above her questioning eyes. "That could be. It's poisonous...Yes, I know...No, as far as I know we don't, but even if we did, it wouldn't explain how it ended up in powder form in my feed bin."

I don't need to hear any more to know it's time to call in law enforcement. While Lucy is still talking with the vet, I dial Wayne Ewing's cell. He answers right away and I quickly explain the situation. Despite the time of night—it's already close to ten—the sheriff promises he's on his way.

When I tuck my phone back in my pocket and turn around, I find Lucy looking at me pissed.

"I was gonna do that."

She doesn't sound happy which doesn't faze me much.

"Don't doubt that. You'd probably have ended up talking to the dispatcher, who'd have sent out the first available deputy, which likely wouldn't have been until sometime tomorrow."

"And?" she challenges.

I shrug my shoulders, I don't see what the big deal is, but the fact I stepped in apparently has her all bent out of shape.

"I have Ewing's direct number, I used it, and as a result he's on his way right now," I explain what makes perfect sense to me.

Lucy mumbles something unintelligible in response as she turns her back and heads for the sink next to the tack room to wash her hands.

"You'd better do the same before you touch anything else," she says over her shoulder. "Doc thinks it may be yew, which is as toxic to people as it is to animals."

I only hesitate for a moment before sidling up to her at the sink.

Ten

"This is getting ridiculous."

I glare at Bo who, for the third night in a row, has chosen to camp out on my back porch with the baby goats.

I hadn't even realized he was there the first night. He was walking the sheriff to his cruiser and I went inside and locked the door. Ewing had suggested we move all the animals out of the barn again so he could come back in the morning to process any evidence in daylight, so it had already been well past midnight and I was wiped.

That was the first time I discovered Bo in a sleeping bag, cuddled up with the goats on the back porch, when I stepped out there at the crack of dawn to let the dogs out. He scared the crap out of me and gave me some excuse of wanting to keep an eye out. *Ridiculous*. Then same thing happened yesterday morning. Again, I told him I was perfectly fine by myself and hoped I got through, but I guess I didn't.

"Morning," he croaks, reaching one hand to rub his bald

head under the beanie he's wearing to keep warm, while he distractedly pats the passing dogs with the other.

"Ugh," I mutter disgustedly. I turn back to go inside, adding right before I shut the door, "Coffee in the pot."

It's the first freaking day of November and—although we haven't had snow since that one storm a few weeks ago—the temperatures have been steadily falling. The weather forecast said it was supposed to go down to twenty-eight degrees last night. Those goats and the hay may provide a little warmth, but you can't tell me the man didn't freeze his balls off out there. It'd serve him right.

I shiver, dropping a pan on the stove. Then I toss in some rolled oats, a pinch of salt, a splash of maple syrup, some cinnamon, and almond milk, adding a sliced banana. That's what this morning needs, a good, stick-to-your-ribs breakfast.

I sip my coffee and stir the bubbling oatmeal, my mouth watering at the smell. I'd almost forgotten about Bo until he walks in the door. He heads straight for the bathroom, giving me a few minutes to get my flare of irritation under control. If I want this to end, I need to stop being reactive and start formulating good arguments.

Bo may be protective to a fault, but he's not unreasonable. He just thinks I am, so I need to show him otherwise.

When he returns, he aims straight for the coffee maker.

"Smells good," he comments.

I almost tell him to go find his own damn breakfast but swallow it down just in time.

"Would you like some?" I offer instead.

The effort costs me and doesn't go unnoticed by Bo. Not much does.

"You sure?" His question is rife with skepticism, which also annoys me.

Heck. Who am I kidding? Everything about this man annoys me.

In lieu of a response, I slap some oatmeal in a bowl and hand it to him, plastering what I hope to be a friendly smile on my face.

"Look," I start after waiting for him to take his first bite. With his mouth full he has no choice but to listen. "I appreciate you looking out for me, but it's really not necessary for you to sleep out in the cold every night."

"Are you inviting me to sleep inside?" he asks, clearly not hindered by a full mouth.

"What? No. I'm not." I press my fingers to my forehead to regain control. "What I'm saying is I've looked after myself for many years. I don't like guns, but I have one and know how to use it. Also, I have two dogs who would likely rip anyone who poses a danger to shreds."

I'm encouraged when he takes another bite of my oatmeal instead of arguing with me and quickly press on.

"I'm sure you have better things to do than waste time babysitting me. I'm sure your mother needs you more." His head snaps up but before he can react, I hammer home my final point. "Besides, I have the alarm system Alex insisted we have installed. In case of a breech, a notification is sent to High Meadow and the ranch is virtually next door."

He pushes away from where he was leaning a hip against the counter, dumps his now empty bowl in the sink, and turns to pin me with a pointed look.

"That only works if you activate the alarm."

I fight not to roll my eyes. Of course. It shouldn't be a surprise he'd know I haven't set it in months. There's been no reason to, although maybe it would've been smart after Dwight Burns showed up unannounced, but I'm not about to admit that to him.

"Which I will do faithfully from here on in," I promise solemnly, making the sign of the cross for emphasis, even though I've never seen the inside of a church.

"Will you—" he starts, when the ringing of his phone interrupts.

To give him some privacy, I take the pan with the leftover oatmeal, grab a spoon, and head out on the back porch to keep an eye out for the dogs. I haven't eaten much before the pitiful bleating of the two hungry goats has me put down my breakfast and prepare theirs.

My hands are freezing as I scoop some of the small pellets into their shallow feeding bowl. Breakfast is kibble because they're hungry enough not to care what they eat. If I'd started with formula—which they still much prefer—they wouldn't even try the dry food. On Doc Evans's advice, I've started weaning them, but it's a slow process. During the days I put them in a small pen on the grass behind the house so they can graze and play, and at night they get their beloved bottle.

The dogs appear from a small cluster of trees on the right and I whistle sharply between my teeth. Both heads snap in my direction as they start trotting home.

"You shouldn't be out here without a coat," Bo's deep voice sounds behind me.

It's all I can do not to roll my eyes. How's that for hypocrisy? It's apparently perfectly all right for him to spend the night on my goddamn porch, but not for me to step out for less than five minutes?

Please, spare me.

If it wasn't for the dogs now wanting inside for their breakfast, I'd stay out here a little longer in protest. Ignoring Bo, I slip past him inside and fill the dogs' bowls.

"I have to go. The sheriff and the game warden are

trying to track down a missing camper near the dam and called us in to help." His scraggly face cracks into a smile and I try not to be charmed, failing miserably as he teases, "I'd love nothin' more than to continue our discussion, but I need to make a quick call to reschedule my mother's appointment at the clinic."

Without any kind of thought process or filter, I blurt out, "I can take her."

What the hell is wrong with me?

The only explanation I can come up with is that I've been pretty bored these past couple of days. Once the sheriff was done looking for evidence and pulling my entire feed bin out of the barn, it took me all of a couple of hours to give the stalls a thorough cleaning, rig up a new bin for the pellets, and put a new padlock on the door. But with Ladybug still being monitored at Doc Evans' clinic and an ongoing investigation into what happened, I was forced to cancel my clients for this week.

I've been twiddling my thumbs.

"Are you sure? It's not why I mention—"

I quiet him with a wave of my hand, noting he looks a little uneasy again.

"Positive." I might as well, I don't have anything better to do. "Tell me when and where."

Honestly? It's probably the least I can do. Not that I needed it, but the man did spend the past three nights on my porch holding vigil.

Besides, maybe I can finally find out what his mother meant with, 'not again,' when she showed up at my door. I haven't found the appropriate opening to ask Bo and he's not volunteering.

Maybe his mom will.

Bo

Fuck.

Last thing I wanted was to put Lucy and Momma in close proximity before I had a chance to clear the air, but if I'd turned down Lucy's offer, it would only have made her more suspicious.

I hope Momma doesn't go spilling the whole sordid story with her usual flair for drama. Pretty sure that won't help my case.

Now I wish I'd tackled this issue head-on instead of procrastinating, using anything and everything as an excuse not to talk to her. Guess I'd hoped maybe I could've gotten her to open up to me a little, get her a bit more invested before exposing the dark stain on my past. It'll probably just give her another reason not to let me in.

Fuck.

"Bo! Watch it!"

I sharply pull back on Blue's reins, causing him to rear up. His left front hoof lands inches from a massive jaw trap that could've snapped his leg in half.

"Jesus!"

I need to start paying attention before I get my damn horse killed.

"I fucking hate trapping," I grumble, taking one last look at the rusty metal claws on the trap before easing Blue around it. "Should be outlawed."

"You won't get an argument from me, but fuck, man... watch where you're going," Fletch grumbles as he moves his ride ahead.

Instead of following him, I dismount and grab a broken tree branch. Not much I can do about trapping in general but I can make sure this one isn't a threat anymore. The jaws slam shut with a loud clang when I touch the trigger plate with the branch, snapping it clean in half.

"Feel better?" Sully inquires when I get back on Blue.

He wears a smirk when I glance over.

"Some."

"She's a handful, that Lucy," he feels compelled to point out. "I can see how she might have you distracted."

"Whatever, man," I try to dismiss him, but Sully's not done.

"I'm guessing you didn't get in there yet? You seem a little tense."

"That's because you're getting on my fucking nerves," I grind out between clenched teeth, annoyed I'm letting him get to me.

"Yeah, you sound a little backed up," he pushes. "Trust me, once you break that seal, you'll find your balance. Although, since we're talking about Lucy, there's a distinct possibility you'll never get in."

It's the hearty chuckle that follows which snaps my control.

"Seriously, brother, fuck the hell off."

"Hey! You two about fuckin' done?" Jonas barks from behind us. "We've got a missing camper out here some-where, who may be injured. Can we try to find him before this rescue turns into a fuckin' recovery?"

Nothing like a dressing down by your commander to slam your head back in the game. Jonas is more a friend and a brother these days, but when he uses that tone, it's like we're back in enemy territory and he's responsible for keeping all of our asses alive.

I mumble an apology, duly scolded, but Sully just grins, pleased as fuck he got me riled. *Asshole*.

My mood hasn't improved much three hours later when we take a break to give the horses a rest and a chance to get watered up.

We've made our way up from the Souse Gulch recreation area to the McGillivray campground along the shore of Lake Koocanusa. The six-and-a-half-mile stretch would have taken us maybe fifteen or twenty minutes on the logging road in a vehicle, but on horseback—taking into account the often-rough terrain—it took us a hell of a lot longer to traverse.

James and Sully are exploring a rock formation a few hundred yards up ahead on foot, while Fletch, Jonas, and I look after the horses.

"So what's going on with you and Lucy? Alex mentioned something."

Fletch grunts and, with a disgusted glare at Jonas, walks off and out of earshot. The guy is like butter around Nella and baby, Hunter, but a cranky bear to the rest of the world.

"Keeping an eye out for her, that's all," I downplay before turning the tables on him. "And how is Alex anyway? Has she forgiven you for selling the colts?"

From his deep sigh, I conclude that issue hasn't been resolved yet.

"Ludwig called last week. He's happy with the colts and is apparently heading this way again next week."

"He wants to buy more?"

"Maybe. Not necessarily from High Meadow though. He's got somebody checking out what's on offer with a bunch of breeders here in Montana, as well as Idaho and Washington. Wants my help filtering through the prospects." He tips back his hat and runs a hand over his head. "Alex is determined to hate the guy, which makes me working with him a bit awkward."

Hating him may be a bit much, but I can see where his woman is coming from. The trainer seems a bit too arrogant, too slick, and too polished. Not someone I'd hang out with for a beer and a good talk.

"He's not exactly the most pleasant of individuals," I defend Alex.

He glances at me sharply. "You too? He doesn't need to be my best friend for me to be able to work with him," he argues a point I'm sure he's brought up at home.

Not sure I agree with it—I don't think I'd be able to—but maybe that's why I don't run my own business and prefer to work for someone else who can worry about shit like that.

"Anyway," he continues. "I'll be traveling around to the different breeders with him in the next week or two, which won't make Alex happy. I know Sully is around at the ranch, but I'd appreciate it if you kept an eye out as well while I'm on the road."

I'm guessing he's asking me to keep an eye on Alex, and suddenly his question about my status with Lucy makes more sense. The two places Alex spends the most time is at the ranch or at the rescue. If I'm involved with Lucy, I'll not only be working at the ranch but would have reason to spend time at the rescue as well.

"No problem. I plan to be around," I assure him.

"Great. Now all that's left is to tell her," he mutters, making it clear he's not looking forward to it.

Kind of like I feel needing to address something I know Lucy might not take kindly to with her.

That is, if my mother hasn't taken care of that for me.

Eleven

LUCY

Wow.

I get equal waves of suspicion and curiosity coming off the small but fierce woman sitting beside me in my truck. It took a bit to help her into the seat and she commented her son's truck was much easier to get into.

That was the first of a number of borderline snarky comments designed to let me know how special her relationship with Bo is. It's almost like she can't help herself, needing to establish top ranking. Well, don't worry, lady, I have no designs on your precious son.

Or so I keep telling myself.

Sure, I enjoyed the few kisses we shared, and I'm not going to deny he makes me feel things I haven't allowed myself to in a long time, but I can't risk getting sucked in any further. My passenger's obvious distrust of me only underwrites that.

"Is that your natural color?"

I glance sideways and catch her blinking her eyes innocently as she indicates my hair, which is currently hanging down my shoulder in a braid.

"It is. I've always been a blonde."

"Hmm."

I bite my lip not to say something snide. If I'd known the woman's appointment was in Kalispell—an hour-and-a-half drive versus ten minutes—I might've thought twice before offering. I want to be ticked at Bo, but I don't really have anyone but myself to blame.

We still have about half an hour to go before we get there. My patience is hanging on by a desperate thread and my nerves are already shot. It won't take much for me to lose my shit on the frail, eighty-some-year-old woman sitting beside me.

I practice breathing deeply through my nose while I count silently and focus on the road ahead, following the instructions from my GPS.

We're driving into the outskirts of Kalispell and I think maybe I'm off the hook when Bo's mother pipes up.

"So who do you favor? Your mother or your father?"

It's on my lips to lie to get her off my back, but then I remember I already told Bo I wasn't sure who my parents were. Can't change that story now.

"I don't know," I tell her, bracing myself for what inevitably is coming.

Honesty is overrated and after almost a decade of lying my ass off, I don't really understand why I suddenly feel compelled to tell the truth. Specifically with this woman—who doesn't seem to like me much—or her son.

"What do you mean you don't know?"

There it is. Moment of truth. Bo didn't push, he's probably waiting for me to share voluntarily, but his mother doesn't hold back.

"Exactly that. I was raised by my grandmother. I only remember her."

Mrs. Rivera turns in her seat to face me, curiosity winning this round.

"She didn't have pictures of your parents?"

"I don't think she even knew who they were."

That clearly throws her for a loop. "How is that even possible?"

I become aware of my hands cramping around the steering wheel, I'm holding on so tight. I carefully release them, wiggling my fingers and taking in a fortifying breath as I prepare to expose another little part of me.

"I was always told she was my grandma. She raised me as if she was and I never had reason to question it. Where I grew up, most people were related in one way or another."

"She's no longer with us?" she asks, her expression is one that suddenly looks a lot like pity.

I think I prefer the mild dislike to this.

"Died twenty-five years ago."

My GPS directs me to turn into the parking lot on the right for the doctor's office. I find a parking spot close to the front doors, shut down the engine, and turn to find Mrs. Rivera looking at me with her mouth slack and her eyes wide. I reach out and grab her hand, which feels cold and clammy.

"Mrs. Rivera, are you all right?"

"Twenty-five years ago? How old were you when she died?" she asks, completely ignoring my question.

"Thirteen, going on fourteen. I was fine though," I add quickly when her fingers tighten around mine. "She'd taught me to look after myself."

By the time I was six, I knew how to look after the vegetables we grew in the small garden behind our trailer. By eight, I took over the laundry, which was done in a large bucket on the small back porch. I was ten when I rode her old bike four miles to the gas station and back to pick her up cigarettes. A year later I was cooking all her meals.

The truth is, while Grams felt herself grow weaker with every passing year, she made damn sure I got stronger.

Mrs. Rivera is quiet and seems pensive as I help her out of the truck and inside the waiting room. No loaded questions or double-bottomed comments. When the nurse calls her name and she doesn't respond, I'm starting to wonder if perhaps she's had another one of those mini-strokes.

"Mrs. Rivera," I prompt as I grab her hand. "They're calling your name."

She turns to me, a gentle smile on her face.

"My mother-in-law was Mrs. Rivera," she says. "Couldn't stand the woman."

She struggles to get out of the chair so I grab her elbow to help her up. When she's on her feet, she pats my hand.

"You can call me Zuri, doll."

Doll?

I'm still trying to figure out what the hell just happened, when I see the nurse and Bo's mother disappear down the hall. One minute she looks at me like I'm about to take off with her life's savings, the next I'm her friend and she gives me a nickname I've kneed grown men in the junk for.

When she walks up half an hour later and hooks her arm through mine, telling me she's taking me out for lunch, there's little I can do but go with the flow.

Zuri may only be about a third of her son's size, but she and Bo are perfectly matched forces of nature. A family of bulldozers. I might have been able to handle one of them, but I'm starting to worry I don't stand a chance against both.

~

Bo

"You better tell her."

I close my eyes and count to ten.

It's the third time Momma brings it up. She clearly has an agenda and won't rest until she gets her way, but she's out of luck on this one. I know better than to let her get involved, it's a death sentence to any kind of relationship I hope to have with Lucy.

That doesn't mean she's wrong, it's just none of her business.

"Not your concern, Momma," I rumble, before taking another bite of my burger.

We're having a quick bite at a family restaurant a few blocks from my mother's building. It's the first chance I have to touch base with her, since I only got back this afternoon.

The team finally found the missing hiker early this morning, after an intense two-day search. He'd attempted to climb along a precarious ridge, lost his foothold, and fell into the ravine below. He was incredibly lucky. If not for the trees breaking some of his fall, he would not have survived. As it was, he shattered one leg, broke his hip, his shoulder and collarbone, and cracked just about every rib on that side of his body. He'd been lying in that gulley for two days, slipping in and out of consciousness.

If not for the ravens circling overhead, waiting for an easy meal, we might not have checked out the narrow ravine.

Even after finding him, it still took hours to get him up to a plateau where the Alert Air Ambulance from Kalispell Regional Medical Center would be able to land. I tried to stabilize him the best I could with the limited tools at my disposal, but the guy still was in a tremendous amount of pain as we hoisted him out of the ravine strapped to a basket. I was almost relieved when he lost consciousness and stopped screaming.

Of course, for us the work isn't done until we get the horses and the equipment back to base camp. Then we have to wait for whatever agency is in charge to debrief, pack up our gear, and head home where we take care of the horses, clean the equipment and get it ready for the next call, and finally write up a report.

We found the guy just after seven this morning, but I didn't leave the ranch to get home for a shower until five thirty.

I'm tired, I'm cranky, and I'm not in the mood to put up with my pushy mother.

"Not my concern?" she chirps back, playing the guilt card. "You're my *only* concern."

"Come on, Ma, that's not what I meant and you know it, but let me make it clearer. What, when, or how I tell Lucy anything is my business and mine alone. I'm a grown-assed man, and I'm not going to have my mother peeking over my shoulder as I'm building something with Lucy. You badgering me ain't gonna change that." I ignore her indignant huff and push on. "I heard you loud and clear—not that I needed you to tell me in the first place—but I did. I'd be much obliged if you'd drop it, so we can have a nice meal together before I go home and try to catch up on the sleep I've been missing these past forty-eight hours."

Dead silence follows, but at least I get to eat my burger in peace. She's still pouting when I kiss her cheek and leave her in her comfortable chair in her apartment half an hour later.

I get back in my truck and for a moment I sit there, contemplating if maybe I should swing by the rescue. A jaw-breaking yawn quickly ends that notion. I need sleep first, if I go see Lucy like this, I'm bound to fuck up something. I need to be on my game.

"Morning."

She squints against the morning light, her puffy face and tangled hair evidence I woke her up.

I sent her a text last night to thank her for looking after my mother and to warn her I'd be coming by today. She replied back with a simple thumbs-up.

"You didn't say you'd be here at the crack of dawn," she grumbles, turning back as she pads on bare feet toward the kitchen.

She's wearing a ratty T-shirt, and another pair of those men's pajama pants. It doesn't matter, slinky nighty or shapeless sack, the jiggle of her ass underneath the thin cotton has me hard in an instant. Lucy is a knockout in every way, but I'm all about her round ass and I can't fucking wait to dig my fingers into that abundance.

"It's seven thirty," I point out as I follow her inside.

"Exactly."

I take a seat at the kitchen table while she stomps

around the kitchen, getting a pot of coffee going. Probably best if I stay out of her way until she gets some morning juice in her.

Five minutes later, she sinks down on a chair across from me, her butt and heels on the seat and her knees pulled up to her chest. She moans as she takes a sip from her mug and I can't hold back a soft grunt. One of her eyebrows lifts high and she regards me with an amused glint in her eyes.

"You okay?"

"Peachy."

The corner of her mouth twitches for a moment before she changes the subject.

"So what brings you out so early?"

"Thought I'd check in; thank you for taking Momma to the clinic, seeing how Ladybug is doing, wondering if the sheriff has been in touch... You know, catching up."

"Well...first of all, you're welcome. Also, Ladybug seems to be doing a little better and Doc says he's gonna keep monitoring her over the weekend, but if she keeps on the way she is we might have her back on Monday. As for the sheriff, he sent a deputy by a couple of times with some follow-up questions, but I haven't heard of any progress being made."

I make a mental note to follow up with Ewing this morning. I know he had his hands full with the missing camper these past few days as well, but I want to make sure he stays on top of this poisoning case too. Ground up plant material from a yew does not simply appear in a food bin on its own.

"Have you been setting your alarm?" I can't help asking.

For a moment she looks mutinous, like she's gearing up to give me a hard time, but in the end, she decides to simply nod and change the subject.

"What about you? I gather you found your missing guy?"

I give her a brief synopsis of the search and ultimate rescue. She hisses between her teeth at the description of the man's injuries and observes how lucky the guy was to survive. I like the way she asks questions without apologizing for her curiosity, but can also listen with interest when I talk.

I never would've thought I'd enjoy the simple act of swapping mundane day-to-day stories over a cup of coffee this much. Guess the right person could make watching paint dry appealing.

All too soon I have to get going. With the team away half the week, lots of work has been piling up at the ranch. I want to make a dent into it, which probably means working late tonight, otherwise I'll be stuck at the ranch all weekend. Normally I wouldn't care, but I've finally found better things I can do with my time.

I get to my feet and Lucy follows suit, trailing me to the front door where I turn to face her.

"I'm swinging by tomorrow at noon. You gonna be around?"

"Any particular reason?"

Yes, there is, but not one I'm going to share on my way out the door. I'll need time, which is why I plan to be back tomorrow.

"Do I need a particular reason?" I lob back with a wink.

Her response is an eye roll, but when I slide my hands alongside her face and lean in, she doesn't resist. Instead, she curls her fingers around my wrists and her eyes drop to my mouth.

Fuck yeah.

I taste coffee on her lips, and a hint of spice that's all

Lucy. Groaning appreciatively when she opens her mouth under mine, I slide my tongue inside. Her much smaller one is no less bold, matching mine stroke for stroke, exploring and testing, until I need to abruptly tear my mouth away.

"Have mercy, Gorgeous."

Twelve

LUCY

"You guys stay."

I leave the windows open a crack for some airflow.

I decided to take Chief and Scout into town. They don't often come with me on errands, but these days I feel a little more secure when I have them around.

Unfortunately, I can't take them into the grocery store, but they should be able to go into at the feedstore I plan to stop at on my way home.

Because I rarely venture out, I know very few people in town with the exception of almost every employee at Rosauers. What can I say? I like to cook, therefore I hit up the grocery store frequently. For the most part, they know who I am, they just don't know what to do with me.

I'm told I don't exactly send off friendly vibes. Alex told me that. Doesn't mean I'm not friendly, I'm just not like Alex, chatting up everything that moves.

I'm more of an observer. For instance, I know the woman with gray streaks in her hair on lane three is Janet.

She works the deli during the week, but on weekends she turns extra shifts on the cash register to pay for her husband's growing medical bills. I also know Rita—who works in produce—gives Janet a ride in to work most days. Neil cuts the best rack of lamb in town and coaches his daughter's soccer team.

I could go on. I probably have picked up some small piece of information about everyone who works here, simply because I've kept my eyes and ears open while staying under the radar myself.

Growing up in the Kentucky hills, you learned quickly to keep your head low and your nose clean. Something I forgot for a while when I first left the holler, but it wasn't long before I was reminded why avoiding attention was a good thing. Nowadays there are only a handful of people I feel comfortable enough with to let down my guard.

Bo has recently been added to that very short list. He's a good man, has been very helpful, and I have no reason to believe he's anything other than trustworthy, but I've been wrong before. Still, I want to do something nice for him, and the only way I know how is by cooking something.

He's supposed to come by at noon today so I thought I'd make some Asian-style fish tacos for lunch. Most of the ingredients I have at the house, but I wanted to pick up a nice piece of haddock, a Chinese cabbage, and some green scallions.

It won't take me long to throw together once I get home.

I select my produce and toss it in my cart, nodding at Rita who is restocking broccoli one bin over.

Next thing I know my cart gets sideswiped, knocking it out of my hands. It topples over sideways, spilling my groceries down the aisle.

"Thievin' bitch!"

I turn my head to find Lester Franklin bearing down on me. Backpedaling, I find the edge of the closest produce bin and dart behind, keeping it between me and the irate farmer.

"Hey!" Rita walks over and steps in the old man's path. "What the hell is wrong with you, Lester? You can't go attacking the lady."

I wince when I realize she knows the farmer's name but calls me, 'the lady.'

"She ain't no lady. Stole my goats, she did. Got the sheriff all up in my business, telling lies. She's a thievin' c—"

"All right, that's enough out of you!" Neil, the butcher, must've heard the commotion and comes marching up, taking a firm hold of Franklin's arm. "Told you last time not to bother coming in when you've been drinking." He starts steering the old man toward the exit. "Come on, best get out of here. Don't make me call the police."

The farmer throws me one last dirty look over his shoulder before the two men disappear down the aisle.

I don't realize I'm shaking until Rita claps a hand on my shoulder.

"Sorry about that. He's never done that before." She looks at my toppled cart. "Let me give you a hand."

"That's okay," I finally manage when I watch her bend over to pick up my groceries. "I've got this."

I can tell from the expression on her face when she looks up at me it was the wrong thing to say.

"My name is Lucy," I blurt out. It suddenly feels important she know my name. "I appreciate your help."

Now I sound clunky and awkward, but Rita smiles at me.

"Glad to finally know your name," she says.

My visit to the feedstore was a little less eventful, thank goodness.

I stayed sharp as I left Rosauers, keeping my eyes open and making sure Lester Franklin wasn't lurking around somewhere. That incident shook me harder than I would've expected. I'm normally alert and vigilant whenever I'm out and about, but I was completely taken by surprise earlier and that scared me.

The boys were good, sticking close by me—despite all the interesting smells in the store—and when I went up to the register to pay for my order, I added a couple of rawhide bones for a treat.

Both dogs are currently chewing said bones on the floor in the kitchen, creating a tripping hazard for me.

"All right, guys, that's enough. Outside with you two."

I throw open the back door, confiscate the bones before they have a chance to sneak them past me, and shove them outside. Moving around the kitchen is a lot easier without the boys underfoot, and it doesn't take me long at all to get the prep work done for lunch.

Yesterday afternoon I spent working on the large, old henhouse behind the barn. Not that I'm interested in chickens, but I figured the pen would be easy to modify so it can house the goats. It would offer them a dry and warm shelter, and a sufficiently large outside run where they'd still be contained and protected.

The main structure was still intact, but the chicken wire needed replacing and the galvanized roof had rusted through in a few places. Instead of housing two dozen nesting boxes, the interior is now one large open space with two levels connected by a ramp, which the goats will love. I was also able to use some old building materials we'd salvaged last year when we cleaned out the wood lot to patch the roof. All that's left to do is put up new chicken wire to secure the outside run and I picked some up at the feedstore this morning.

It's nice out, one of the last mild spells before winter sets in for good. Bo mentioned he'd drop by around noon, which leaves me about half an hour to try and get a little work done on the run.

The roll of chicken wire is a pain in the ass to wrangle by myself. I need more than one pair of hands to uncoil it and keep it straight so I can staple it to the existing posts. Swearing up a storm, I shove another bleeding finger in my mouth. One of several so far caused by those damn sharp cut edges.

"Gloves might've been an idea."

I startle and let go of the piece of wire I was trying to stretch tight. It coils up with a violent snap and I swallow a juicy curse. Then I turn my head to find Bo riding up, my traitorous dogs trotting beside his horse's large hooves.

I'd heard them bark in the distance a couple of times, but I didn't pay much attention. They sounded more playful than alerting. Clearly, they're getting too used to Bo's coming and going at the rescue. Apparently even when he approaches the farm from the rear.

"The ones I have are too big. They don't make 'em for this size."

I hold up my child-sized hands to illustrate.

◁∾▷

"I'll find you some."

Sometimes I wonder if she is more capable than is good for her. Although I'd never dare say that out loud.

So much for my grand entrance, she didn't even see me coming.

I swing a leg over the saddle and dismount Blue. I notice Lucy eyeing the full saddlebags hanging on either side and the rolled-up blanket I strapped to the horn. The food packed in there is part two of my plan, but I need to convince her to go with me first.

That's going to be the tricky part, because instead of letting her saddle her own horse, I need her to get on Blue with me. There's a spot half a mile back where a rock plateau overlooks a drop in the water of the creek, creating a small waterfall. I figure if I can get her there, I'll get her mellowed up with the food in my saddlebags, and then drop the bomb. If I'm extremely lucky, she'll take it in stride, but if she doesn't, at least she won't be able to take off on horseback.

I walk right up to her, take her injured hand in mine and close my mouth around the bleeding digit. Her eyes slightly widen and her breath hitches as I let her finger slide from my lips.

"You ready?"

Her slightly dazed look is replaced by confusion.

"Ready? For what?"

I point at Blue. "We're going for a ride."

"Oh. You just said you'd be by; I would've saddled Ellie if I'd known."

"No need." I wrap her hand in mine and start walking. "Blue can handle us both."

"But—"

She swallows the rest of her protest when I move her in front of me and grab her by the hips.

"Up you go."

Instinct takes over as she reaches for the horn and throws a leg over the saddle when I lift her up. Before she can change her mind, I shove my boot in the stirrup and swing myself up behind the saddle. Not the most comfortable position with the edge of the cantle pressing into my business, but it's probably better Lucy doesn't feel my hard-on poking her in the backside. Not yet anyway. I wrap my arms around her, one anchoring her in place and the other to grab Blue's reins.

"Trust me," I whisper in her ear when I feel her body go tight.

Then I give Blue my heels and steer him in the direction of the creek that runs along the back of the rescue. Both dogs trot alongside the horse, happy to tag along.

"Bo, where are you taking me?"

"The creek. Check the saddlebags, I brought lunch."

"A little cold for a picnic, isn't it?" she observes sarcastically.

"Doesn't have to be," I suggest.

That seems to take the wind from her sails and the rest of the ride to the creek is silent. First thing I do when we get there is build a small fire right on the edge of the creek.

"You know, I was gonna feed you fish tacos for lunch," she comments when I spread out the blanket on the rock plateau and gesture for her to sit.

"We can have them for dinner."

I'm hoping she'll still be willing to feed me after my confession.

The food I brought is from a restaurant down the block

from me. I had them wrap up some easy finger foods; ribs, chicken wings, veggies and blue cheese dip, and potato skins. I also packed a couple of bottled waters, canned beers, and I thought to bring a roll of paper towels. No muss no fuss.

Lucy chuckles when I finish unpacking my saddlebags.

"What?"

"Nothing," she quickly responds. "It's perfect."

"So..." I finally start when she has her mouth full of chicken wing, trying to capitalize on the fact she can't respond.

Damn, you'd think I was better prepared, spending as much time as I did figuring out what to say. She pulls up one questioning eyebrow as she chews. May as well rip that fucking bandage off.

"Twenty years ago, I was arrested for statutory rape."

I feel the instant chill as her eyes widen and her mouth freezes mid-chew, and turn my head toward the water, unable to watch the disgust that's sure to follow.

"They showed up with handcuffs at St. Luke's in Boise, Idaho, where I just started working as a surgical nurse. Didn't exactly make a good first impression."

That's an understatement; I lost my hard-fought job before the cops tucked me in the back of the cruiser, and thought my life was officially over.

"I met Melissa in a bar," I explain. "I assumed she was legal and never thought to question her when she said she was nineteen."

What I don't share is that she was a small blonde spark plug like someone else I know—which is probably why my mother responded to Lucy the way she did—and a lot of fun for a month or so.

"It was fun for a while, but I ended up breaking things off before they got too serious."

Closer to the truth is, I made the mistake of bringing her over to my mother's for dinner and gave Melissa the wrong idea. She was talking kids before the night was out and there was no way I was even ready to joke about shit like that. With my new job about to start, I decided to end it a few days later. She did not take that well.

I'd been shocked to find out she was only sixteen instead of nineteen, which she told me she was. The small apartment she took me to a few times turned out to belong to a friend, and she actually still lived with parents she claimed not to have.

"She didn't much like that and—"

"Wait. For real?" Lucy interrupts.

I glance over and am stunned to see disbelief etched on her face.

"Please don't tell me she reported you as revenge for breaking up with her *after* she lied to you about being of legal age?" She sharply shakes her head. "Hell no. That's not right."

Anger, disgust, even disappointment were reactions I would've expected, but not this. She seems almost upset on my behalf.

"I was twenty-four."

I'm not sure why I'm defending her, but the truth is, I've always struggled with the fact I should've known better. She was just a kid for cripes' sake, even when I thought she was nineteen I was still the adult of the two.

"So? What the hell does that have to do with anything? Did you force her?"

"Hell no."

Now she's starting to piss me off.

"Of course you didn't. So, what happened? The little cow make you do time?"

One moment I'm getting steamed up, the next she makes me chuckle.

"No time. I had a good lawyer, the son of a friend of Momma's."

The guy had been a godsend. If not for him I would've been dependent on some public defender.

"He was good. Managed to find witnesses willing to testify Melissa had been flashing a fake ID and lying about her age everywhere. Charges ended up being dropped, but where there's smoke there's fire—at least that was the consensus around town. I had no future there, so I enlisted. Got out of Dodge."

I don't regret it. It wasn't the life I'd envisioned for myself when I graduated college, but right here on this rock sharing a great view and good food with Lucy, I can't say I'd want it any other way. Life turned out all right for me.

"Wait a minute, is that why you were so hung up on age? That explains what your mother meant when she wanted you to remember what happened last time."

I lean over and tug on a strand of her long blond hair that somehow freed itself from her braid.

"Looks *and* smarts."

She grins at my cheesy compliment and I can't resist stealing a quick kiss.

I was so fucking sure I'd have to chase after her. Instead, she wraps a hand around the back of my neck and pulls me back for a full-on, open-mouthed kiss that has me sing all verses of "Amazing Grace" in my head.

Go figure.

Thirteen

LUCY

I catch a glimpse of my reflection in the bathroom mirror and do a double-take. I almost don't recognize myself.

I'm smiling.

Shaking my head, I shove the dirty towels in the hamper and carry it to the laundry room. I've been on a roll since waking up at six this morning. I loaded the dishwasher, cleaned out the fridge, stripped the bed, mopped the floors, and took down the temporary pen for the goats on the back porch. I've been full of energy.

Now, I rarely sit still, but I don't usually tackle my chores with this level of enthusiasm. I suspect Bo's surprise picnic up at the rapids, working side by side to fix the outdoor pen for the goats, the fish taco dinner that followed, and all the kisses in between, left me energized.

Part of me was frustrated when he kissed me goodnight after dinner, but I was relieved at the same time. With what little he knows; he seems to understand I'd probably get spooked if things moved any faster. My dating experience can be whittled down to less than a handful of attempts, all resulting in utter failure.

The most disastrous one was shortly after Alex and I moved the rescue here. The guy seemed nice, but turned out to be a murdering psycho, once again proving my poor judgment when it comes to men. I vowed that had been my last and final attempt at any kind of relationship with a man.

Of course, since then I've had plenty of dealings with good men—decent men—most of them part of the High Mountain Trackers team. Including Bo, but it's one thing to like him, even get along with him, but starting up any romantic entanglements requires a whole different level of vulnerability I'm not sure I'm able to risk.

I want to—hell, I was ready to climb him like the tree he is last night—but seeing as kissing is already further than I've allowed myself to go for longer than I care to remember, it's probably wise to go slow. However, that almost alien sexual energy has left me restless, which is what I've been trying to burn off all morning.

"All right guys, let's go check on the goats," I tell the dogs, already waiting by the door again.

The babies are down to three bottle feeds a day, which is so much easier to handle. I can feed them simultaneously, cutting the time it takes in half, and the rest of the time they munch on hay or pellets. They've reached that age where they are super playful and I could sit and watch them all day long.

Yesterday, with Bo's help, I built an outdoor platform for them with an old, rusted water trough as a base and left-over barn boards lashed together topping it. We turned some of the boards into a ramp with one-by-one inch cross-braces to prevent their little hooves from sliding, and they love going up and down the contraption.

I shrug on my jacket and shove my feet in my boots. This morning the fields were white with frost and the temperature is not supposed to go much above freezing today. When I open the door, the dogs scoot out in front of me, just as my phone vibrates in my pocket. I don't recognize the number.

"Hart's Horse Rescue."

I'm met with silence on the other side.

"Hello? Who's this?"

"Erm...I'm looking for Lucy Lenoir? Am I pronouncing that right?"

The voice is a woman's, I'd guess my age, maybe older.

"This is she, and yes, you pronounced it just fine. How can I help you?"

I pull the door shut behind me and sink down on the top step, tugging my jacket under my butt.

"My name is Jenny Mills. You don't know me, but your name was given to me by Sheriff Ewing?"

It's asked as a question and I'm scrambling to place her name, which sounds vaguely familiar.

"It's about my daughter," she adds.

Amelia Mills. The girl Bo and his team found now almost two weeks ago. The rape victim I'd offered to help.

Suddenly I feel inadequate and unsure.

"Ah, yes, Mrs. Mills. I'm so terribly sorry for what happened to your daughter."

"It's Jenny, and thanks."

She sniffles and sounds like she's wiping her nose. I imagine not only the girl, but her entire family is struggling with the aftermath.

"Jenny, how can I help you?" I prompt her gently.

I could tell her what I might be able to do for her daughter, but as with any kind of victim of trauma—direct or indirect—it's important they actively pursue their own recovery.

"I was told you had experience with this kind of thing."

It's a pretty typical coping mechanism to avoid naming the trauma in an attempt to make it less significant than it is, but that often times only emphasizes its impact. If the mom is doing it, it might send a signal to her daughter that what happened to her is not open for discussion, which would only hamper her recovery.

I decide to call a spade a spade. My first step in hopefully helping Amelia.

"Mrs. Mills. Jenny," I quickly correct before continuing in a gentle tone. "I assume when you say 'this kind of thing' you mean rape?"

"Oh, I can't stand it. It's such an ugly word."

"Yes, it is," I agree with her. "But it's also an ugly reality Amelia lived through that she can't change just by avoiding the word. I know it's the last thing you would want, but you might be making it harder for your daughter to talk about what happened to her. Cover that kind of trauma up and it will fester with far more detrimental consequences."

It's something someone once shared with me and as much as it made sense, I never felt I had any other choice than to cover things up. Which is probably why I'm still as fucked up as I am. Then again, I didn't have the support of family and community this girl does.

"She won't talk," the woman whispers, clearly emotional.

"That must be hard," I sympathize. "I'm not a psychologist or psychiatrist, and I can't make you any promises, but if you are willing to be patient I'd like to try and help you with that."

Ten minutes later, I tuck the phone back in my pocket. Jenny is stopping by with Amelia tomorrow afternoon. We'll see how the girl responds to the animals, but I'm guessing she'll trust them before she'll trust me, which is fine by me. It'll give us something in common.

⁓

Bo

"One forty-seven eighty-five, please"

The clerk at Managhan's Furniture starts packing up the new quilt and sheet set.

"Redecorating?" she asks, eyeing the fat candle I set on the counter.

I mumble something unintelligible while I pull my credit card from my wallet and hand it over. Mainly because I don't know how to answer.

I'm trying not to look too deeply into why I'm suddenly shopping for new linens for my bed. The old set was fine, although maybe a little threadbare and faded. Not that I give a rat's ass, but my mother made a comment yesterday.

I'd picked her up for lunch and groceries yesterday, and we had just ordered some Mexican at Rosita's downtown when she brought up Lucy, suddenly singing her praises. Apparently, Momma had not only misjudged her age, but her character as well. When she told me she found out Lucy had been on her own since thirteen, my stomach clenched.

I know she'd been raped at some point in her life, she

made that clear, but not how old she was when it happened. Now I'm thinking she may not have been much older than that girl we found.

Anyway, I was a little lost in thought when my mother suddenly suggested it was time I get some new sheets for my bed. She reminded me she'd bought the old ones for me years ago. I never gave the sheets I was sleeping on a second thought, but suddenly I felt the need to replace them.

As to why I tossed the candle in my cart, beats me. I picked it up, sniffed it—it smelled like lemon and coconut—and for some reason it reminded me of Lucy.

Fuck. It's all about Lucy; the candle, the sheets, the pile of old newspapers collecting dust I tossed out last night, washing the piles of dirty dishes in my sink, scrubbing the bathroom top to bottom. All of it's about her, or about me making a good impression on her.

I've had one or two women in my apartment before, and I've never given a flying fuck what the place looked like. They didn't either, that wasn't what they were there for. That's not how I see Lucy and it's important for me to show that. With a candle, new sheets, and a clean apartment, among other things.

Tossing my purchases on the passenger seat, I climb behind the wheel and pull out my phone.

I didn't see Lucy yesterday—all part of my plan to take things at a pace she can keep up with—but tonight, I'm hoping to take her out for a meal and bring her back to my place for a movie.

"Hey..."

I can't help but smile at her tentative greeting.

"Hey, yourself. How's your day so far?"

It's only nine thirty, but I'm sure she's been at it since dawn.

"Good. I'm heading out to pick up Ladybug shortly."

"That's great news. Do you need help? I'm in town running a few errands but am about to head to High Meadow, I can stop by."

Never mind Jonas mentioned to be there for a ten o'clock meeting when I called to tell him I'd be in a little later this morning.

"No, that's okay. Alex is coming with me. Between the two of us, we'll be fine."

"Sure?"

"Yeah. Nothing we haven't done a hundred times before," she reminds me.

The truth is, she's probably better and more experienced with horses than I am.

"All right then. I was calling for another reason though. I'd like to come and pick you up for dinner in town, nothing fancy. Maybe a movie at my place after?"

The silence stretches so long I'm about to give her an out when she finally responds.

"Yes, to dinner, but can we play the offer of a movie by ear?"

"Yeah, we can, as long as you know the offer was for a movie only."

"Oh, yes, of course, I—"

"Maybe some kissing," I continue, cutting her off. "A little innocent petting, clothes on, unless you prefer them off, in which case I might be persuadable."

The rich sound of her laughter feels good. It had been my intention to try and lighten up the moment for her and I'm glad it worked. Last thing I want is to have her feel like she's pressured into something she's not ready for.

"That actually sounds like fun," she admits with a smile in her voice.

"Six okay?"

I'm suddenly in a hurry to nail this down.

"See you then."

I drop my phone in the console and look over at the plastic bag with my new bedding.

I'm so full of shit.

~

"I'm hoping to be back by next weekend, but don't quote me on that."

Ludwig is arriving tomorrow and Jonas just went over their itinerary, which is supposed to take them through three states. Four days seems a bit unrealistic, but what do I know.

"James will take lead on any HMT business, should anything come in. If things are under control on the ranch, think about taking Dan along on a call. Time that boy got his feet wet, although maybe..." He turns to face me. "If there's time, I want you and Fletch to run him through some drills this week. Drop him off in the mountains, see if he can make his way back."

"What if he doesn't?" Sully wants to know.

"Send up the bird to check on him."

"Nothing like throwing the kid to the wolves," I comment.

"Hardly a kid," Fletch contributes. "He's older than any of us were when we were sent into the mountains of Afghanistan. He'll be fine. A little toughening up will be good for him."

In my opinion, the kid is tough enough. The past few years he's been looking after his very ill mother while working the sometimes-long hours of a ranch hand.

Recently he was also given more responsibility with the handling of the stallions and his new role of supervising a few of the newer hands. I do think, however, the kind of exercise Jonas is suggesting will boost Dan's confidence as a new member of the team.

"All right," Jonas continues. "I think we covered it all. Don't forget my dad can be an asset, but he needs to be kept in check. Oh, and, Bo, you'll keep an eye on things at the rescue?"

I nod. He doesn't mention Alex but I know he's referring to his request from last week.

"Good. Then we're done here," he announces.

"Hey." Fletch catches up with me in the yard. "Tonight, let's set up a hunt for Dan. Lay out some tracks for him to follow?"

"Got plans tonight. Tomorrow good?"

He shrugs. "How about I'll set him up one tonight, you do tomorrow?"

"Works for me."

I keep walking to the barn, Fletch keeping pace.

"So..." he drawls, his head down as usual, but he shoots me a sideways glance. "What kinda plans ya got tonight?"

"Dinner and a movie."

No use trying to keep secrets here. This place is like one fucking giant grapevine.

"Better be with Lucy," he grumbles, "or I'm gonna have to kick your ass."

I snort. For fuck's sake, I expected interference from Sully, at the very least an opinion from Jonas, and of course Thomas had something to say on the matter, but I never thought a grouch like Fletch would have an interest in my love life.

"Yeah, Lucy. Who the fuck else?"

He grunts, following me into the tack room.

"Anything else?" I snap, getting annoyed.

"Tread lightly."

I can't for the life of me understand why everyone thinks I'm blind to what appears evident to everyone else; that woman is hiding pain under that brass and bristly exterior of hers.

"Yeah, I know, Fletch."

"Just making sure," he grumbles, as he walks into the barn.

Christ, what a bunch of old hens.

Fourteen

LUCY

"You guys better be on your best behavior."

Chief's ears twitch, his soulful eyes looking up, but Scout doesn't even glance at me and wanders off following her nose. Normally both dogs would be off and running, but I've noticed the shepherd has been hanging back a bit recently. Maybe his age is slowing him down some; he is after all the older and wiser of the two.

He sticks by my side as I make my way to the barn. I'm getting ready for a busy day, starting with getting Ladybug's stall ready for her. The entire barn was cleaned after the sheriff's office was done with it—every stable mucked, and feed trough and water bucket scrubbed—but I haven't put clean straw down in her stall yet.

I should have enough time before Alex picks me up. We're supposed to meet Doc at the clinic in an hour to load up Ladybug and bring her back home.

Sliding open the barn door, I'm struck by the silence. With Bella the goat now reunited with her kids in the old chicken run, and the horses and donkey all out in the back field, where they have a shelter, the barn is sitting empty. At least it will be until Ladybug gets here. For company, I may put Daisy in here with her.

I head up the ladder to the loft and toss a bale of straw into the barn below. While up here I do a quick scan and make a mental note to put in one last order before winter hits.

Climbing back down, I haul the bale to Ladybug's stall and cut the twine. Half of it for her stall and the other half for the one next door where I'll house Daisy. It'll only be for a week or so, until Ladybug is sufficiently recovered to join the rest of the herd.

We usually have a bunch of brooms, shovels, and hayforks neatly leaning in the corner by the tack room, but with all the recent activity in here from the sheriff's department, it's a bit of a mess. Half the tools have toppled over and I quickly restore order. Unfortunately, I can't find the good hayfork, so I have to use the old one with the bent tine, which is a pain in the ass.

Once I've spread the straw in both stalls, I grab a lead from the peg on the wall and head out back to fetch Daisy. Not a fan of the cold, she's already coming toward the gate when I walk up.

"You're a spoiled little girl, aren't you?" I tell her as I clip the lead to her halter.

She trots ahead as far as the lead will allow, apparently eager to get inside where it's warmer. When I have her settled in with some fresh hay, I close the barn and whistle for the dogs.

I've just herded Chief and Scout inside when Alex pulls up. I hold up a finger for her to wait and duck inside to grab my ball cap. The wind has picked up and I don't want to have my hair blowing in my face.

"You look upset," I observe when I get in the passenger seat and take a gander at Alex's pinched face.

"That's because I am," she states, looking over her shoulder as she backs up her truck.

"How come?"

"I got into it with Jonas this morning. Did I tell you he sold Missy's colt?"

"Yes, you did. To a new business associate of his? Something about a multi-disciplinary training program?"

I admit, I was listening with half an ear at the time, but I got the gist of it.

"Exactly. Well, the guy—some fancy trainer from Kentucky—is apparently flying in and Jonas is hitting the road with him tomorrow. They'll be gone for days, checking out potential additions to the program in three different states, and I did not find out about it until this morning." She shoots a pointed look my way. "He claims he mentioned it. He didn't. Not to me anyway. So yes, I'm upset."

I'm having a hard time staying focused. The moment she mentioned a fancy trainer from Kentucky, my mind locked in on that. Kentucky is home to a lot of fancy trainers; she could be referring to any one of them. While my head is fighting the onset of panic with logic, I break out in a sweat, despite the chill in the air.

"Understandable," I mumble, trying to be a good friend.

Alex seems happy just venting, which is a good thing, since I can't seem to come up with anything more helpful or supportive to impart. While I make appropriately sympathetic sounds, I'm contemplating the likelihood that after almost ten years my past has finally caught up with me.

By the time we have Ladybug loaded up in the trailer, I've almost convinced myself I'm being ridiculous, but Alex must've noticed my internal struggle.

"Everything all right with you?" she asks when we start driving home.

"Yeah, fine, why?" I blurt out.

Dear God, can I be more obvious?

"You seem a little...preoccupied."

"Sorry. Yeah, just a little worried about a client of mine."

It's not exactly a lie, although I'm using it to distract Alex.

I have been worried about Samantha. Haven't seen or heard from her since her husband showed up at the rescue. I left her a message cancelling her session scheduled for the morning after Ladybug got ill, but she didn't get back to me. Nor has she answered any of the other times I've tried contacting her.

I'll try one more time, and if she doesn't answer, maybe I should contact Bo's friend, Detective Williams.

"This is Midnight, and that there is Mocha."

The sullen girl tries hard not to respond to me or the baby goats, but Midnight's persistent pleas for attention finally break through.

Her mom, Jenny, is sitting on the porch where I carefully suggested she stay and enjoy the cup of tea I made her. It was obvious as soon as the two arrived, I wouldn't have a chance to try and even connect with the girl as long as the mother was around.

Poor woman, I feel for her. She's clearly desperate to help her daughter, but is hovering, answering for the girl, putting words and thoughts in her mouth and it's only making Amelia more resistant. I'm guessing perhaps before this horrific experience, the relationship between these two may have already been strained. It seems to be a common issue between adolescent girls and their mothers, and Amelia's ordeal may well have widened that gap.

She crouches down to pet Midnight when Mocha sees his opportunity clear and jumps on Amelia's back. The giggle that escapes her sounds so childlike and, for a moment, the angry teen makes way for the innocent child underneath.

Wow.

"Who's that?"

Her voice is soft, hesitant, and I try not to pump my fist at the fact she's actually talking. It's only the first tentative step in what will be a very long and arduous journey.

"Her name is Bella," I respond, looking at the goat poking her head out of the shelter. "She's their mother, but they had a rough start in life and she needed help looking after them. Which reminds me, they need their bottle. Do you think you could give me a hand?"

The girl can't hide her reaction of eager anticipation but quickly masks it with feigned disinterest as she shrugs.

"Sure, whatever."

She's tough as nails. Or that's what she'd like me to believe. I'm sure it'll take some time to win her trust but I'm hopeful the animals will help me pave my way.

Low intensity exposure, high quality impact.

～

I'm not in a good mood when the first thing I see driving up to Lucy's house is fucking Reggie Williams standing on the damn porch.

Either this is some bogus follow-up call by Williams, or something else has happened and Lucy called him instead of me. Not sure which one pisses me off more.

"She's just in the shower," he announces as I get out of my truck and make my way up the steps.

The smirk on his face is enough to have me clench my fists.

Yeah, I know he's fucking with me, I may not trust him, but I know Lucy. It doesn't make me any less pissed.

"What the hell, Williams?"

The words are barely from my mouth when the door flies open wide and Lucy steps out. The dogs focus immediately on Reggie, checking him out thoroughly, but Lucy's eyes are on me.

"I was actually in the middle of blow-drying my hair when he showed up," she clarifies. She must've heard Reggie's bullshit story.

She explains calling him to see if he perhaps knew why her client was suddenly unreachable. It had been his choice to show up on her doorstep and his idea to hang around when Lucy mentioned she was in the middle of getting ready for a date with me.

"Hey," the asshole says, his hands up defensively. "I was just jerking your chain. I had good reason to stop by."

"I'd like to hear it," I grind out, hanging onto my last thread of patience.

"After your call about Samantha," he addresses Lucy first, "I went by her apartment to check on her, but she wasn't there." Then he turns to me. "No one has seen her there recently. So, I drove by Mr. Burn's place of business to have a word with him. According to his foreman, he's in Panama dealing with an emergency with one of his projects there."

"Panama?"

Lucy doesn't know what Sully dug up for me as leverage on the man, but I did share with Reggie, which is why he makes a point of mentioning it.

"Yeah, Dwight's worked on a few projects there these past few years," Williams volunteers. "I've got someone trying to verify he's indeed out of the country and I'll be looking to find out Samantha's whereabouts, but in the meantime, I wanted to make sure you've got some security in place, just in case."

"It's covered."

I don't give Lucy a chance to respond because, security system or not, I plan to make sure she stays safe.

Reggie looks from Lucy's scowling face to mine and shakes his head as he backs down the steps.

"I'll leave you to it, now that's taken care of. If I find out anything, I'll be in touch."

The moment he backs his car away from the house, Lucy turns and walks inside. Afraid she'll shut the door in my face, I follow right on her heels.

"Don't talk about me like I'm not there."

She's waiting in the living room, her hands in fists on her generous hips. I'm a little distracted by the picture she makes. I don't think I've ever seen her wear anything but jeans or those ratty old flannel pajama pants. Definitely not a dress.

It's a denim shirt dress, or whatever the hell they call one of those numbers; long sleeves, collar, and buttons all the way down the front. By all accounts, it shouldn't be sexy, but she's wearing it with a wide leather belt, accentuating her hourglass shape, and well-worn cowboy boots on her feet. Add to that the mass of wavy blond hair hanging down below her shoulders and she's about the sexiest thing I've ever seen.

"Did you hear me?" she snaps when she thinks I'm not paying attention.

Fuck, I'm paying all kinds of attention.

"I did. I was simply making sure Williams understands your security is taken care of because keeping you safe is all I fucking care about."

She was primed for a fight, which is why I'm giving her the honest truth. Now I watch all the fight drain out of her, leaving her looking a little unsure.

"I...oh."

"Do you need to feed the dogs before we go?" I prompt her.

Mostly because if we stand here any longer, I'll happily forfeit the best damn grilled steak in the county for dinner of another kind.

She shakes her head. "No, they're taken care of."

"You've got everything you need?"

"Let me grab my phone."

She darts into the kitchen and is back two seconds later, a small backpack slung over her shoulder. She heads straight for the door.

"Coat," I remind her, grabbing her coat off the rack.

I hold it open, wait for her to slide her arms in the sleeves, and then I turn her around, tugging the edges closed under her chin.

"By the way, you look great."

She blinks a couple of times and, for the first time, I

notice how long her lashes are. Or maybe it's because I've never seen her wear makeup before. She doesn't need it, but it touches me she put that much effort into a date with me.

Unable to resist, I take her inviting mouth, tasting deep before I withdraw, holding her plump bottom lip between mine.

"Gorgeous..." I sweep the pad of my thumb along her cheekbone where the skin is slightly flushed. "If we don't get out of here now..."

No need to finish that sentence, the implication hangs thick in the air.

Lucy nods, turns away from me, and yanks open the door.

~

"*Bourne Identity*."

I shake my head.

"No way. *Mission Impossible* is far superior."

She scrunches up her nose.

"Can't stand Tom Cruise. Give me Matt Damon any day of the week."

"You're telling me you'd pick *Good Will Hunting* over *Top Gun*?"

She moves her empty plate out of the way, biting her lip as she plants her palms firmly on the table and leans forward.

"In. A. Heartbeat."

I grin at her theatrics. This lighthearted side of her is new, at least it is to me, but it doesn't surprise me she has one. She's often funny in a grumpy, sarcastic way, but as I'm discovering she can be playful too.

"You wound me," I retort, covering my heart with my hand.

Her eyes sparkle as she sits back. "I'm sure you'll survive."

Our banter is interrupted with the appearance of our waitress at the table.

"Can I get you anything else? Coffee? Dessert? Our special today is a pecan pumpkin cheesecake."

I glance at Lucy, who shakes her head and presses her hands against her stomach.

"Oh, I wish I could, but I'm afraid I'm stuffed."

"We'll have the bill and add two dessert specials, if you could pack those to go?"

The young girl smiles at me.

"Absolutely. I'll be right back with those."

After settling the bill—Lucy is smart enough not to argue with me on that—I lead her outside and help her into the passenger seat of my truck. Not because she needs my help, but because I don't want to pass up on an opportunity to touch her.

During dinner we were able to keep the conversation light and away from the reason for Reggie's visit earlier. It doesn't mean I wasn't thinking of it, and somewhere between ordering our appetizers and paying the bill, I'd already come to a decision.

"Hold on to these." I set the bag with our dessert on her lap and get behind the wheel. "Hope you don't mind a small change of plans."

I feel her eyes on me as I pull out of the restaurant parking lot and turn the truck toward my apartment building.

"Like what? We're not going to your place?"

"We are, but we're only staying there long enough for me to pack a bag."

"Because?"

Her tone is instantly suspicious and I'm starting to feel a distinct chill coming from her.

"Because if I had my way, I'd pack you up and move you in with me where I know you'll be safe, but I know that's not an option," I quickly add when she's about to voice a protest. "You have animals that need looking after as well, so I think we'll both be more relaxed if we watch a movie at your place."

She's quiet, which means she's processing, until I pull the truck into the designated parking spot behind my building.

"And you plan on staying the night?"

"That part is not negotiable. I can crash on your couch," I reassure her, even though I'd rather be sharing her bed. "It will be an improvement to the cold boards of your back porch."

She doesn't exactly agree, but she's not arguing either.

We walk into my apartment and I let her roam around while I duck into my bedroom to throw some stuff in a bag. It only takes me a few minutes to shove some clean clothes and toiletries in my old duffel before grabbing my laptop from the study. When I walk into the living room, I find her standing by the couch, the fat candle I bought this morning in her hands.

"Not what I expected. Smells nice though," she comments, giving it a sniff before she sets it back down on the coffee table.

Somehow, I get the sense she knows I bought the damn candle for her. Unsure how to respond, I grunt and grab her hand, pulling her to the door. I don't want to risk her wandering into the bedroom, noticing the brand-new sheets —still sporting the package creases—I quickly threw on the bed before I picked her up.

"So...*Bourne Identity*?" she asks, nodding at the TV screen.

When we got to the rescue, she showed me the spare bedroom, despite my assurances the couch would be fine. I ended up helping her check on the animals before she told me to find a movie while she changed into something more comfortable.

To be honest, I'm a bit disappointed to see the dress go, but figure it's a good thing she's comfortable enough to change into those ratty pajama pants with me in the house. The fact she plops her butt down on the couch beside me makes me feel even better.

"Your TV, your call," I explain. "But next time, if we're at my place, get ready for Ethan Hunt."

She mock shivers and makes a face. "I'm gonna need a good scrubbing in the shower after."

I'm sure she means it as a joke and not a suggestion, but I can't resist tucking her under my arm and whispering in her hair, "That can be arranged."

Instead of stiffening up—which I almost expected—she rests her head back against my shoulder and tilts her face up.

An invitation if ever I had one.

Bending my head, I go in for a kiss when the glare of headlights hits the wall behind the TV.

Shit. What now?

I have Lucy tucked under my arm and on the move with me when I hear a pair of footsteps coming up the porch. When I pull open the front door, Ewing is just lifting his hand to knock. He briefly bends down to greet the dogs, who pushed their way outside, but I don't like the serious look on his face when he straightens and focuses on Lucy. Something's wrong.

"Bo, Lucy."

"Wayne. What brings you here?"

My tone is sharper than I intended but it doesn't seem to faze the sheriff, who still isn't looking at me.

"I have a few questions for Lucy."

"And it couldn't wait until morning?"

Now I get his eyes.

"Trust me, I'd rather be home right now."

"What's going on?" Lucy pipes up beside me, drawing the sheriff's attention again.

"Lester Franklin was found dead this morning."

I recognize the name of the farmer who shot at Lucy, and a cold chill runs down my spine. I don't like the sound of this.

"Dead?"

Lucy presses her hands against her chest and I tighten my hold on her shoulder.

"Murdered."

Fifteen

LUCY

"I don't understand."

I scramble to try and wrap my head around this.

Franklin was found dead this morning after an anonymous tip came in to the sheriff's office. Ewing is not sharing how the man was killed, so my imagination is working overtime. Even more so since he seems to expect me to have information for him.

"The anonymous tip led us to check into an altercation at Rosauers Saturday morning. Do you know anything about that?"

I feel Bo go rigid beside me. He'd followed me into the living room and sat down on the couch, close enough our bodies were touching from shoulders to knees. I was grateful for the silent support because the sheriff's visit has shaken me.

"What the hell are you talking about, Wayne?"

Bo's tone is hostile and the question sounds more like a warning. My hand automatically goes to Bo's knee in an attempt to contain him. I never mentioned the run-in I had with Franklin, but in my defense, there was other stuff going on that had my attention the rest of that day.

I wonder who might've been the anonymous caller, it would've had to have been someone who was in the store at the time. Neil? Rita? It doesn't make sense.

"Lucy?" the sheriff prompts, ignoring Bo's reaction.

"I...I wouldn't call it an altercation." I hate how I immediately sound defensive, like I have something to hide. "It felt more like an ambush. I hadn't even seen him until my shopping cart got sideswiped, sending my stuff flying. It startled me, and then he started yelling at me. I mean, it took me a while to process what was happening, and by then Neil —he's the butcher at the store—was already leading him out of the store. I don't think I even said anything."

"What about after? Did you have any contact with him?"

"No. I mean the man nailed me with buckshot the first time we met, then called me out in the middle of the grocery store the next time. Why the hell would I seek him out?"

Ewing leans forward, his elbows on his knees.

"You tell me."

"You've gotta be fucking shitting me," Bo curses as he gets to his feet. "Not another word, Luce. Not without a lawyer and not until the sheriff tells us what exactly brings him here."

Whoa. A lawyer?

Ewing hangs his head down and I'm not sure how to take that.

"The tip we received suggested you might have knowledge of what happened to Lester." He lifts his head enough so he can look me in the eye. "My job is to follow all leads, however unlikely."

"Glad you're at least admitting that," Bo grumbles as he starts to pace.

Ewing's only reaction to Bo is rubbing his hand over his face before he straightens up, his focus on me.

"Hope you understand with that anonymous call on record, I had no choice but to follow through. For what it's worth, my report will show that I believe there is no credible information suggesting you have any knowledge of, or involvement in the murder of Lester Franklin."

"Damn right she doesn't."

Bo clearly isn't letting the sheriff off the hook that easily, but I've had enough. Last thing I want is to draw any more attention to myself. I get to my feet and put a restraining hand on his arm, but address Ewing.

"I appreciate that, Sheriff. Sorry I couldn't be more helpful."

Unfortunately, when I close the door behind him there is no sense of relief. Why would someone bring up the incident at the grocery store? Was that intended to put the focus on me? And if so, for what reason?

"Un-fucking-believable," Bo grumbles, walking toward me and wrapping his big arms around me and squeezing a little too hard.

For a moment I indulge, grateful for the unconditional support he offers. I'm not sure I deserve it, but I'll take it.

"He was just doing his job," I soothe, patting his imposing chest. "Now, how about that movie? I could use a drink with my Jason Bourne," I add to lighten the mood.

Fifteen minutes later, I'm curled up on the couch beside Bo, a beer in my hand, and Matt Damon taking up my screen, but my mind is still occupied with the sheriff's visit.

"I can hear you thinking."

I turn my head to find Bo staring at me.

"I can't shut it off," I admit. "I keep wondering who would've made that anonymous phone call. Were they trying to point the finger at me? The only person I'd consider pissed off enough to do that is dead."

"Don't forget Burns," Bo suggests.

"Doesn't that seem a little far-fetched though?"

The movie long forgotten, I tuck my legs under my butt and turn my entire body toward Bo before I continue.

"It would mean Burns somehow knew Lester Franklin, knew about my issues with him, and witnessed the incident at the grocery store. But not only that, how would he have known where to find Lester's dead body? That's the part I can't square away."

"Unless he killed him."

I shake my head. I'm not buying it. Sure, Burns was pissed. Perhaps pissed enough to poison my animals, but I don't believe for a second he would go to such lengths to implicate me.

Bo pulls his phone from his pocket.

"What are you doing?"

His soulful eyes fix on mine as he puts the phone to his ear.

"Reggie? Yeah. I think you and the sheriff need to compare notes."

He goes on to briefly relay the sheriff's earlier visit before he asks, "Were you able to confirm Burns's whereabouts? Or his wife's?"

"Ex," I mumble, correcting him.

Bo shoots me a glance from underneath his heavy brows before returning his attention to the phone call.

"I see. I still think you should talk to Ewing... Okay."

After a curt goodbye, he tucks the phone back in his pocket.

"Burns was confirmed on a flight to Panama yesterday afternoon."

"So it couldn't have been him," I conclude.

"That depends. We don't know what the time of death was."

Oh. I didn't think of that. When the sheriff mentioned they found his body this morning, it didn't occur to me he might've been dead for a while already.

"And I guess a phone call could be made from anywhere."

"Yeah." Bo reaches for me and rearranges me, tucked against his side. "Now, do you think you can quiet your mind long enough to watch this damn movie? If this Matt Damon guy doesn't put you to sleep first."

"Wouldn't be the first time he stars in my dreams," I mumble.

Bo's low growl has me grinning as I snuggle against him.

⁓

Bo

I doubt she even knows I'm here.

Her hair is piled in a ratty nest on top of her head, haphazardly held in place with what looks like a chopstick. She's still wearing the pajama pants and shirt she had on last night when she fell asleep on the couch and I carried her to bed.

Her face is puffy, like she slept hard, and she squints against the morning light as she shuffles straight to the coffee maker. She startles when she realizes coffee has already been made. That's when her eyes open and find me sitting at the kitchen table.

"Morning."

"Hmph..."

Definitely not a morning person. I try to curb my grin but Lucy catches it, narrowing her gaze sharply before she returns her attention to the coffee.

I quickly finish the message to Reggie I started, asking for a progress update. I didn't sleep a whole lot, ended up moving from the guest room to the couch, so I'd be closer to Lucy's bedroom, but still sleep didn't come easy. I probably would've done better if I'd slipped into bed with her, but who knows what that might've triggered for her.

"Work?"

Lucy takes the seat across from me, her eyes a little clearer in her face.

"Just checking in," I tell her by way of explanation as I put my phone down.

"Hey," she suddenly says, her eyes darting around. "Where are the dogs?"

"I let them out. Hope that's okay? They were begging by the door."

"Thanks. Yeah, of course. I should probably get their breakfast ready."

She seems a little rattled this morning and I wonder if it's finding me in her space.

"What about you? Did you want breakfast?" she asks me as she gets up.

"We forgot the cheesecake in the fridge last night," I point out. "I'm sure it'll do fine as breakfast."

She shoots me a toothy grin right before she ducks into the fridge. Guess I'm not the only one who'll eat dessert for breakfast. My mind instantly floods with ideas on how I could use sweet treats to make waking up in the morning more appealing for Lucy.

When she slides one of the takeout containers and a fork in front of me, I wrap my hand around her wrist and tug her down on my lap. Not giving her a chance to react, I cup my other hand around the back of her head and pull her closer, taking her mouth.

"That's better," I mumble against her lips. "Morning, Gorgeous."

"Morning," she echoes.

Scratching at the back door has her scrambling off my lap to let in the dogs.

After we have our cheesecake and the dogs eat their breakfast, Lucy heads for the shower and I step outside. Reggie sent a two-word reply; *Call me.*

"Compared notes with Ewing last night," Reggie says when he answers my call. "Other than Burns and the victim's shared dislike of Ms. Lenoir, there is no obvious relation between the men. Nothing that would get me a warrant to dig through Dwight's phone or financial records."

"That's fucking great. So you're expecting me to believe someone poisons Lucy's animals and implicates her for murder all in the same week is all a coincidence?"

"Look, for what it's worth, neither Ewing nor I are treating anything as a coincidence. We're cops, we're trained not to believe in coincidence. One thing though, brother, with Burns in Panama and Franklin dead, there's no reason to think Lucy isn't safe."

That may be enough for Reggie but it sure as hell isn't for me.

He mentions he hasn't yet had any luck locating Samantha, but he still has some leads to run down. We end the call with Reggie promising he and Ewing will keep each other up to date and he'll call me if there is anything to report.

I notice Lucy watching me through the kitchen window when I swing around.

"Any news?" she asks the moment I walk in, easily guessing who I was talking to.

I relay the gist of the conversation but omit Reggie's view on her safety. I don't feel the same confidence, and frankly, I don't want her too confident either. Better to stay vigilant until all of this has been cleared up.

"Be careful and keep the dogs with you at all times," I instruct her when she walks me to my truck ten minutes later.

I tried to get her to come to the ranch with me, but she's got her hands full here and I really want to catch Jonas before he leaves today. Unless we're called in for search and rescue, I hope to spend as much time at the rescue as I can, which I would like to explain to my commander in person.

"I'll be fine," she repeats what she told me earlier.

I guess it's encouraging she's not accusing me of over-stepping. I'd much rather she willingly participates than fight me tooth and nail every step of the way.

"Indulge me."

She rolls her eyes but lifts her face when I lean in for a kiss.

"I'm only a few minutes away," I remind her when I get behind the wheel.

She nods, pushing the door closed, but I immediately turn on the ignition to lower my window.

"Call me for anything."

"Good grief, Bo. Go already. I'm fine, I'll keep the dogs with me, I'll even bring the shotgun into the barn if it makes you feel better, and I'll arm the alarm when I'm in the house by myself. Did I cover it all?"

I reach out the window, lift her chin with my finger, and give her a hard kiss on the lips.

"Smart-ass."

~

"We'll move her here."

About the reaction I expected from Jonas.

I just finished filling him in on what has been going on, and I figured he'd be a fan of locking Lucy down. He doesn't know her the way I do though, and too heavy a hand will have her running for the hills.

"That would actually complicate things from a logistics perspective. The animals at the rescue are gonna need looking after. She's got two baby goats who still get formula three times a day. Simpler for her to stay right there."

He peers at me from under the rim of his hat, a skeptical look on his face.

"What you're really saying is you don't wanna piss her off," he assesses.

I briefly consider his comment before speaking.

"Yes, that's what I'm saying."

His laugh booms as he rounds his desk to clap me on the shoulder.

"Welcome to the club, Rivera."

"I'm interrupting something."

Jonas and I both turn to the door to see Ludwig walk into the office.

"Nah," Jonas is first to respond. "Rivera here is quickly learning what goes into keeping a woman happy."

I grin and shake my head, incurring the tease before I fire one right back at him.

"Luckily, I'm not taking lessons from you or I'd be in hot water now, wouldn't I?"

Jonas flips back his hat and runs his hand over his face.

"Don't remind me." Then he looks up at Ludwig. "What about you? You married? Involved?"

"Married. It's work," the trainer directs at me, showing off his capped teeth. "That doesn't change."

Great, now I have this slick operator giving me relationship advice. I need to get out of here.

"Good to know." I turn to Jonas. "Anyway, I'd best get working on those training exercises for Dan."

"Yeah, we should probably get going shortly as well," Ludwig suggests as he steps aside to let me through. "I've got Marco waiting outside."

"No problem. Give me five minutes to grab my gear," I hear Jonas say behind me. Then he addresses me, "And, Bo, we'll be in touch, yeah?"

I give him a thumbs-up before stepping outside.

I notice Alex is in the corral working with a skittish paint pony. Thomas is leaning against the fence, watching, with someone I assume is Ludwig's guy. I've never seen him.

Thomas turns when he hears me approach.

"Bo, how's your mother?"

"Saw her Sunday. She's good."

The guy beside him turns too, giving me a once-over. I take stock of him as well while I listen to Thomas with half an ear. The guy wears a ball cap instead of a proper hat, but at least it's not one of those sissy Tilley hats like Ludwig wears.

"Was thinking of giving her a call, actually. There's a

Thanksgiving social at the Legion in town, weekend after next, I thought she might enjoy."

When what he says registers, I accidentally inhale spit and start coughing to clear my airway. Thomas starts pounding on my back.

Jesus. I don't know whether to laugh or cry.

"Fuck, Thomas. You asking my permission or something?" I grumble when I can finally get some air in my lungs.

"Nah, simply a heads-up, son."

I grunt before addressing the reason I walked over here to talk to him about in the first place.

"I was supposed to set out a trail for Dan to track after work today, but Jonas says he had to take Gemma to the doctor. When he comes back could you ask him to call me? I can't wait around for him. I've gotta get back to the rescue."

"Sure, I'll pass it on."

"Appreciate it."

I nod at Thomas, tip my hat to the guy, and lift a hand to Alex who catches sight of me and waves. Then I turn and head for my truck. I'm halfway there when Thomas calls after me.

"Best take good care of that girl!"

Sixteen

Bo

I'm enjoying the view. Both the one around me as well as the one straight in front of me.

Fine, maybe the sight of Lucy's ass bouncing in the saddle wins out over the landscape. Yup, definitely enjoying that.

"What about here?"

Lucy points at a branch hanging low enough it barely clears her head. I'll have to duck to get under.

"Sure."

I watch as she pulls some hairs from her head and wraps them around the slim branch.

"Cheeky," I tell her.

It had been Lucy's idea to add an additional challenge to the tracking exercise I planned to set up. I intended to lay down a simple trail with the horses for Dan to follow, but she thought it would be more fun for him to turn it into more of a 'treasure' hunt by leaving a variety of clues from different species along the way he would have to collect and identify.

She collected goat droppings, a raven feather, donkey hair, shed snake skin, a chicken bone, and a dog turd, which she's been leaving along the trail we're setting out. Tossing in a few human hairs would throw him off.

"Change the term *animals* to *species* in his instructions and we're covered," she suggests.

Very cheeky.

When the buildings of the rescue come into view, I check my watch to see it took us forty or so minutes to get back down the mountain. We'd gone up the existing trail along the creek to the southeast boundary, where a previous owner had built an underground shelter.

The location borders High Meadow lands and I figured it will make a good spot for Fletch to drop Dan. He can lead him in—blindfolded and on the back of a four-wheeler—on the old logging path on ranch property. Dan will be left with instructions on what he is to look for and a time limit of three hours to find his way to the end point, which is the rescue.

As we approach the barn, I call Fletch.

"Whenever you're ready. Tell him that aside from horse tracks, there is evidence for seven other species he needs to collect along the way."

Fletch chuckles. "Putting him through his paces. I like it. I was too easy on him last night. Kid did pretty well, he's got potential."

"Wasn't my idea, Lucy came up with it. We'll see if he can find them all."

"How long does he have?"

"Three hours."

"Even if he makes it in two, he'll have to do part in the dark," Fletch observes. "That'll mess with his orientation."

"I know," I confirm.

Another deep chuckle.

"I'll make sure he has a flashlight. Give me half an hour to get him up there."

"Roger that."

I catch up with Lucy and quickly dismount, following her into the barn with Flint, one of the rescue's horses. A sedate, big old guy, no longer suited for heavy work, but still good for an occasional stroll. I tie his lead to one of the stall doors and remove his saddle. Then I carry it into the tack room, bumping into Lucy who is coming out.

"Are we gonna put them out or do you want them in here?"

"Back in the field. I need to haul a couple of bales of hay for the feeder in their shelter, though. Not a lot of grass left and with snow expected toward the end of the week, I should probably start feeding them on the regular."

"I can help with that."

The dogs run ahead of Lucy, who is leading both horses, while I follow behind balancing three hay bales on a wheelbarrow. What this place needs is a John Deere Gator. Something that'll make it easier for Lucy to haul hay all damn winter. I'll have a talk with Pippa. There's an old Gator behind the shed at High Meadow, along with a few other broken-down vehicles we haven't disposed of yet. She might be able to get that thing back in working order. I'm sure Jonas won't mind.

She needs a new pitchfork too, the one I grabbed from outside the tack room has a bent tine.

"How long do you think it'll take him?" she asks as we walk back to the house.

I have to shorten my stride to allow her to keep up with me.

"Fletch should be doing the drop-off right about now." I check my watch; it's four thirty. He'll only have an hour of daylight left at most. "He's got three hours but I don't think he'll need it. We'll see."

"Okay, good. That gives me time to make beef chili. He'll be hungry."

I shake my head as I let her go up the porch steps ahead of me. Don't particularly want Dan hanging around any longer than necessary. He'll finish the exercise and I'll get someone from the ranch to swing by and pick him up.

"He can eat when he gets home."

She swings around, looking annoyed.

"He'll be cold, tired, and hungry. Least we can do is feed him."

Like hell. Last night's plans were interrupted, and I fully intend to make good on those tonight, which won't work if the kid hangs around. Unless, I can get a head start on those plans before he gets here.

"Fine. We'll order pizza," I announce, putting my hands on her hips and backing her up to the front door.

"But I was going to make chili, I already took the beef from the freezer."

"It'll keep."

Her mouth thins stubbornly so I bend my head and kiss her. She doesn't give an inch at first, planting flat hands on my chest but not quite pushing me away, until her fingers slowly curl into my shirt and her mouth opens.

With my tongue slipping between her lips and my hand covering her ass, there is no space left between us. There's no way she can't feel the outline of my cock straining against my fly, but she's not flinching. In fact, I'd

174

swear she presses even closer and I growl deep in my throat.

Then one dog barks, followed by the other, and reality crashes home.

"I should feed them," Lucy mumbles, disentangling herself from me.

"Fine, we can continue this inside."

I reluctantly let her go as she turns to unlock the front door and take a moment to cool my jets. When I follow inside, I almost run into her back.

She stands frozen on the threshold of the living room and almost jumps out of her skin when I drop a hand on her shoulder.

"Everything all right?"

~

Lucy

I do my best to keep a straight face.

Ever since we came home, Bo has kept a very close eye on me. I don't think he believed me when I told him everything was fine.

The truth is, I'm probably just paranoid, but everything that's happened in the past couple of weeks has me on edge. When I walked in the house earlier, I watched the dogs make a beeline for the kitchen. Both of them stopped in front of the sink, their noses high as they sniffed the air and the hair on my neck stood on end.

I noticed it right away; the blinds covering the window over the sink were all the way up.

They're never rolled all the way up. The sun comes up on that side of the house and I don't want it blinding me when I stumble around the kitchen in the morning, so I end up leaving the blinds half-closed all the time.

It brought me right back to another time, another house, and another kitchen.

In an instant, the hot buzz in my blood Bo left with his kiss was replaced with a sharp chill. Bo's question if I was all right snapped the freeze and I rushed into the kitchen to return the blinds to their half-closed position. Then, with shaking hands, I fed the dogs and pulled the ingredients for my chili from the fridge. By the time I dared look at Bo, he was sitting where he is now—at the kitchen table—closely observing me.

"This will only take a minute," I tell him, rinsing the beans.

I have onions and beef browning in the Dutch oven and the scent of the rich spices is filling the air. All I have left to do is toss in the rest of the vegetables and beans and turn the whole thing to simmer. Chili tends to be better the next day when the flavors have had more of a chance to blend, but that's why I always make tons.

When I drop the lid on the pot, turn down the burner, and swing around, Bo is right behind me.

"Now are you ready to tell me what that was all about?"

No. I'm not ready to go down that rabbit hole.

I've already convinced myself Bo must've rolled up the blinds this morning before I got up, and I simply didn't notice until now. I don't want to explain what caused my mini freakout. I'm afraid if he finds out he'll want a name, but even without he's going to dig around and put me right back on the radar.

I've fought too hard to build some kind of life that

could sustain me, in more ways than one, to risk it over my own paranoia. I'll stick as close to the truth as I'm comfortable with.

"I zoned out. I haven't been sleeping great. First it was the goats, then Ladybug, and now this murder. I guess it's all getting to me."

The look on his face softens as he takes a step closer, lifting his hand to my face to tuck a strand of hair behind my ear.

"Yeah, I get that." He looks over my shoulder at the stove. "Any more you need to do here?"

"No, it just needs to simmer."

The words are barely out of my mouth when he grabs my hand and starts walking toward my bedroom.

"Wait a minute...what's—"

"You need a nap."

"It's the middle of the day," I protest as we enter my bedroom. "I have a pot on the stove and Dan will be here soon."

I feel a light breeze coming in from the partly opened window when he stops me by the side of the bed. Then, with his hands on my shoulders, he urges me to sit on the edge.

"You've got plenty of time. I'll wake you up when he gets here."

I shake my head. "I couldn't sleep if I tried."

"Sure, you can," he insists, as he climbs on the bed, lies back and pulls me down with him.

"What are you doing?"

I try to lift my head, but he rolls on his side and props himself up on an elbow. Then he presses his index finger against my lips. His touch and those dark eyes hovering over me spark a heat deep in my belly and reignites the buzz in my blood.

"Shh."

My skin tingles as he traces my face with his fingertips, his gaze following their path. I feel seen, and yes, exposed, but in the most delicious way possible.

Sleep? That's a joke. There's no way I could sleep when even his slightest touch is lighting my body up.

I want him.

My life is in chaos, I'm jumping at shadows, and by all accounts this is the worst possible time to open up to someone, but fuck it...I want this man.

So when he lowers his head and aims a kiss at my forehead, I lift my face and slide my hands around his neck, catching his mouth on mine. To his credit, he tries to restrain himself, but that doesn't last long when I swing my leg over his, using the leverage to flip him on his back.

His pained groan rumbles down my throat as his hands find purchase on my ass. With my mouth fused to his, my tongue tasting and probing, I roll my hips seeking friction on the hard ridge of his cock against my aching core.

I'm no longer thinking of the past and I don't allow myself to think of the future. I exist only now; with this man whose need-filled groans and claiming hands cause a storm of sensations raging through my body.

"I want you," I mumble against his mouth, sinking my teeth into his lush bottom lip.

"Fuck, Luce..."

His fingers dig into the globes of my ass as I rub my body against him restlessly.

"I *need* you."

The next moment I'm on my back and my arms are being stretched above my head. Then his hands roam my body before shoving up my shirt. He yanks down my bra and latches on to my nipple, drawing me deep. The pull is so intense, my back arches up from the mattress.

"Please, Bo..."

"Easy, Gorgeous. I've got you."

One hand slides down to my waistband and with deft moves, he undoes my button and zipper before slipping his fingers inside. His moan when he finds me slick vibrates against my skin. Lost to the barrage on my senses, I hiss when he slips a finger inside.

"Too much?" he asks softly, freezing his movements as his breath ghosts over my skin.

"Not enough," I return, moving my legs restlessly.

"Give me your mouth," he orders on a growl as he pumps his finger inside me, slipping a second digit alongside. "And ride my hand."

I'm not sure who I am anymore as I let go of all control and allow Bo to play my body masterfully. The sound I hear is my own keening when the tight coil of my need is released in a breathless free-fall.

I wake up when the dogs start barking some time later. It takes me a moment to become aware I'm curled up on my side, Bo's rough hand covering my breast and his hard body pressed against my back. Then I scramble out of bed, my heart pounding.

"It's Dan," Bo claims, much slower to swing his legs out of bed.

I'm frantically trying to straighten myself into something presentable, but my hands are shaking.

"How would you know?" I snap.

I'm feeling vulnerable and I don't do well with that.

"Because I could hear him walking up to the house." He

drops a kiss on my head as he moves past me to the door. "Take your time."

I'm not going to allow myself to process what happened earlier in my bed. Not now. It'll have to wait for a quiet moment when I can be alone. There's simply too much to sort through.

Bo is stirring the chili on the stove, and the High Meadow lead ranch hand is leaning against my kitchen counter sipping a beer, when I walk in. Dan pushes off and stands straight as soon as he sees me.

"You made pretty good time," I comment, checking the clock.

It had taken him a little over two hours. An hour less than Bo said he was allotted.

"Thanks."

He grins a little sheepishly. Nice guy, but seems a little shy for someone his age. Or maybe he's just quiet. Can't be easy taking care of a loved one who is fighting to stay alive.

"We'll have to see if you picked up all the clues we left," Bo mentions.

"Be my guest, I left them all on the porch," Dan indicates. "Some of them weren't suited to bring indoors."

I smile. Guess he found the poop.

"Let's go check it out."

We file out onto the porch where Dan displayed his clues on the railing.

He has both the goat droppings and the dog turd, both wrapped in leaves. Next to it the raven feather, snake skin, chicken bone, and donkey hair. Six out of seven, not bad.

"Sorry, kid. You missed one," Bo points out.

Dan shoves a hand in his jeans, a grin on his face.

"Oh, you mean this?"

He pulls a strand of long blond hair from his pocket and hands it over to me.

"Yours, I believe?"

"Good catch," I tell him.

Bo shakes his head.

"Well, I'll be damned."

Seventeen

Bo

"You're kidding?"

Lucy beats me to it. She's clearly as shocked as I am.

"Afraid not." Speakerphone gives Reggie's voice a slight echo. "We missed it on the flight manifest."

"And voluntarily? You're sure?"

"That's what she said on the phone."

I'm not sure whether I buy into the whole 'reconciliation' Burns claims. The man apparently found out from an employee that the police came looking for him and contacted Reggie to 'clear the air.' As it turns out, Samantha went to Panama with him.

"You spoke with her?" Lucy asks sharply.

"I did. She was with him."

"FaceTime?" she pushes, and I can see what she's getting at.

"No. He called on a landline from a resort in Rio Hato, Panama."

"And you were satisfied it was her?"

I can hear Reggie is getting annoyed when he comes back with, "Been doing this work for a while now, Miss Lenoir. I can assure you it was her."

It's obvious from the look on Lucy's face the answer doesn't quite satisfy her. Her eyes meet mine over the kitchen table, where we were just having breakfast.

"I hope you're right, Detective, but take it from me, abusers like Burns will do anything to try and regain control over their victim. They'll lie, manipulate, blackmail, threaten, overpower, restrain, and yes, they'll kill too."

After a pregnant pause, Reggie bites off a muffled expletive followed by, "I should'a picked up on that. You're a victim too."

She flinches ever so slightly but immediately straightens her shoulders and lifts her chin.

"The appropriate term is survivor, and I have no idea what you're talking about."

She's lying and we all know it.

Half an hour later, I watch Lucy and Alex walk toward the back field. The farrier is scheduled to come today and look after all the rescue's nine horses, plus the donkey. The horses will need to be brought into the corral and from there rotated through the barn where the farrier will set up shop.

The past two days have been pretty uneventful, and I ended up doing a few minor repair jobs around the house to keep myself busy while Lucy went about her normal routine. She seems to have retreated a bit since Tuesday night after Dan left. She went to bed almost immediately and pointedly pulled the door shut behind her. Other than a few pecks I managed to steal, there've been no passionate kisses or heated touches, and each time I try to bring it up, she evades the subject.

Then yesterday afternoon, she had a session with the young girl we rescued a few weeks ago. The kid seemed a little freaked to see me there so I stayed in the house and out of sight until they left. Understandable, I'd seen her at her most vulnerable and she probably didn't want to be reminded of that.

When I was trying to get to sleep on the couch last night, it occurred to me that maybe Lucy was feeling vulnerable too. She'd let go the other night. Let me see her need which, I'm sure, she's not used to sharing. Part of me expected her to straight out reject me at some point, but that hasn't happened yet.

It's been tough, taking a step back to give her space when I've been trying to get closer. With Alex here all day with the local farrier, I'm going to take the opportunity to get out for a bit. I'll stop by my apartment to grab some clean clothes and I also want to check in with Momma. I haven't seen her since Sunday and I'm sure she'll need me to pick her up a few things. Maybe Lucy will miss me.

The first stop I end up making is at the sheriff's office. Ewing is on the phone behind his desk when the deputy shows me in. I take a seat and wait for him to finish his call.

"Rivera, what brings you here?"

He sounds tired. Looks it too, with dark circles under his eyes. I don't envy him his job and I'd probably feel for the guy if I weren't still pissed off at him.

"Following up to see if you're any closer to finding Franklin's killer. If you figured out who your anonymous caller was."

It would be good if Lucy didn't have that case hanging over her head, take some of the stress off her. That's one thing I can do, keep the pressure on the sheriff.

Ewing shakes his head, pinching the bridge of his nose between his fingers like he's staving off a headache.

"I've got more questions than answers. Nothing on the caller, it's a dead end, but that was the lab on the phone just now. They were swamped and took a while to get back to me on a few pieces of evidence we collected. Those are leads I now have to run down. Unfortunately, one of the items they came back on was a plastic baggie of powder found in Franklin's shed. Turns out it contains ground yew berries."

The look he fixes on me is somber, pretty much matching my mood. That is not good news. Instead of absolving Lucy, it further ties her to this case.

"You've gotta know you're barking up the wrong tree, right?"

It takes him a while to respond, which doesn't make me feel any better.

"I can only go where the evidence leads me. The good news is, they were able to extract a few fingerprints off the murder weapon. We'll run those through the various databases and hope for a hit."

"Murder weapon? You never did say what killed him."

"Penetrating neck trauma severing the jugular vein, according the coroner."

That would've been messy.

The sheriff leans forward with his elbows on his desk before he elaborates.

"Someone stabbed him in the throat with a pitchfork."

~

Lucy

"Ladybug looks good."

I unclip the lead from Hope's halter and step aside as she and her colt trot into the field toward the others. Ladybug already rejoined the herd after Alex let her go.

"She does. She was pretty lucky. I still can't believe she was the only one affected. It could so easily have been Hope and her colt, or Ellie."

We installed padlocks on the tack room and the feed box. The simplest would've been to put a lock on the barn door, but neither of us were comfortable doing that. In case of an emergency, you want to be able to get to the animals fast. We had a neighboring rancher in Billings who lost a couple of his horses in a stable fire when first responders encountered a locked and bolted barn door. He learned the hard way, and I don't think either Alex or I are willing to take that risk.

We slowly start walking back to the barn. Joe Blackwell, the farrier, already left and there is only a bit of tidying up left to do. A good thing, because I'm tired. Insomnia has been plaguing me and I feel like I'll never catch up on my rest.

I must've sighed louder than I intended because Alex swings her head around to look at me.

"Is everything okay with you?"

Normally my automatic response would be to tell her I'm fine. Knowing Alex, she wouldn't believe me and give me a stern look, but she wouldn't pry. She asked me once when she first hired me what happened to me. I'd still been so jumpy and afraid of my own shadow; it must've been obvious. I told her I couldn't ever talk about it, and if that was a deal breaker I'd be on my way. She said it wasn't a deal breaker and she wouldn't pry, but that if ever I needed to unburden, she'd be ready to listen.

I'm not sure I'm ready to dig up the past, but I don't want to give her my standard response either. I'd like to share some of what weighs me down though.

"Not really."

She stops in her tracks and stares at me with her mouth open.

"I did not see that coming," she remarks.

"If you make a big deal out of it, I'll go back to my usual answer," I warn her.

Her hands fly up defensively. "Gotcha. No big deal. But can I ask what's wrong?"

I chuckle humorlessly.

"Easier to ask what's right. I did something stupid," I confess. "I let Bo in and now I can't get him out."

I start untying one of the ropes we used to secure the horses in the center aisle between the stalls. Alex tackles the other side.

"Why do you need to get him out?"

I wish there was a simple answer.

"Because a lot is happening, I feel overwhelmed, and it's too tempting to let him carry the weight."

I roll up the rope, take the one Alex untied, and return them to the tack room. Alex follows me.

"Let him. Bo has a good set of shoulders; he can handle it. More importantly, he wants to."

I know he does, which is part of the problem. I get the sense he'll do anything for me.

"I can't risk it, Alex. He already knows too much and it's keeping me up at night."

We walk out of the barn and I close and latch the doors. Then we head for the house.

"He cares about you, and that's a good thing, Lucy," Alex assures me, keeping pace.

Yeah, I can see she would think that, but I know better.

"I feel like things are catching up with me, you know? This sense of doom... I can't seem to shake it. I can't afford to let my guard down."

The dogs start barking and run ahead toward Bo's truck coming up the drive.

Alex grabs my arm, holding me back.

"Yes, you can. You have an entire special ops unit at your back, my friend."

Up ahead I see Bo pulling in beside my wheels and get out. Then I watch as he rounds his truck to the passenger side. What on earth?

"Is that...?"

It's not hard to recognize the short spark plug he helps out of the vehicle. She barely comes up to his shoulder as he leads her up the steps.

"Zuri," I answer Alex's unfinished question. "Bo's mother."

We catch up with the pair on the porch.

"I tried calling," Bo explains with an apologetic shrug of his shoulders.

I immediately grab my phone from my pocket because I didn't hear it ring. It's dead, probably because I was up half the night watching YouTube videos and playing Sudoku.

"Gas leak in Momma's apartment," he adds, holding up a large bag of Chinese takeout.

"I'm telling you it's that new tenant. Tonya thought he was charming. I knew right from the start he was up to no good."

"Ma, the man is eighty-eight and uses a walker. He's harmless."

Bo sounds exasperated. I'm guessing this isn't the first time they're having this discussion.

"He wears white wingtips and his eyes are too close together," she insists stubbornly.

Beside me Alex stifles a chuckle, and I have a hard time not bursting out laughing myself.

"Why don't you come in?" I quickly invite Zuri. "I'm ready for a drink, would you like something?"

She shoots her son a sharp look before turning to me with a wide smile.

"Won't say no to that."

I hear Bo's heavy sigh as I lead his mother inside and straight through to the kitchen.

"I should get going," Alex announces, following us in.

"One drink," I plead with her.

The idea of being alone with Bo and his mother in my house feels a little overwhelming, so I'd love it if she hung around a bit for support. I try to convey as much with my eyes, which she seems to pick up on.

"Sure."

It actually turned out not to be half as bad as I expected. Bo assured Alex he brought enough food for us all and she ended up staying for dinner.

Zuri had us in stitches with some funny stories about her neighbors. Her sharp tongue and thick sarcasm are hilarious, but I'm pretty sure I don't ever want to end up on her bad side. I thought high school was brutal, but apparently the seniors' home is no better.

Some say life is an arc rather than a circle. The theory being that different phases growing up return in opposite order once a person is past their prime. By that model, my guess is Bo's mother has hit the senior equivalent of a teenager: rebellious, stubborn, angsty, with an often-inappropriate sense of humor.

I notice Bo has been quiet most of the night, occasionally cracking a smile at his mother's antics, but mostly silently observing. Mainly me. I've felt his eyes on me and caught him looking a few times. Again now, as he helps his mother into her coat.

He received a text notification from building management fifteen minutes ago the problem was found and fixed, and it was safe for tenants to return home. Since Alex was about to leave anyway, she offered to drive Zuri into Libby. I thought for sure Bo would pass on the offer but surprised me with his easy acceptance.

"Call me when you get in."

"Yes, *Mother*." Zuri's eye roll is over-the-top dramatic and has me laughing out loud.

While Bo hustles his mother outside into the snow that's just beginning to fall, Alex holds me back.

"Are you gonna be okay?"

I honestly hadn't thought much about our earlier conversation—credit to Zuri for being a great distraction—and I still don't have a clear answer for her.

"I'll figure it out."

"Yes, you will," she says with a smile, showing more confidence in me than I feel.

I stand in the doorway, rubbing my arms against the cold, and watch as Bo helps his mother into Alex's truck.

"You're gonna catch a cold," he grumbles, climbing up the steps as Alex drives off.

I scoff. He's one to talk, all he's wearing is a short-sleeved shirt. At least I have a sweater on.

Once inside, I head for the kitchen to tidy up. It's a little early to be heading to bed, even though I wish for the refuge my room offers. I get the sense Bo's had something on his mind and he's waited for us to be alone to tell me, whether I'm ready to hear it or not.

"I saw Ewing earlier."

My hands still in the soapy water in the sink, I turn to look at him. He's casually leaning with his hip against the edge of the counter beside me, but there's nothing casual about the expression on his face. As I feared, this is not going to be good.

"They found the poison in Franklin's shed. Ground yew berries."

My initial reaction is relief, knowing the person who poisoned my horse no longer is a threat, but it's quickly followed by guilt for even thinking that. Then I notice Bo eyeing me carefully.

"Is that bad?"

"Depends on how you look at it," he says before elaborating, "I think what's important is how it might look to someone investigating Franklin's murder. The poison would make for a possible motive."

A chill runs down my spine. Yeah, this is bad.

"Is that what the sheriff thinks?"

"He says he has no choice but to take the evidence at face value."

I'm not sure if I'm supposed to be reassured by that. Looks like tonight will be another sleepless one.

How did things start coming apart all of a sudden? How did I even end up in this position? I'm starting to wonder if I should think about disappearing again. I don't want to, I like the life I've built and the people in it, unlike the last time I reinvented myself.

"I see."

My voice sounds dull—almost resigned—even to my own ears.

"Don't jump to conclusions," Bo urges, taking a step closer, as if he knows I'm ready to bolt. "Ewing is still waiting for some evidence that is sure to take the focus off you. Fingerprints, on the murder weapon. His own pitchfork."

There's a sudden ringing in my ears as goosebumps break out on my skin.

No, it can't be.

Eighteen

LUCY

I hear him.

The surge of fear manifests as nausea, and I have to clamp my hand over my mouth to stop the egg roll and sesame chicken I had for dinner from making a return.

It was just a footstep on the gravel outside the barn—a single one—and yet I know to the very fiber of my being it belonged to him. Even after all these years, my senses are so attuned to him, I can taste his proximity in the air.

I deluded myself into thinking two thousand miles and a new identity would be enough to shake him.

It's not. He's right here.

My complacency will cost me, as I knew it would. I let down my guard, loosened the hold on my thoughts and feelings. I opened up, allowed myself to dream, and now I'll pay for it.

Sinking down in the corner of the stall, I try to silence my own breathing and heartbeat, which sound loud in my ears.

I'm convinced he can hear me. He always seemed to be able to find me.

I squeeze my eyes shut when I hear the squeal of the rusty hinges on the barn door as it's pushed open. It seems so much louder than normal, not that it does much good since there's no one else to hear it. Then it slams shut and I hold my breath as I wait for his footsteps.

Instead, I hear that deceptively soft voice.

"I know you're in here, Maggie. I remember your smell."

I start trembling at the sound of my name.

The baby goats, oblivious to the impending threat, think this is a game and jump up against me. The impact has me teeter backward and I reach behind me to stop my fall, encountering the handle of my pitchfork.

Then his head appears followed by his torso as he hangs over the stall door to check inside.

"Ahh, there you are."

The triumphantly cruel smile on his face tells me his revenge will be worse than anything he's put me through so far.

I don't think, I react, wrapping my hand around the long handle. Then I turn my body, holding the pitchfork in front of me like a shield. I close my eyes and in one move I surge to my feet, and drive the tines up into his chest with a scream drawn from my soul.

I wait for the pounding of my heart and rushing in my ears to subside.

Then I hear it, a wet gurgle, and I open my eyes. He's still standing, blood bubbling from his mouth, the pitchfork poking obscenely from his chest.

But instead of the handsome face of evil I was expecting, it's the weathered mug of Lester Franklin, his eyes wide in shock.

And I scream again.

~

Bo

The first scream wakes me up and startles the dogs. The second scream has me tripping over them in our combined efforts to get to her.

The dogs won, barking, and already scratching her bedroom door by the time I got there.

"Stay!" I boom at them as I fling her door open.

Last night, I watched her disappear to her bedroom and I was worried. She'd looked rattled and I cursed myself for mentioning the murder weapon. She didn't need to know that. It paints too vivid and horrific a picture of Franklin's demise.

I'd been standing in the kitchen, watching her door, wondering if I should go after her but decided against it. Now, watching her writhing in bed, the hair on my neck on end from her terrified whimpers, I curse myself for not making sure she was okay last night.

"Lucy, baby. Hey, wake up, Luce, you're having a bad dream."

Her hair is messy, strands sticking to her tear-streaked face as she rolls her head from side to side. I sit on the edge of the bed, put a hand on her shoulder, and shake her gently.

Suddenly her eyes pop open wide and her fist comes swinging up at me, catching me right on the chin.

"Umph..." I grunt with the impact that knocks me back. "Oww!"

Lucy shoots up in bed, cradling her hand, as she looks around her in confusion.

I test my jaw with one hand, while I reach for her injured fist with the other.

"Let me see."

The skin on her knuckles isn't broken but it looks like it's swelling a bit. Doesn't surprise me; that was a decent hit and I have strong bones.

"You've got quite the right hook."

"I'm sorry..."

She tries to wipe the hair from her face with limited success, so I do it for her, carefully pulling the strands away from her cheeks. With the pads of my thumbs, I wipe at the tears under her eyes.

"Don't be. I should've been more careful." I press a kiss to her forehead and push myself up off the bed. "I'm gonna grab some ice for that hand," I announce, walking out of the room where the dogs are surprisingly still sitting on the threshold. "Okay, boys. You can go."

They don't need to be told twice and I can hear Lucy mutter a greeting as I head to the kitchen.

To my surprise, I find one actual gel pack in the freezer, and I reappropriate half a bag of frozen corn. I find dishtowels in the third drawer next to the sink and pull out two to wrap the ice packs with.

I pass the dogs on my way to the bedroom. They appear to be heading back to their beds in the living room. Lucy is just coming out of the en suite bathroom. It looks like she splashed some water on her face and she's cautiously flexing her hand.

"I've got something for that."

She eyes me uncertainly when I make myself comfortable in her bed, my back against the headboard and my legs stretched out. I pat the mattress beside me.

"Hop in."

She hesitates for a moment and I'm almost expecting her to kick me out, but then she surprises me when she climbs in beside me. I take her hand and apply one of the icepacks to her knuckles.

"Hold that on there for as long as you can."

I press the second pack against my jaw, while reaching for Lucy with my other hand. Tucking her close, I encourage her to lean against me and wait until she settles in.

"Now," I start. "Want to tell me about it?"

"Not really," is her instant response.

"Luce, your screams took ten years off my life. I know something I said last night upset you. I know a lot is going on and you've been under a lot of strain. And I also know there's a history you don't talk about, stuff from your past you're not sharing. I think the weight is crushing you, and I'm worried."

Her eyes had been aimed down at her hands, but with my last comment she tilts her head up and looks at me.

"I'm fine."

It's a futile attempt at evasion and she knows it.

"People who are fine don't wake up at a quarter to four in the morning, screaming like Satan himself just showed up at their bedside."

No sooner have the words left my mouth when I feel her body start to shake against me.

"Lucy?"

"Tomorrow," she whispers. "I'll tell you tomorrow...in the daylight."

I'm about to protest when she suddenly drops her

icepack on the bed and turns her body toward me. Then she proceeds to climb on my lap, straddling my hips.

"Please make me forget."

Something tells me I'm being manipulated, but I'm not sure I care at this point. Patiently waiting for her to be ready hasn't gotten me very far. Perhaps I'll have more success getting inside her body than I have getting in her head. Who knows? Maybe once we find that physical connection, it won't be so easy for her to brush me off.

My cock is already on board with the plan, straining against my fly.

"You've gotta be sure," I prompt her, tossing my own icepack on the nightstand.

"Never been more sure about anything in my life," she replies, her eyes already on my lips and her mouth closing in.

Looks like this is fucking finally going to happen.

~

Lucy

Any lingering shakes dull with the pressure of his fingers digging into my thighs and the deep probing strokes of his tongue in my mouth.

The foggy remnants of my nightmare—spurned by past and present fears—slowly dissipate as unbridled pleasure builds deep in my belly.

"Yesss," I hiss as his hips buck off the bed, grinding the hard ridge of his cock against the ache between my legs.

In one move, he whips my nightshirt over my head before claiming my mouth again. Then he cups my breasts in his hands, the rough palms scraping my sensitive nipples.

Ahh, yes.

My own hands get busy, one pulling on his shirt while I try to work my pajama pants down my hips. Not an easy task since I have one leg on either side of Bo. A frustrated growl escapes me and the next moment I'm lifted up, jostled around, and deposited on my back on the mattress. Bo stands at the foot end of the bed, eyes narrowed and nostrils flaring, as he pulls his shirt off.

My eyes dance over the gleaming dark skin pulled taut over strong muscles and thick veins. A collection of tribal tattoos covers his chest and shoulders and on one side, reaching all the way down to his wrist. That draws my attention to where his hands make quick work of unbuttoning his fly and pulling his jeans down his thighs.

While my focus is still on his fully erect cock, he reaches for my waistband and strips my pajama pants clean off me. Then he grabs my ankles, sinks down on his knees and pulls me to the edge of the mattress, throwing my legs over his shoulders. Shoving his hands under my ass, he lifts me off the bed and goes down on me like a starving man.

Bo initiated most of our shared kisses but so far hasn't really pushed for more. I'm the one who seems to be looking to take things further. I realize that's probably by design; he's been careful with me, waiting for me to give the green light, and now that I have there's no doubt as to who's taking the lead.

I'm a rag doll as he bends and arranges me, his hands and mouth reducing me to a whimpering ball of need. But instead of making me feel powerless, I feel treasured, worshipped, and stronger for it. My hands slide off his bald head, slick with sweat, as I hold on for dear life. Blood is roaring in my ears, muffling the desperate sounds coming from my mouth as I'm reaching to come.

All of a sudden, his mouth disappears, then his fingers, and my eyes fly open.

"Don't stop."

"Not a fucking chance in hell," he mumbles.

He gets to his feet and reaches for his jeans. Producing a condom, he rips the foil pack with his teeth, and I watch almost breathlessly as he rolls it down his length. Planting one knee on the mattress, he leans over and kisses my belly before rolling on his back and scooting up so he's leaning against the headboard again. Then he crooks a finger.

"Hop up, Gorgeous. Put me out of my misery."

I notice his fist wrapping tightly around the base of his cock as I scramble up the bed. His jaw clenches when I brace my hands on his chest and lick a path from his belly button up to the hollow at the base of his throat.

"Hmm, salty."

"Luce..." he warns with a growl.

Oh yeah. I feel powerful.

I swing my leg over and lean forward, shifting until I feel the bulbous head of his cock brush my folds. Starting to sink down, I have a brief moment of panic when I feel myself stretched to the point of pain. I dart a look at him and focus on his warm dark eyes.

"It's been a long time," I admit, but I get the sense he already knows that.

"That's why you're setting the pace."

I can tell it costs him, beads of sweat break out on his forehead as he tries not to move when I ease myself down, in very small increments, until he is rooted inside me. The feeling of fullness is overwhelming but I'm not scared. I realize Bo could easily hurt me, but I also know he won't.

Already he's shown me a different side to sex than what I've been used to. Foreplay was never part of the act, so the soft touches, the kissing, the whispers, the eye contact, are all new to me. Deriving pleasure from giving it an alien concept until I could feel Bo hum his appreciation while his mouth was between my legs. I hope one day I'll be able to give him a blowjob and enjoy it, but I'll have to work my way up to it.

"Killing me, here, Lucy..."

I lift my hips and let him slide out of me a little, before lowering myself. Then I do it again, and again, until my body falls into a rhythm that takes control. I close my eyes, letting myself move and feel. My arms rise up over my head, stretching for the ceiling as I bounce and roll my hips so I can feel every inch of his cock.

"Magnificent."

My eyes snap open, finding Bo's face tense, a muscle ticking in his jaw, but he looks at me as if I'm the most beautiful thing he's ever seen. No one's ever looked at me like that.

Emboldened, I lock eyes with him as I lower my hands and cup my breasts, fingers plucking and rolling my nipples. My mouth falls slack and a hot coil tightens low in my belly as my movements become erratic and I lose my rhythm.

"*Shit*," I mumble, and instantly his hands grab my hips and lift me up.

Then I'm rolled on my back, Bo hovering over me.

"Do you trust me?"

"Yes," is out of my mouth before I realize what I'm saying.

But there's no turning back as Bo spreads my legs wide, fits his hips between, and drives himself inside me with a power that takes my breath away. Rooted deep, he grinds himself against me, hitting all the right spots and the next instant I'm soaring, flying apart in a million fragments.

Moments later, Bo throws his head back with a roar, the tendons in his neck stretched to the max, as his body jerks with the force of his release.

~

I sit up in bed when he walks in buck naked with two steaming mugs of coffee. I appreciate the view but I moan with pleasure as I take my first sip. He chuckles as he assumes his position with his back to the headboard.

"The dogs?" I ask.

"Outside."

After we wore each other out, we managed to get another hour or so of sleep. No dreams either, but when I woke up a few minutes ago Bo was already awake, waiting. I was able to delay with the justification I needed some caffeine first, but I'm afraid I'm out of excuses.

"Whenever you're ready," Bo prompts.

I'm struggling with how much to tell him. Even if I just tell him about the dream, it will prompt questions. He's going to want names and that's something I won't give him. I've learned enough about Bo to worry he will want to slay my demons for me. He won't realize he's dealing with pure evil and I'm terrified he'll get hurt. I couldn't live with myself.

"I was in the barn," I start. "In a stall with Midnight and Mocha. I think I was putting down fresh straw."

I avoid eye contact and try to keep any inflection out of my voice. Bo occasionally grunts as I describe what I remember, taking care not to reveal too much. Still, as expected he has questions.

"Who was it? You say he was someone from your past. Your rapist?"

My entire body flinches at the barely contained rage in his voice.

"I don't know."

It's not a lie, I've long suspected it but I don't know for a fact.

I jump when I feel his hand on my shoulder.

"Jesus, Luce. I'm sorry. I'll control myself; I promise."

He tugs me tight to his side, pressing his lips against the side of my head.

"*Sorry...*" he repeats on a whisper.

He's a good man and I believe he really cares about me. He said in so many words he wants me to share the weight of my past. God, if only he knew how much I want that.

"I don't mean to be so secretive," I tell him. "It's how I've kept myself and everyone around me safe."

I take in a deep breath for courage and start at the beginning.

"There were two of them..."

Nineteen

Bo

Fucking hell.

I was able to sit through Lucy telling me how she was making a few bucks a week mucking stables on a farm near her house. A few months after her grandmother's passing, she was walking home one night, when they jumped her and hauled her into the trees.

That's when I jumped to my feet and started pacing back and forth, so Lucy suggested we move to the kitchen. Closer to the coffeepot. We brought the dogs in and filled up our mugs.

Lucy seems more comfortable, sitting at the table and sipping her morning brew. Her eyes follow me as I continue to pace.

"I never saw them. They pulled what felt like a pillowcase over my head and knocked me out with something. Only reason I know it was two of them was because I wasn't out that long and when I came to, one was on top of me and the other was yelling at him to hurry it up."

With rage rippling under my skin after hearing that, I don't understand how she can sit there so calmly.

"Tell me they caught the bastards."

She glances at me, a little smile pulling at her lips.

"My home was the holler where I'd grown up. Only time we saw the cops was when they came to pick someone up, so I was taught not to trust them."

When she mentions a holler, my mind immediately goes to the southern Appalachians. In those regions the term is used for a small valley in the hills with a collection of modest, even ramshackle houses, often with only one dirt road leading in and out, where everyone knows everyone and no one trusts strangers.

"You're telling me no report was ever made? No charges laid?"

I can't seem to hold back the sharp edge to my questions, making them sound more like accusations. It doesn't go unnoticed by Lucy, the flash of hurt in her eyes like a punch in my gut. I'd better check my temper if I want to have any chance at earning her trust.

"That didn't come out the way—"

She waves her hand, cutting me off.

"It doesn't matter. Trust me, I've kicked my own ass plenty over the years. Would've made a world of difference if I'd gone to the cops." She wipes her hair back off her face and almost absentmindedly starts braiding it. Her hands probably need something to do. "As it was, I didn't. I managed to make my way home and didn't tell anyone. Not then. The farmer's son came looking for me when I hadn't shown up for a few days. He told me I wasn't safe by myself and took me back to the farm."

She pauses, and I'm not sure if she's done or just needs a

moment to gear herself up to continue. I sit down across the table and lean forward.

"Did the family take care of you?"

She laughs derisively and it sends a shiver down my back. I've heard her laugh, normally the sound is warm and melodious, but it's cold and harsh now. I take it to mean she was not looked after and I get the sense I'm not going to like this part of her story any better.

She lets me take her hand across the table and, gently running my thumb over her bruised knuckles, I'm reminded how small and delicate she is under those tough layers. While I wait for her to speak, I imagine creative ways I'm going to kill each and every fucker who ever hurt her.

Fucking cowards, two of them jumping a little girl. Those sick bastards need to pay for what they did.

"They took me in and I was grateful. It was just the farmer and his two sons. Their mother died the year before and the old man was ailing. So I didn't think anything of it when I was expected to lend a hand around the house. At least not at first, but soon I was doing all the work. Cleaning, laundry, cooking. I took care of the chickens, milked the goats, looked after the vegetable garden."

"Child labor," I comment and she nods.

"The first time I complained, the brothers made me watch as my grandma's house burned to the ground. Everything I owned was in there. I was barely fourteen and mostly sheltered from the real world, I believed everything they told me."

She lets her eyes drift over my shoulders and cautiously pulls her hand back from under mine, cradling it in the other one on her lap.

I honestly thought that was the worst of it. Boy, was I wrong.

"The first one to come into my room was the older brother a few months later," she continues in a monotone voice. "He told me I was lucky, that I ought to be grateful I had a roof over my head and food in my belly. That I was soiled, that no one else would want me anyway."

I have a visceral reaction to the horrific picture she paints, but through the red haze, the blood thundering in my ears, one thing she mentioned stands out.

"He knew. That son of a bitch knew!"

As I shove my chair back and surge to my feet, Chief starts growling in the living room. But Lucy hasn't moved, her eyes are still fixed on a distant point behind me. She's back there somewhere, reliving those horrors.

*The first one to come into my room...*he hadn't been the only one.

Suddenly I don't need to hear any more. I round the table, go down on my knees in front of her, and take her hands in mine.

"No more, Lucy. That's enough." My voice sounds raw. "Fuck, I'm sorry I pushed."

To think that for too many years I felt I'd gotten a tough deal. My God, even if I'd gone to jail it would've been a walk in the park compared to what this woman lived through.

"I'm already back there," she whispers. "Let me finish."

She forges ahead and I don't do anything to stop her. The least I can do is hear her out, even if I'd rather stab pencils in my ears.

~

Lucy

"The older of the two moved away a few years after."

Funny, I'd always thought the older one was the more vicious of the two, but once he was gone the younger brother became more ruthless.

I'm almost grateful Bo keeps his head down. If I had to look into those warm, compassionate eyes, I'd never be able to finish my story and I don't ever want to go back there again. I spent a few years in therapy, ripping the scab off that wound every fucking appointment, and it's no more pleasant now.

This'll be a one-and-done trip down memory lane and that is it.

"When he left, I was told I needed to start helping with the horses. That became the highlight of every miserable day. It's where I found my strength, those horses saved me."

What I don't add is that they save me still. Every day.

His long fingers give my hand a squeeze but he doesn't look up. I so badly want to sink down on the floor with him, let him hold me together as I fall apart, but then I won't be able to finish.

I'm almost done. *Almost.*

"Then, one day, I passed out mucking out the stable, just as the younger brother walked in with the vet. I hadn't been well for a while, and that morning I'd started cramping heavily and bleeding more than was normal."

I still remember the pain in my stomach being so intense I wasn't able to stand straight, but I was told to suck it up. If it hadn't been for the vet showing up when he did, I doubt they would've taken me to the hospital and I would've bled out.

"Turned out it was a ruptured fallopian tube. As the result of an ectopic pregnancy."

His head snaps up and he stares at me for a beat before he gets to his feet. Then he starts pacing again, his hands in white-knuckled fists by his side.

"I guess they couldn't control the bleeding and they had to take the uterus as well."

"Oh, Luce," he mutters, stopping in front of me, but I wave him away and rush to finish my story.

"Day after surgery, the staff had me out of bed and walking. The day after that I snuck into the nurses' locker room, stole clothes and some money, and walked right out of that hospital. I'm not proud of some of the things I did to survive but I did. I got as far away from—" I'm narrowly able to swallow information I didn't want to share. "As far away as I could."

Those first few years, I never stayed in one place for long, picking up odd jobs along the way, and when I couldn't find work, I'd steal what I needed. I mucked stalls, weeded gardens, cleaned, harvested, and cooked—whatever was needed—and never owned more than a rusty bike and whatever I could carry in the old backpack I pulled out of a dumpster.

And then I met James.

"I'd found work at a stable as a groomer. The manager was a kind man, a former jockey who'd ended up in a wheelchair after an accident on the racetrack. He formed an interest in me."

Bo snorts loudly.

"Not like that," I hurry to clarify. "He was interested in my potential. I was good with the horses, he encouraged me to take on some more responsibilities—cooling down the animals after exercise and eventually exercising them. He used to say my size combined with my affinity and ease with horses made me good jockey material. I ended up becoming his protégé. I moved into his cottage on the grounds, and he became like a father to me over the next few years. I'd grown to trust him enough I even shared some of my background with him."

I loved him. The only man I'd ever known who made me feel safe. Who didn't exploit me but showed me what I was worth.

"Then, one day, I was on the exercise track riding Magic when his owner showed up. He'd do that occasionally but this time he wasn't alone; the second man who got out of the truck was the farmer's oldest son. It had been almost eight years since I last saw him, and two states over, but I had no trouble recognizing the man. I ran, didn't stop to see if he'd recognized me, I just took off."

I can still taste the bile burning my throat at the sight of him.

"My friend caught up with me at the cottage, where I was tossing my belongings in my backpack, and demanded to know what was going on. I made the mistake of telling him."

I signed his death certificate that day.

"He wanted me to go to the police, but I pointed out it was three against one. They'd never believe a nobody like me over people of their standing. He ended up loading me in his truck and driving me to the next largest town. There he gave me a stack of money, put me on the first Greyhound bus out of town, and told me to call him once I settled into a new place."

I remember getting as far as Omaha, Nebraska the next day, when I caught a news story on the small TV hanging on the wall of a roadside diner we stopped at for lunch. I was eating a cheeseburger at the time. Hell, I even recall the waitress's name. That moment is seared in my brain.

"He was dead the next day. Not even twenty hours after he put me on the bus, he was killed in what they called a freak explosion at the time, but was later discovered to have been intentional. It didn't matter, I'd known right away helping me had cost him his life. That was ten years ago."

Bo reaches out and tilts up my face, his thumb brushing my cheek. His face is blurred and I realize I'm crying.

"Luce..."

"Lucy Lenoir isn't my real name," I confess, letting him wrap his arms around me.

"Figured as much, baby."

I press my face in his chest, stifling a sob.

"I saw it in an obituary in the newspaper once. I paid someone to fake a birth certificate. It seemed like a good name."

"It's a great name," he rumbles against my ear.

"Bo?"

I tilt my head back and look up at him.

"Right here, Gorgeous."

"He was the man in my dream."

"The guy who showed up at the stable?"

I shake my head.

"No, it was the younger brother."

Twenty

Bo

"I can make it run."

I grin at Pippa's insulted tone. My comment that I wasn't sure anyone could get that old Gator going had the desired effect.

"It's for the rescue. It'll make Lucy's life so much easier."

"Awww," Pippa teases. "You're sweet on her."

I glance out the front window at the corral where the subject of conversation is exercising Ladybug in the snow which fell overnight. First time since the horse was poisoned.

After this morning, both of us needed a physical release. Her choice had been to put the horses through their paces, and I opted to chop some firewood. Lucy lasted longer. After almost two hours of wielding the axe, my arms felt like they'd fall off, and there was almost enough wood to last the winter, so I went inside and putzed around on my laptop instead.

"For a while now," I admit.

"I think we all knew that, Bo. I just wasn't sure you'd ever get around to doing something about it."

She snickers when I grunt. Then I promptly change the subject.

"Is your husband around?"

"In the office. He's prepping some paperwork for Jonas, who's apparently scheduled to be back tomorrow."

Perfect. I can maybe catch him alone. Thanking Pippa for agreeing to look at the Gator, I end the call and dial Sully.

"There was an explosion at Wilton Stables near Lexington Kentucky in December of 2012," I barge right in when he answers. I give him a synopsis of the article I just found on my laptop. It hadn't been that hard to pull it up, even with the minimal information I had.

"A former jockey by the name of James Rodriguez was killed."

I hear the tapping of keystrokes and I know he's looking it up.

"Initially thought to have been an accident, authorities are now convinced the blast was intentional," he reads to me.

"Bingo."

"Why are we looking at this?"

"I'm looking into something for a friend."

"A friend?" he echoes back doubtingly. "What does this 'friend' want to know?"

"I need a name. Someone who was a business associate or acquaintance of the owner. I'm looking specifically for an individual who was at the stables with him the day prior to the explosion."

"You're not asking for much, are you?"

"It needs to be discreet."

I'm not sure what I'll do with the information when I get it, but I want it. I want to know the names of these people who took advantage of a young, innocent girl in the most depraved ways.

He scoffs, "Of course it does."

"It's important or I wouldn't ask."

It's quiet for a beat before Sully responds.

"I know that, Brother. I'll do my best. Now, have you spoken to Jonas at all?"

"Briefly the day before yesterday but not since. Why?"

"He's heading back here tomorrow."

"Yeah, your wife mentioned something."

I watch Lucy dismount Ladybug in the corral and walk her out through the gate. It's snowing again and getting pretty thick. I can barely see the barn from here.

"They're bringing back four more yearlings for the program. I'm prepping the paperwork for the horses to be flown out at the end of next week and, apparently, Ludwig is staying to work with them here until then. Then we're gonna need to get Doc Evans to come in and get the animals certified before Friday. It's gonna be all-hands-on-deck because Jonas is going to be busy with Ludwig."

I just see Ladybug's swishing tail before she disappears into the barn.

"Wait, isn't he supposed to head out for the Annual Winter Auction in Utah on Wednesday?"

He'd planned to drive down with two three-year-olds.

"With James, yes. So James is driving out on Wednesday, and he's taking Dan. Jonas plans to fly out to join them on Friday morning, leaving at the same time Ludwig is flying home. But that means it's you, me, and Fletch left to keep business going here."

Shit. After hearing Lucy's story, I don't want to leave her alone at all but I may not have a choice.

"Sure thing. Why don't I check in tomorrow?"

"Sounds good, and I'll see what I can find out on this explosion."

By the time I get off the phone, Lucy has been inside the barn for close to ten minutes.

"Come on, boys," I call for the dogs, who are ready by the front door before I can shove my feet in my boots.

Outside the wind is fierce, blowing the snow almost sideways. I could've used my big parka but it is back at my apartment and this lined corduroy jacket isn't quite cutting it in this weather. I flip up my collar, shove my hat on tighter, and duck my head against the wind as I make my way to the barn.

Ladybug is in her stall, but I don't know where Lucy is. My first instinct is to check the tack room but she's not there either.

"Lucy?"

I stop at the bottom of the ladder and peer up to the hayloft. Not a sound coming from up there. Despite feeling the first hint of foreboding, I force myself to methodically search every one of the six stalls in the barn.

I'm about to climb up to the hayloft when I realize the dogs didn't come into the barn with me. They're still outside, which very likely means Lucy is too.

When I push open the barn door it's almost ripped from my hand by a gust of wind. *Jesus, it's blowing.* I'd better make sure it's latched properly.

When I turn around, I catch sight of Scout sniffing around by the chicken coop—or goat pen as it's been repurposed—but no sign of Lucy.

"*Lucy!*" I yell as loud as I can, my hands cupped around my mouth.

Problem is, snow tends to absorb sound and if you add the wind to it, I'd be surprised if it carried at all. Scout heard it though. He runs over, jumps up, and immediately walks back toward the pen, stopping halfway to look back at me.

"What is it boy?"

I follow him and am surprised to see the door to the shelter partway open. I duck my head inside and the coppery smell hits me a fraction of a second before the gruesome sight registers.

It takes me a moment to realize I'm looking at only one goat. The momma goat, Bella. It's hard to tell what got her but whatever it was did a number on her. No sign of the little guys, or Lucy for that matter.

Then I hear barking.

~

Lucy

I have no idea how Midnight ended up under the shelter in the back meadow, but that's where I found him. Right beside Daisy, munching on some of the hay I'd put out there before the snow hit.

I knew something was wrong when I came out of the barn and almost tripped over Mocha. But when I bent down to pick him up, he took off, which is when I saw the door to the pen was partly open. I'd been so sure I closed it after I fed them earlier.

Mocha was already halfway to the back field before I

caught up with him. I managed to scoop him up and tucked him under one arm when he loudly bleated his protest. To my surprise, a responding call came from the field.

I'm on my way back when Chief comes running up to me, barking.

"Hey, buddy. Did Bo let you out?"

The dog dances around my feet looking for attention but I don't have a hand free to pet him.

"Are you okay?"

I look up to find Bo striding toward me, his face a tense mask. He looks pissed.

"Yeah, I was chasing down the babies, they got out. I probably didn't put the latch on properly. Bella probably took off too, better put these guys away and—"

I stop my nervous rambling abruptly when I notice Bo seems to be staring at Midnight. Then he reaches for him.

"What is it?"

The moment Bo has a hold of the goat I see it; blood on my hand. Not just a little bit either.

"Oh my God. Is he all right?"

He was wet when I picked him up—they both were—but I figured that was from the snow.

"We'll check him in the barn. Let's get out of this weather."

Bo leads the way and holds the door open for me to go ahead as he whistles for the dogs. Inside, I quickly put Mocha down and notice that hand is bloody as well. It's impossible to tell where the blood's coming from—both of them have dark hair—but I can't find any injuries on Mocha and he doesn't really look hurt. Neither does Midnight for that matter. Bo is next to me running his hands over the goat.

"I don't get it. The blood has to come from

somewhere."

Bo sends me a look I can't quite place as he lets the little guy go. The two immediately dart off, playing as they usually do.

Then it occurs to me; Bella is still out there.

The moment I start moving toward the door though, Bo is on his feet. Then he steps in front of me, blocking my way, and shakes his head.

"Bella?"

"Something got her, Lucy."

Oh no...poor Bella.

"Let me see."

I try to slip by him but he puts a hand on my stomach.

"Not a good idea, Luce, it's ugly."

"Bear?"

Even as I suggest it, I know it's pretty unlikely, most bears would be in hibernation by now. Maybe a mountain lion, but I haven't seen evidence of one around.

"Too late in the season. Why don't you stay here and I'll go have a better look? I was more worried about finding you earlier."

I surprise myself when instead of arguing with him, I sit down where I stand and catch the first little goat that darts by, snuggling him tight.

I'm still not used to having someone worry about me. It feels good.

Tough not to think about Bella, but I try to distract myself by playing with her babies. Thank God whatever killed her didn't get them. Weird, when you think about it. The little ones would have been the more obvious prey. I'd like to think that despite her rejection of her kids at first, she still had enough motherly instinct to put herself between them and a predator. I'm still sad, but it makes me feel a little better.

But then Bo walks in a few moments later, his phone to his ear but his eyes on me.

"Reggie. Yeah, man. I need you to come over to Lucy's place. We've got another problem."

He sinks down on the ground beside me—surprisingly graceful for such a large man—and wraps his free arm around my shoulder, and I know this is not going to be good.

"Someone killed her goat."

Someone?

Bo's arm tightens around me in anticipation, just as I'm about to jump to my feet.

"A knife," I hear him say. "No, I didn't touch it."

Who?

So many thoughts roll through my head, but nothing makes sense. Lester is dead. He may have poisoned Ladybug but he couldn't have done this, so someone else must've killed Bella. Why would two different people hurt my animals?

Could it be Burns? Not unless he's back from Panama, and even then, if it's true Sam is back with him, what reason could he have?

My mind starts going in another, even darker, direction but Bo seems to sense it and presses a kiss to my temple.

"Don't overthink. Let's just wait for Williams, he won't be long."

Easier said than done. It actually becomes impossible to think of anything else, and that feeling of doom closes down on me like a vise.

The dogs start barking about fifteen minutes later,

moments before we hear a vehicle drive up and stop right outside the barn.

"Keep the dogs in here."

I shiver involuntarily, missing his warmth the moment he gets to his feet.

It feels like an eternity, but it's probably no more than ten, maybe fifteen minutes later when Bo walks in with Detective Williams in tow.

"Detective," I mumble in greeting as Bo helps me to my feet.

"Ms. Lenoir, I'm sorry for your loss."

I'm not sure why that sentiment suddenly has tears brimming in my eyes. It's not like he's notifying me of the death of a loved one. Then again, I guess in my world she was. A goat—if it wasn't so sad it might be funny. My family is a collection of rejected and abused horses, a small donkey, a couple of dogs, and three—now two—pygmy goats.

"Are the little guys okay?" Williams asks.

"Yeah, they were lucky."

"Good, because that was a pretty brutal scene. Bo tells me you had to chase them down? How'd you find out they were missing in the first place?"

I tell him how I bumped into Mocha outside the barn and that's when I noticed the door to the pen open. As I'm talking, Bo closes in beside me, sliding his hand up my spine and curving his fingers around my neck. Quiet, supportive, and I find myself leaning into his hold.

"And you didn't go check it out?"

"No," I snap, feeling a bit defensive. "I was too busy chasing after that one." I point at Mocha. "He took off and when I caught him out back, I noticed his brother in the shelter with the horses. Bo was already here when I got back."

"I understand you were outside most of the afternoon. You didn't see anything or anyone?"

"No. I was exercising the horses in the corral; I would've seen anyone coming up the driveway. I guess they could've approached from the back since you can't really see the pen from the front, but I never saw anything. I didn't notice anything going into the barn either."

Williams exchanges a look with Bo. I'm not sure what message is being relayed but Bo seems to press even closer. Then Williams sticks a hand in the front of his winter jacket and pulls out a plastic bag. It holds a bloody knife.

"Do you recognize this?" he asks.

The image of my kitchen blinds rolled up all the way flashes before my eyes. It had been one of the many small ways the brothers would torture me.

I've always struggled with early mornings, in part because my eyes are hypersensitive to light when I first wake up. I'd walk into the kitchen with the low morning sun glaring in through the window. My eyes would burn and tears would start running down my face.

That's why my mind went there when I walked into the house last week and saw my kitchen blinds up. I'd almost dismissed it as a fluke until now.

"That's my chef's knife."

Twenty-One

Bo

The snow has stopped when we step out of the barn.

Lucy and Williams are each carrying a goat and I'm leading Ladybug to join the other horses out back. Lucy was adamant she didn't want any animal left to fend for themselves so Midnight and Mocha are coming back to the house. Ladybug will be safer from any kind of predator with the herd.

I suspected the knife might be hers when Reggie pulled it out. The first time I looked into the pen I hadn't noticed it, I'd been distracted by the carnage, but I spotted it when I looked a second time. Whoever killed the animal left the knife embedded in an eye socket as a pretty significant statement.

It wasn't easy, listening to my friend grilling Lucy, but as he pointed out to me earlier in the goat pen, he'll be able to get to the truth faster if I let him do his job. He also warned me he'd be calling in Ewing since it's clear something is going on—too much to be considered a coincidence—and Lucy is at the core of it.

"Let's go, boys," I tell the dogs, who ended up following me.

Ladybug is heading for the hay feeder and the rest of the herd, and I turn back to the house with Scout and Chief on my heels. I find Lucy and Williams on the back porch, setting up the makeshift pen she had out here before.

"Want me to go grab some straw?"

I notice as Lucy turns to glance at me, she looks worn out and her voice is flat when she answers.

"Would you?"

Turns out she needs some hay and food for the goats as well, but twenty minutes later the goats have all they need. I'm standing by the front window watching Reggie lead the sheriff to the barn. Lucy is in the kitchen, making a stack of sandwiches in an effort to stay busy. She's been very subdued and I'd love to try and get her talking, but I figure there'll be more questions for her when those guys get back here. She can probably use the breather.

"I keep that knife in here," she explains later, as she pulls open the top drawer and takes out a knife guard. "It belongs in here."

"And the last time you saw it?" Reggie asks.

He pulls a pair of gloves from his pocket, slips one on and gingerly takes the knife guard from Lucy, then he inverts the other glove over the sheath to protect any prints.

So far Ewing has taken a back seat for the most part. It's a little weird, the detective and the sheriff sitting at the kitchen table eating Lucy's sandwiches while conducting what, at times, sounds more like an interrogation to me.

"I can't remember exactly. Maybe a week ago? I thought it was in the dishwasher."

"For a week?" Ewing pipes up.

I open my mouth to call a halt to this at the same time Lucy slams her mug down on the counter with such force, the ear breaks clear off in her hand.

"Yes, for a week! I live here by myself so it takes me longer than that to fill a load. Why would I lie about that?"

Agitated, she lobs the broken ear in the sink with a sharp clatter.

"We're just trying to understand," the sheriff placates her, but she's not having any of it.

Things have just reached their limit for Lucy, but in the next moment she manages to bring me to mine.

"Then understand this; there's a reason I was taught not to trust cops and this is it. Can't you see someone is trying to set me up? Now I *know* he was in my house last week. He took my knife."

"What do you mean in your house? Who was in your house? When?"

My mouth is spewing out the question as my mind is trying to make sense of what she said.

"Last Tuesday," she says, her fire already dimming.

I remember we'd come back from setting up a trail for Dan. I'd found her frozen to the spot in the living room when I walked in.

"Something spooked you."

She nods, letting her eyes drift over my shoulder. "The kitchen blinds were rolled up."

I remember asking her what was wrong and her telling me she hadn't been sleeping well, had too much on her mind. I took her at her word and didn't pry, didn't push. I should've.

Frustration has me lash out.

"Why the fuck didn't you tell me?"

She startles at my barked question and Reggie reaches out to put a restraining hand on my arm. That ticks me off even more and I shake him off, focusing on Lucy.

"How the hell am I supposed to look out for you—protect you—if you keep shit like that from me?"

"I never asked you to look out for me!"

Her mouth is set in an angry line yet her eyes are shimmering with unshed tears, and I'm instantly regretful. Yelling at her is not going to change anything, but when I make a move toward her, she warns me off with raised hands.

"Why don't you tell us about the blinds," Ewing intervenes, his voice soothing as he draws Lucy's attention.

Angry at myself for losing it on her, I take a few deep breaths as I force myself to simply listen.

According to Lucy, the kitchen blinds are always half closed on purpose. She mentions she has some eye condition that makes her sensitive to light first thing in the morning.

Well, that clarifies why she looks like she has trouble waking up.

She explains she noticed it the moment she walked in and panicked, thinking someone had been in the house, but then she convinced herself it could've easily been me.

"I never touched them," I volunteer.

"Any sign of forced entry?" Williams asks.

Lucy shakes her head. "I'd locked the front door when we left, but hadn't set the alarm." Then she throws me a quick glance. "And I'd left the bedroom window open a crack."

I remember I'd offered to go ahead and fetch the horses from the back field and asking her if she'd locked up when she joined me in the barn. By the time we ended up in

Lucy's bedroom my mind had been firmly on other things. Fine protector I am.

Reggie is already over by the sink, donning a pair of latex gloves he pulls from his pocket, and giving the blinds a closer look.

"Were you planning to wipe those for prints?" Ewing asks. "Because it's probably easier just to take the whole thing down. I can drop it off at the lab, let forensics do it."

"Are you done with me?" Lucy addresses the sheriff. "I'm not feeling well."

Shit. She looks like she could keel over at any minute, she's so pale. But when I step closer, she starts moving away from me toward the short hallway that leads to her bedroom.

"Sure," Ewing tells her. "We'll call if we have more questions."

With a quick nod at the sheriff, she disappears, and a moment later I hear the bedroom door click shut.

Lucy

I flop facedown on my bed and pull the pillow over my head.

Should I have told them?

That would've meant dragging up my entire sordid history once again. Even if they believed every word, it would still be a long shot to convince them of the possibility one of the brothers suddenly found me after more than a decade, only to mess with my kitchen blinds. They'll think I'm the one who's crazy.

Hell, it sounds far-fetched to me. I wouldn't put it past either one of them to harm the animals, but it still doesn't explain what happened to Lester Franklin, it's not like he was a friend of mine, like James was.

Also, I would have to come clean about living under a fake identity with forged papers I paid a mint for, and that could get me in serious trouble.

Then again, what if it *is* one of them? Am I playing into their hands by not saying anything?

I don't know what the right thing is and it's giving me a headache. Damned if I do and damned if I don't.

With a frustrated groan, I roll out of bed and walk into the bathroom, where I hope some Tylenol and a shower may help clear my head.

When I emerge fifteen minutes later, with my hair twisted in a towel and another wrapped around me, Bo is sitting on the edge of the bed.

"I'm sorry," is the first thing he says, taking me by surprise.

He was pretty angry with me earlier and not entirely without cause, I can see that now, but at the time I didn't think he'd believe me.

"I shouldn't have yelled, but why would you keep something like that from me? Especially after you had that nightmare and shared your history with me."

I sit down beside him, focus on my bare feet, and notice how much smaller they are than Bo's boots. Still, despite the fact he could crush me like a bug and looked angry enough earlier to try it, I don't feel the slightest threat from him.

"Would you have believed me then?" I turn it back on

him. "You wouldn't have known a knife was missing and Bella was still fine then. It would've sounded crazy."

To his credit, he doesn't argue my point, although he doesn't concede it either.

"Maybe, maybe not. No way to know now."

He lifts a hand to my chest and brushes away a few lingering drops.

"Are they gone?"

"Yeah. They took the blinds and the knife guard as well. They're sending over a tech to dust the window in here tomorrow. Hopefully they'll come up with something. In the meantime though, I'd like you to pack a bag."

"Why?"

It's an automatic response because, to be honest, I feel a little skeeved out thinking someone was in my house, let alone in my bedroom. I can't leave the animals though. Especially after what happened to Bella.

Bo lies back on the mattress, taking me with him. Then he rolls on his side to face me.

"Because you can't stay here. Hear me out," he quickly adds, covering my lips with a finger before I have a chance to protest. "There's a guest cabin at the ranch. You can bring the dogs and I'm sure we can find a place for the goats. It's all-hands-on-deck at the ranch this week and it'll make me feel a whole fuck of a lot better if you were close."

"But I can't leave Daisy and the horses," I point out. "And I have Amelia Mills and her mother coming again on Tuesday."

"You should probably cancel Amelia either way, Luce. At least until we figure out what the hell is happening."

That kind of confirms what I was thinking, but I hate the idea of losing that tiny thread of connection I started forming with the girl. I also don't want to risk adding more trauma, should something else happen at the rescue when Amelia is there.

"As for the rest of the animals, they're safe enough if you're not here. It seems obvious whoever is doing this hopes to implicate you, and with you gone it wouldn't make sense to hurt your horses. But if it makes you feel better, once I have you installed at the ranch, I'll come back with Fletch or Sully and install some trail cams around the pasture."

"They need a steady supply of fresh hay."

Bo smiles, probably sensing a victory, and leans in to brush my lips with his.

"Consider it done."

Alex is waiting on the small front porch of the cabin when Bo pulls the truck up.

It's already pretty late and I feel bad she waited up for us.

The back seat of the truck is crowded with both the dogs and the kids sharing the narrow bench. I glance over my shoulder, hoping the goats hadn't chewed on or shit all over the fabric.

"Oh my, look at those cuties."

Of course, Alex already has the back door open to greet the animals before I'm out of my seat. Chief and Scout hopped right down, while Max—the ranch's Bernese mountain dog—jumps with his front paws up on the bench and gives the newcomers a good sniff.

"Dan got a stall ready in the barn for these two," Alex shares, grabbing Mocha under her arm.

I lean in and lift Midnight out. Bo grabs the bag with

their feed and bottles from the back of the truck and hooks it over my shoulder.

"Why don't you go get them settled in. I'll look after the rest of the stuff."

Alex and I start walking toward the barn. The outside light over the barn doors as well as the floodlight over the corral are on, so we're not stumbling around in the dark. All three dogs stick close, sniffing the occasional marks in the snow but never venturing far.

It's so cold the fresh snow crunches under my boots. I hope the cabin has heat, I'm about ready to crawl into a warm bed, I'm exhausted.

"You didn't have to wait up for us."

Alex turns her head to look at me.

"Of course I did. I don't sleep much when Jonas is gone anyway," she admits.

I'd been shocked to see it was already after eleven on the dashboard clock by the time we had everything loaded up. It had taken me a while to get all the gear for me and the animals together and packed. In the meantime, Bo had called ahead to the ranch to clear things with Alex. He'd also given Detective Williams a heads-up so they'd know where to find us if they had any more questions.

"Well, I appreciate you letting me stay here."

"Of course. Anytime. That cabin's been empty since Sloane moved out last month. She got a place in town." She grins at me. "Decided living this close to Uncle Sully put a bit of a damper on her love life."

"I can see how it would. Is she seeing someone?"

"Not that I know. Although, I've wondered if perhaps there wasn't something going on with Dan. They definitely notice each other."

I follow her into the barn, where she enters the first stall on the right. It looks to be about twice the size of the ones back at the rescue. A chuckle escapes me when I walk in.

Someone—I assume it was Dan—used straw bales, a couple of old tires, a few boards, and an upside-down bucket to build a jungle gym of sorts for the goats against the back wall of the stall. The moment I put Midnight down, he hops on the bucket and without hesitation traverses a steep incline along a narrow board to a stack of bales. His brother is not far behind.

"This is awesome." I turn to Alex. "Did you ask him to do this?"

"Nope. This is all him."

I make a mental note to do something nice for Dan.

Satisfied the goats are secure for the night, we close the barn and head back in the direction of the house.

"Bo gave me the gist of what happened," Alex starts tentatively. "I'm sorry about the momma goat. He says you guys think someone was in the house?"

"Yeah."

It warms me he would say both of us thought someone was there. It's an indication at least he believes me. I feel a little guilty for not elaborating—Alex deserves to know—but I really don't want to go over the whole thing again tonight, or I'll never get any sleep.

"Tomorrow is soon enough," she says, proving herself to easily be the better friend. "Go get some sleep."

I moan when I walk into the cabin and find it cozy warm. It's nothing special; a large square room housing a basic kitchen, an old Formica kitchen table, and a plaid, threadbare couch and well-worn coffee table facing a wood-burning stove. The dogs have already taken up domicile on their beds Bo tossed on the floor in front of the stove, which is radiating all kinds of heat.

Bo comes walking out of one of the doors on this side of the cabin—bedroom and bathroom, I assume—and heads straight for me.

"Get out of those, it's warm in here," he mutters, pulling off my beanie and unzipping my parka.

Normally I'd probably swat at him but I'm tired and my hands are half frozen, and frankly, it makes me feel good to be looked after. At least when Bo does it.

"Did you want something to drink? Are you hungry? You haven't eaten. Alex put some basics in the fridge."

I shake my head, I'm barely able to stay on my feet. This entire day suddenly hits me like a ton of bricks.

"Too tired."

"I can tell. You're a little unsteady." Next thing I know I'm swept up in his arms. "Let's get you to bed."

The last thing I remember is his warm body curving against my back.

Better than a heated blanket.

Twenty-Two

Bo

I crack an eye when I feel a small hand slip inside my boxer briefs.

Apparently, someone else is already awake. I'm surprised, given Lucy's allergy to early mornings, but I don't have any problem with it.

"Morning to you too," I groan as fingers curve around my morning wood.

I glance down just in time to watch Lucy slip the tip of my cock between her lips.

Have mercy.

I don't want to think too hard about how she became so skillful with her mouth and hands, so I close my eyes and focus on the sensations as I blindly reach down for her. But the instant she feels my fingers sliding into her hair she freezes.

"Lucy?"

The next moment she abandons my cock and scrambles off the bed, making a beeline for the door. Before I can figure out how to react, I hear the shower turn on in the bathroom next door.

I figured, after getting a general sense of the abuse she suffered, she would have triggers around sex. I was actually quite surprised by her enthusiasm the night of her dream and again just now. Both times she initiated sex and I don't have a problem with her taking control. She probably needs to, although I'm only guessing at that.

The truth is, I have no clue what she needs or doesn't need. Her reaction just now proves that. Unless I want to risk triggering her again, I either have to become a passive participant—and I'm not really on board with that—or I need to understand what her triggers are. Last thing I want to do is upset her.

Only way to find out is ask her, so I swing my legs out of bed, shrug into my jeans, and pad into the kitchen. Even though the sun won't be up yet for a while, I suspect she's going to need some caffeinated reinforcement.

While the coffee is brewing, I toss a few logs on the glowing coals in the wood stove. It's cold. Last night's condensation has frosted the bottom half of the windows. Looks like winter has arrived, which usually means work slows down a bit. First though, we'll have to get the horses moved to pastures closer to the ranch, where they'll have shelter from the worst of the weather.

After yesterday's dump and the descent into the deep freeze last night, I suspect we'll be riding out sooner rather than later. I wouldn't be surprised if we roll out today since we'll be short a few bodies starting Wednesday, when Dan and Fletch are off to the auction. I'm not looking forward to leaving Lucy, but at least she won't be alone here at the ranch.

I pour coffee in two mugs and take them into the bathroom with me. Lucy is still standing in the tub under the shower, her back turned to me. Her entire posture—the hunched shoulders, arms wrapped around herself—screams defeat. I don't like it, that's not the woman I know.

The decision comes easy. Setting the mugs on the vanity, I kick off my jeans and boxers, and step into the tub with her. The water is almost scalding hot and I quickly reach around her to adjust the temperature.

She doesn't move. Not even when my arms encircle her, pulling her flush against me.

"What happened?"

I expect her to need some prodding, so I'm taken by surprise when she comes back right away.

"I made a mistake."

"Didn't feel like a mistake to me."

I purposely focus on the incident earlier, rather than the entirety of our relationship which I'm afraid she might be referring to. But I'm encouraged when she explains.

"I thought maybe I could do this, have a normal relationship, but I'll never be rid of my past."

I want to be careful how I respond. My instinct is to disagree with her and make promises I likely won't be able to keep, which will only hurt my credibility. So, I take my time weighing my words.

"I think it's reasonable to assume whatever happened to us in the past plays a role in how we react to our present and adjust for the future. That goes for positive experiences as much as it does for negative ones."

She slowly turns in my arms and lifts her face. I notice her eyes are shiny. Then she places her hands on my chest and tilts her head slightly, showing me she's listening.

"It's clear something happened just now that took you out of the present and back to the past," I forge ahead, encouraged. "I can only guess at what it was, but perhaps if you identify it, we'll be able to adapt for next time."

Her eyes drift away from me and lock somewhere on the tile wall behind me.

"And also," I press on, a little worried I'm losing her. "What is a 'normal' relationship anyway? A relationship is a connection created between two unique individuals. None of us are alike, and the only thing we share is that we're human and therefore we're flawed. There is no *normal* in a relationship, there is only what we make of it and what we take away from it."

Her gaze is once again firmly focused on me.

"I was raped," she states in an amazingly strong voice, and I work hard not to wince at the harshness of her words. "I don't like doggie style and I don't like my head held during a blowjob. The first because I can't see who's behind me, and the second because I can't breathe."

Fucking hell.

My efforts to keep a straight face fail miserably. I want to put my fist through a wall but instead I bury my face in her hair. I realize this may be as much of a test for me as it is for her, because my words become meaningless if I'm the one who can't move on from her past.

So I inhale her scent, draw from her strength, and lift my head with a grin.

"How do you feel about up against the shower wall?"

For a moment, I'm afraid maybe I took it too far, but then a grin slowly spreads over her face as her hands slide up and around my neck.

"I don't know, it'll be a first for me."

An invitation if ever I heard one.

"Hop on up."

I catch her with my hands behind her legs as I press her back into the wall and cover her mouth with mine.

She feels so damn good; her sexy padded body a perfect pillow for mine, silky water-slicked skin for my hands to explore, and the sweet, wet heat of her mouth to claim. She gives as good as she gets, her tongue dueling, fingers clawing, and rocking against me until the crown of my cock breaches her pussy.

Fuck.

She groans her protest when I pull back.

"Condom," I mumble against her lips.

"I'm safe," she whispers back, rolling her hips.

"Shit, Luce. I'm clean."

Our eyes meet as I hook my arms under her knees and spread her wider.

Then she sinks her teeth into her plump bottom lip as I fill her in one stroke.

Sexiest damn thing I've ever seen.

~

Lucy

I swear it feels like everyone can see I'm walking bowlegged.

"Come sit by me."

Thomas pats the seat of the chair beside him. I smile and take him up on his invitation. Bo grumbles behind me since he's now relegated to the only other available seat at the table, across from me.

We'd barely come out of the shower when Sully knocked

on the door, telling Bo breakfast was ready and to get our asses in gear. I only had time to throw on some clothes and was forced to twist my wet hair in a braid, before Bo was rushing me out the door.

"Coffee?"

"Please."

I never had a chance to take a sip of the coffee Bo brewed back at the cabin.

Ama, James's wife, hands me a cup and I eagerly gulp down half of it, so she sets the coffeepot in front of me on the table.

"I'll just leave it here," she comments dryly.

There's a clatter of china and cutlery as plates of scrambled eggs, toast, bacon, and hash browns do the rounds around the table. Thomas, Alex, Sully, Ama, James, Pippa and the baby, Dan, and then Bo and I easily fit around the large dining table in the main house.

"Fletch is on his way," Sully announces. "There's another storm heading this way and it's expected to dump upward of ten inches between midnight and tomorrow morning. We've fallen a little behind and it's catching up fast. We've got some damage to the fence on the field behind the barn and one of the corrugated roof panels blew off the shelter in yesterday's storm. Someone needs to go out and check the shelter back here." He points out the kitchen doors to the empty field beyond the garden. "And check this fence line."

"I'll check the back field here," Bo volunteers.

Dan pipes up right after. "I'll take care of the shelter roof and the fence by the barn."

"I'll give you a hand with that," Fletch announces as he walks into the kitchen.

"Good," Sully approves. "I'm going to want Phantom,

Blitz, and the team horses stabled, but we also have those four young horses coming in sometime today. That's a lot of horses inside and we're already down one stall with the rescue goats, so we'll have to be creative. Our horses can be in their regular stalls—we'll need to get those ready—but I don't think it's smart to cram those yearlings in too."

"I can move around some barriers in the breeding barn to create makeshift stalls for the four newcomers. They're here only temporarily anyway," James suggests.

"Leave the barn to me," Alex volunteers, "I'll get it ready."

"I can help," I offer.

I might as well make myself useful, although I'm even more worried about my own horses at home now.

"We're going to need to put up some trail cams on the herd at the rescue," Bo brings up to Sully, as if he could read my thoughts.

"Okay. Repairs first, then James, Dan, and I can bring our animals home, and you and Fletch go put up the cams at the rescue."

"And I'll keep the homestead safe," Thomas contributes.

"You mean fall asleep on the porch, old man?" Ama teases.

"The dogs'll wake me up."

Ten minutes later, the table is cleared, dishes stacked in the massive dishwasher, and other than Ama and Thomas, everyone bundles up and heads outside.

I give Pippa a hand with the baby, holding little Carmi so her mom can get dressed herself, when I catch Bo looking at me, a worried look on his face. I guess that's going to be a conversation for another time. This morning's topic was quite enough for one day, although Bo did a good job of making me forget about it for a while.

The baby talk will have to keep for another day. I have no idea if Bo wants children, but he knows I can't have them. I've come to terms with it over the years, but it's probably a good idea to figure out how he feels about it before my hopes bloom and my heart gets more invested.

I press a kiss to Carmi's downy forehead and hand her back to Pippa.

"Are you good?" Bo's deep voice rumbles beside me.

"Yeah, I'm fine. I'd better go feed my goats."

I throw him a little smile and he responds by planting a kiss on my lips.

"Stay close. Call if you need me, I've got my phone on me."

I mock-salute him and Thomas starts cackling in the doorway behind me.

"Women generally respond better to requests than orders," he advises Bo.

"Thanks for the wisdom," he fires back with a grin. "So, how's that working for you?"

"Not too bad. Where is your mother anyway?"

Bo stalks off, shaking his head, which clearly pleases the old man to no end. He takes a seat in the rocking chair on the porch, pulling a fat cigar from his jacket pocket. Looks like he'll be here for a while.

"You boys stay with Thomas," I order Chief and Scout.

They've taken a liking to him and drop down on the porch by his feet without protest, as I start down the steps.

"Hey, Lucy..."

I look over my shoulder at Thomas, who jerks his chin toward Bo's retreating back.

"He's like a son to me. You could do worse."

Throwing him a smile, I continue toward the barn.

I could do a whole lot worse.

Twenty-Three

Bo

I find Lucy in the stall with the goats.

"I'm heading out with Fletch to set up those cameras. Anything you need from the rescue?"

She immediately jumps to her feet, brushing straw off her clothes.

"I can come help."

I cup her face between my hands and brush a kiss on her lips.

"Fletch and I are like a well-oiled machine, Gorgeous. Stay. I bet Ama wouldn't say no to some help though; she's got a lot of hungry mouths to cook for and an obstinate teenager to chase down."

Not a lie, I heard Ama hollering on the phone. Her and James's daughter, Una, has morphed from a sweet, funny kid into a stubborn, defiant adolescent. Not unlike her mother at that age, according to James.

But my real objective is to keep Lucy occupied here. I don't want her to tag along to the rescue because I hope to get Fletch to help me clean up the goat pen. Reggie called earlier to let me know they're done with the place, and I really don't want to leave Bella in there to rot. Luckily, it's been cold enough she shouldn't stink that much but I'd like to deal with her before the ground freezes.

I get a suspicious look from her. She knows damn well I'm manipulating her, but still can't resist the lure of working in the industrial grade kitchen in the main house. I know when she's stressed she cooks, she's told me as much herself. Plus, I've seen her eye the massive dual-oven, seven-burner range which to her is probably like the 6.2-liter HEMI V8 engine in the new Ram 1500 TRX is to me; the stuff dreams are made of. Except the truck would put too big of a dent in my nest egg at a tidy ninety grand or so, but it could withstand the price of a range like that. I'm not sure when Lucy's birthday is, but Christmas isn't that far away and I'd love to make a dream come true for her.

"Fine, but don't think I don't know what you're doing," she says with a deep frown.

I don't bother playing innocent and instead hook my arm around her waist, hauling her flush against me. Then I kiss her, doing my best to wipe that frown off her face. I know I've accomplished my goal when I feel the blunt tips of her fingers dig into the back of my neck.

"Don't you guys have a fucking cabin here? Use it," James grumbles, leading his horse past us out of the barn.

The guys are saddling up to go fetch the herd before they lose all daylight. The days are getting so much shorter and this one has slipped away from us. So, with the impending snowstorm moving a little faster than expected and lots left to do, tensions are mounting.

I grin down at Lucy, who looks a little uneasy with the interruption.

"Ignore him. He has a daughter determined to get on his last nerve, which is more punishment than any father deserves."

My comment earns me a faint smile. Not much, but I'll take it and capitalize on it immediately.

"I should get going. Fletch is waiting and, believe it or not, he *can* get even crankier."

As evidenced by the dirty look and mumbled expletives when I climb into the passenger side of his truck a couple of minutes later.

~

"Fuck, that thing stinks."

Fletch covers his nose and mouth with the collar of his jacket.

He's not wrong. Despite the cool temperatures, the goat has started smelling like a combination of body fluids and rotten eggs.

"They sure did a number on her," he adds. "Seems angry, doesn't it?"

Hadn't thought about that, but looking at the way the animal was carved up I'd have to agree.

"Yeah. You'd almost think this was more than merely an attempt to scare Lucy," I suggest.

I'm not a profiler but it doesn't seem too far of a stretch to think whoever did this imagined cutting and mutilating a person, not a goat.

"Definitely working out his anger on someone," Fletch appears to agree.

An image flashes in my mind that turns my stomach.

"I'm gonna find a shovel."

I'm gonna hurl if I don't get out of here.

The barn looks undisturbed and I turn to the corner by the tack room where Lucy keeps the tools. She's got a couple of brooms, an old hay fork, and two shit shovels. Not exactly prime tools to dig a hole, but it'll have to do unless I can find an actual spade.

I hand Fletch, who followed me in, the shovel.

"It's the best I can find for now. See if it's any use while I go check if she's got something better in the shed by the house."

"Gonna need a flashlight too."

I point at the one on the nail next to the door.

"Grab that one."

It's dark out and snow has started falling. Luckily, we opted to put up the cameras first, before we tackled Bella, figuring we'd make the most of the remaining daylight.

The outside lamps must be on a sensor because both the floodlight above the barn doors and the porch light at the house are on, which is enough to light the way.

Lucy admitted she's not in the habit of locking the door, let alone setting the alarm, when working around the property, but she made sure she locked it up tight before we left yesterday. I got the keys and the alarm code from her so I can get in to grab the shampoo she forgot, but first I need to get into the shed to see if I can find a decent shovel.

Unfortunately, access faces the rear of the house, which means it's pretty dark and I can't see a hell of a lot, even with the doors wide open. Turning on the flashlight on my phone, I shine it into the shed, seeing the regular stuff: a rusty mower, wheelbarrow, a couple of buckets, a rake, old clay pots, and a half-empty bag of soil.

But aside from the spade I spotted in the corner, my attention is drawn to a plastic lawn chair, an upside-down bucket beside it. It's not the only bucket, or lawn chair for that matter, but there's something about the way the two are positioned. When I shine my light on the floor in front of it, I notice a pair of boot prints in the dirt, suggesting someone might have been sitting there. Keeping vigil, watching and waiting.

I can feel the hair on my arms stand on end.

Then I back out of the shed, close the doors carefully, and turn off the flashlight on my phone before dialing Reggie Williams for the second time in as many days.

~

Lucy

"Hey, buddy."

I pull off my gloves and shove them in my pocket before crouching down to scratch Scout's head. He jumped down from the porch at the main house when he saw me coming. I just finished giving Midnight and Mocha their bottles—I can manage them simultaneously now—and was hoping to clean up at the cabin before seeing if Ama could use a hand.

Thomas waves from his rocking chair, a sleeping Max at his feet. The man must have a built-in heater, I swear he's been out there most of the day. Chief is lying down at the top of the steps, his head propped up on his crossed front paws—a preferred pose—with his ears up and alert, eyes on me, and tail wagging furiously. How can I resist?

"Ready to join an old man for a drink?"

I climb up the steps and sit down next to Chief, who quickly moves his chin to rest on my leg. I'd enjoy helping out in the kitchen, but I wouldn't mind shooting the breeze with the old man for a bit. I like Thomas, he's quite a character and as straight as they come. Salt of the earth, as my grandma used to say.

"I'd love to, but I should probably get cleaned up." I demonstratively sniff my braid and pick out a few pieces of straw. "*Eau de* goat and physical labor."

"Doesn't bother me none," Thomas says with a wink.

"Maybe not, but I'd rather not be the one smelling rank at the dinner table later."

"Fair enough. Maybe I'll pop inside for a little nap before dinner then."

He slowly gets to his feet, his knee popping audibly. I do the same with a smidgeon more ease, as the front door opens revealing Ama.

"Good, you're standing," she addresses Thomas. "I was coming to check if you were still breathing, but if you're still on two feet, I guess that answers my question."

"Your concern just warms the cockles of my heart," he fires back without hesitations.

"I don't even know what those are," she grumbles as she passes me on the steps. "And if you're coming in to look for dinner, you're shit outta luck. My brat of a daughter has gotten herself stranded in Kalispell, when she wasn't supposed to go there in the first place, and now I have to go fetch her and drive her back without strangling her. Doc Evans called Alex to help him with a horse that got itself tangled up in barbed wire so I don't know how long she's gonna be, but when the boys get back you guys can order pizza or something."

Thomas winks at me after Ama storms to the SUV parked closest to the house and peels out of here.

"Spirited girl, that Ama. Not one to mess with."

"Maybe after I have a shower, I can see if there's something I can throw together for you."

"No need." He waves me off. "I reckon I can still operate a can opener, even if it's been a few years."

Then with another wink he heads inside with Max on his heels. My boys look at me expectantly.

"Come on, guys. I'll feed you."

The dogs follow me and we're about halfway to the cabin when Scout stops a few feet in front of me. He leans forward, his ears flicking back and forth as he emits a low growl. Chief follows suit and both seem fixed on the cabin that belongs to Dan and his mother. When I turn to look at it, I notice the curtains on one of the windows moving like someone was peeking outside. I bet Gemma is wondering what's keeping her son.

"Come on, boys, that's just Gemma. Let's go."

I slap my thigh a few times as I start walking and they quickly catch up with me.

"Lucy?"

I turn around to see Gemma outlined in the door opening. I quickly backtrack and walk up to her porch. The woman is seriously ill, maybe she needs something.

"Hey, is everything okay?" I ask.

"I'm so embarrassed," she mutters, swaying on her feet. "I tried calling Dan but I guess he's out of range somewhere."

"He probably is. They left about twenty minutes or half an hour ago, fetching the horses from the back pastures before the snow hits tonight." The words haven't left my mouth and the first flakes start to fall. "But can I help?" I add.

Gemma holds up a hand wrapped in a kitchen towel.

"I was cutting vegetables for soup and...well, I guess maybe I shouldn't be using knives anymore either. I nicked myself good but it won't stop bleeding, and I can't reach the first aid kit because Dan put it in the cabinet over the fridge, and I'm too dizzy to get on a stool, and I can't get hold of Ama..." The poor woman bursts out in tears, sobbing as she finishes her rant. "And I'm sick and tired of being a pest and a burden."

I'm good with animals, not so much people, but my heart is breaking so hard for Gemma, I'm choking up myself.

"Nonsense. Come on, let's get you looked after."

The cut turned out to be not too bad and with a little firm pressure, a Band-Aid, one of those finger condoms I found in the well-stocked first aid kit, and a few encouraging words, Gemma was back in the kitchen, wearing her usual stoic smile. In her shoes, I don't know if I'd have the strength to stay standing.

In our cabin, I take a moment to feed the dogs and make sure they have fresh water before I head to the bedroom. I strip, grab clean clothes from my overnight bag, and am about to head for the shower when I remember Bo was supposed to pick up my shampoo. I already tried to wash my hair with regular soap this morning and it wasn't a great success. I'd rather wait 'til Bo gets back.

I play back my brief interaction with Gemma as I put some clean clothes on. Must be tough to lose your independence like that, her cancer has really stripped her of her abilities. Same goes for Thomas, although he is of an age where you'd expect that, I know it wasn't too long ago he ran a small ranch by himself, but that was before his heart started acting up.

Maybe I should quickly check on him. Make sure he

didn't hurt himself opening cans and is bleeding on the kitchen floor since he's alone.

"Be good, boys. I won't be long."

I shove my feet in my boots, shrug on my heavy winter coat, and tug my beanie over my head since it's snowing, before I walk out the door.

It starts as a little niggle of unease between my shoulder blades, but by the time I walk past Gemma's porch I feel daggers in my back.

It feels like I'm being watched.

I stop and do a quick scan of my surroundings, but with the blowing snow it's hard to see anything. For a fraction of a second, I'm tempted to knock on Gemma's door, but I don't want to freak her out when I may be imagining things. It's been a hell of a few weeks and after what happened to poor Bella yesterday, I feel knocked off-kilter.

I'm halfway to the porch when headlamps light up the snow leading up to the house and I can hear the sound of a heavy engine. I turn to look, see if perhaps Bo and Fletch are back, but it's a truck and trailer driving past and stopping by the barn below. I don't have time to see who's in the truck because suddenly I see him.

Lit by the lamp post by the corral, he is leaning against the fence, one heel up on the bottom rail, his arms crossed over his chest. Even with his face obscured by the brim of his hat, I can feel his cold gray eyes on me.

I know it's him.

He points two digits of his right hand at his eyes, before aiming only the index finger straight at me. I'm frozen, vacillating between running for the house or for Bo's truck, when I watch him push off the fence and walk down to the barn where he is greeted by Jonas with a handshake and a clap on the shoulder.

In my pocket my phone pings with a message. I pull it from my pocket and read the display. It's from Bo.

Who is Margaret White?

I take one last look at the group of men by the trailer and duck in the shadow of the house for cover.

Then I run.

Twenty-Four

Bo

"And the plot thickens."

Reggie crouches down, shining his own flashlight on the shed floor. He brushes at some darker smudges and sniffs his gloved fingers.

"Ashes," he mumbles, before reaching under the lawn chair and pulling something from under one of the legs.

The squashed butt of a cigarette.

"Lucy doesn't smoke, does she?"

"No. Neither does Alex."

Tucking it in a small evidence baggie he shoves it in his pocket.

It didn't take him long to get here. When I called him, I caught him leaving the Lincoln County shooting range right behind the regional airport, about ten miles up the road.

"Where is Lucy anyway?"

"She's at High Meadow. I thought she'd be a bit more comfortable there after yesterday. I'm glad I pushed for that; I wouldn't want her to see this. She's safer where she is."

He nods and gets to his feet, backing out of the shed.

"Well, those are size thirteens," he says, pointing at the prints before he pats his pocket. "And if we're lucky we can get some DNA from this. We need some good leads. Nothing we have so far makes any sense. Wayne Ewing called when I was on my way up here, the print they found on the pitchfork not only matches the prints on the chef's knife from Lucy's kitchen, but links to a missing person's file, which popped up on AFIS. In 2008, a woman in her early twenties went missing from the obstetrics ward at Webster County Memorial Hospital in West Virginia."

My entire body goes rigid, which doesn't go unnoticed by Reggie.

"The sheriff is knee-deep in a pileup on the highway near the suspension bridge, but I told him I'd ask Lucy if she knows anyone by the name of Margaret White. Now I wonder if maybe you do."

I wonder that myself. But far be it from me to share Lucy's story before I have a chance to talk to her first.

"The name is not familiar," I tell Williams. No word of a lie, but my friend still looks doubtful. "I can ask her if you'd like."

"I was going to ask her myself as soon as the tech gets here to grab those prints, but that might be a while. What the heck, why not? I'm dying to know."

I already have my phone in my hand and quickly type out a text—this way she has some warning and doesn't get blindsided by a phone call—before hitting send. It earns me a glare and a shake of his head.

"Thought you meant calling."

"She's more likely to answer a text than a call. She keeps her ringer turned off, and besides, she's got her hands full helping to get the horses at the ranch to shelter before this storm hits full force."

If it hasn't already. The wind is picking up, blowing the snow sideways like it did the other day, and I wonder how Fletch is faring trying to dig a grave with a shit shovel. I find out a few minutes later when he comes walking up to the house, his head tucked down so his hat shields his face from the storm, cursing and swearing.

"The fuck, Bo. Way to leave me hanging while you shoot the shit with your buddy here."

He brushes past me and heads for the shed.

"Hold up," Reggie orders. "You can't go in there."

Fletch turns on his heel and tries to stare Reggie down, who doesn't budge.

"I've got a rotting carcass to get in the fucking ground and I ain't doin' it with my bare hands. I need a fucking tarp or something."

I can tell Fletch is close to his breaking point. He's got a wife and baby waiting at home with a winter storm raging. I get it.

"There's a tarp on the back porch, I'll go grab it and give you a hand."

The tarp was put up to shelter the goats from the worst of any precipitation, and it takes two seconds to tear down. Fletch is already stomping back to the barn, Williams watching him go.

"The goat?" he asks.

"Yeah. We've gotta get it done or it'll only get worse."

"Hmmm. Too bad I have to wait here for the tech, otherwise I'd give you a hand."

"You're full of shit," I tell him, as I start heading after Fletch.

"Hey, I've got a job to do here, but that ain't it," he yells after me.

As I rush to catch up with my brother, I check my phone to see if there's a reply from Lucy, but there isn't.

The plan is simple, spread out the tarp outside the goat pen, drag the carcass onto the tarp, and wrap the mess inside. Should be a piece of cake. *Right*. Except I didn't account for the disgusting gore an eviscerated body leaves behind. The kind that can only be scooped up with a shovel.

Lucy's shit shovel does double duty, and is definitely going to need a solid cleaning after this job. I do as well, the putrid smells released by moving the goat cling to the insides of my nostrils, as I'm sure it does to the rest of me.

"Why don't you head home?" I tell Fletch when we get to the house.

I can see lights moving around in the shed where I assume Reggie and the crime scene tech are busy.

"I can take Lucy's truck or grab a ride with Williams."

It's parked out front and I have her keys, but since Reggie will want to talk to Lucy anyway, it's easier if I hitch a ride with him. That way I'm sure I'm present when he does.

I check my phone again after Fletch drives off. Still no response. It's been close to an hour. I try calling but it rings and rings before bumping me to voicemail. It bothers me she's not answering. I guess it's possible she put down her phone somewhere and forgot about it. It wouldn't be the first time.

Rather than worry for however long it'll take the cops to be done here, I call the main house. I'm almost ready to hang up when Thomas answers, sounding a little out of breath.

"Is Lucy around?"

"You caught me dozing on the couch, let me get my bearings."

I wait patiently while he moans and groans getting to his feet, I suspect. Then I hear him moving through the house.

"No, no one's here. Alex is out with Doc Evans, Ama left to pick up Uma in Kalispell, and from the looks of it, the boys are just coming back with the herd. Oh, and I see Jonas is back. He's out by the barn with a couple of guys. Boy, it's really coming down out there, isn't it?"

More information than I want and nothing I'm interested in. He doesn't mean anything by it so I hang on to my patience.

"Thomas, what about Lucy?"

"Oh, right. Erm, she stopped by to pick up the dogs on her way to the cabin. She said something about feeding them and having a shower because she smelled. I told her she smelled fine by me."

The relief is instant. Good. She's probably just in the shower.

～

Lucy

It's all over.

The rescue, this ranch, even the town of Libby had started to feel like my sanctuary—my safe place—and I should've known it couldn't last.

Against better judgment I formed connections, built trust, even developed feelings. I allowed myself to believe I could have a life here, a family of sorts, maybe even a loving relationship.

That illusion evaporated tonight.

It was hard enough telling Bo as much as I did, but I kept the one last connection to my past to myself; my name. I guess it didn't matter since he somehow found out anyway. He knows my name and there's only one way he could've found out; from the man I just saw greeting Jonas Harvey like a long-lost friend.

How did he get here? How did he find me?

I feel like I'm in the middle of some elaborate plot I'm the only one in the dark about. Does everyone know? Can I trust *anyone*? Or is he playing me; showing me he has the ability to infiltrate and manipulate my life, that he won't hesitate to hurt or kill to control me.

His fatal flaw, however, is thinking I'm weak. I'm not. I'm determined enough to get away and leave everything I've come to love behind if I'm forced to, to keep them safe. I'm much stronger than I was when he knew me, both physically and mentally.

Still, my chest is burning as I fight to take in each breath, the effort of trudging through the snow making my legs feel like noodles, but I can't afford to slow down. The one stroke of luck is the fact the snow is still coming down hard, quickly obscuring the prints I leave behind.

Every now and then I risk a glance over my shoulder to see if he's getting close, because there isn't a doubt in my mind he's coming after me. Whether alone or with help, I honestly don't know at this point, but I purposely stay off the trail and opt instead for the trees and their thick underbrush to make it harder for anyone to track me. Branches hit my face and snag in my clothes, but I ignore them, letting adrenaline drive me on.

I need to get away as far and as fast as I can, but first I need to get to the rescue and the emergency escape pack I stashed. It gave me a sense of security to know that if anything ever happened, all I had to do was grab that backpack and I'd have everything I need. This is what part of me has always been prepared for.

What changed over the past few years is the attachment I feel here; to the place, to the people, and to my animals. My poor dogs, Midnight and Mocha, and my horse, Ellie. *Jesus*, my heart hurts. Alex and Bo.

I swallow hard to keep down the sob trying to escape my chest. It's wasted energy right now. I need to get to the river, follow it upstream to where the creek branches off onto rescue property. My objective is to get to the place Bo inadvertently took me less than a week ago.

The old underground shelter.

A few years ago—it was only a few months after Alex and I moved here—this shelter was at the center of a massive manhunt for two escaped terrorists. The FBI ended up stripping the place, which was used as a hideout and weapons storage, but left the underground structure. I figured what worked for the terrorists might work for me in case of an emergency, so I stashed my backpack and stored a few supplies to sustain me for a while should I ever have to make a run for it.

Looks like that time has come. Fight or flight, but flight has been so ingrained in me I don't know how to do anything else.

I don't stop moving until I catch a glimpse of the river through the trees. The water continues to flow, it's still too early in the season for it to freeze over. It will be cold, but my best chance of getting away is if I can wade along the shallower river's edge to the mouth of the creek. From there, it's not far to the property line and the shelter beyond.

That is, if hypothermia doesn't get me first, but I feel I have to go in the water to throw off the dogs if they're using them. It may be optimistic to think I could outwit a team of professional trackers determined to find me. It's probably a futile attempt, but I have to try.

I'll allow myself a minute to catch my breath before I brave the water. I'll give myself a heart attack otherwise. Stopping at the edge of the water, I look back in the direction of the ranch. It's hard to see anything through the curtain of snow, but I'm keeping an eye out anyway. Hearing anything isn't much better. The accumulating white blanket muffles any sounds, and other than my own labored breathing and racing heart, I can't hear anything either.

When my heart is no longer galloping and I've stopped gasping for air, I brave the river. It doesn't feel so bad, until the water slowly soaks into my jeans, socks, and boots. The last are water repellent but not water resistant, so submersed they don't stay dry or warm. The water itself isn't below freezing yet, but once I get out, my wet feet will be at higher risk for frostbite.

I stop moving when I suddenly feel a vibration in my pocket.

Shit, my phone. What was I thinking? That is the easiest way for them to track me.

Clearly, I'm not thinking straight, letting panic take over. I know better than that. Hell, I planned better than that. Quickly I pull my cell from my pocket and check the screen.

You can't hide.

The message is from an unknown number and I don't hesitate to lob the phone to the middle of Fisher River. Let them think I drowned trying to cross.

Grinding my teeth against the cold, I wade through the water up to my knees, far enough out from the bank, but not too close to the drop-off into deeper water. I lose all sense of time, keeping my mind focused on putting one foot in front of the other until I find Swamp Creek.

I'm relieved when I see the dip in the shoreline marking the mouth of the creek, but when I turn the corner, I can see the shallower water up ahead is covered with a thin layer of ice. I could probably break it up as I walk through, but that would leave easy tracks as well. Better to get on shore.

By now my feet are numb, making climbing up the steep snow-covered bank even more of a challenge. After slipping and sliding for a bit, I finally manage to get up on the bank.

Next step is get to the shelter, lay low while I dry out and warm up, and make a plan where to go and how to get there. The Canadian border is not that far, only seventy-two miles, but I'd need some wheels.

I wonder if I still know how to hot-wire a car?

Twenty-Five

Bo

The roads are a fucking mess.

On the short drive from the rescue to High Meadow, we've already encountered two cars and a pickup in the ditch. Now we have a fucking semi with the cab hanging onto the base of the driveway to the ranch with a single wheel, but the trailer twisted on its side in the ditch. The driver seems to be unharmed, standing beside the cab and talking on his phone.

"Goddammit. It's gonna be a long night full of idiots like this one."

Reggie manages to pull across the road and slip his department-issued sedan around the grill of the semi, parking it to block the driveway.

"I'm sorry, brother, I've gotta get this truck situation sorted before we have bigger problems. You're gonna have to walk the rest of the way."

"Do you need a hand?"

"Nah. In this kinda weather it's gonna take forever

before we can get a tow for this guy. I'll probably just set up some flares and put in a few calls. Go ahead, just let people know the driveway is blocked."

The first thing I notice is the trailer parked next to the barn and it's already covered in a respectable layer of snow. Looks like Jonas and Ludwig got back not long after Fletch and I left.

The light inside the barn is still on and I see some movement. Probably one of the guys, or it could be Lucy looking in on the goats. Either way I head there first.

As I approach, I notice a few of the horses in the paddock seeking shelter next to the barn. Good, the boys are back. It's turning out to be some storm, it's probably not safe for anyone to be out in this.

I stomp off the snow clinging to my boots when I walk in and immediately look to my right into the stall housing the goats. Both kids are balled up side by side in a corner, asleep, but there's no sign of Lucy.

"Hey."

Dan is leaning over the half-door a few stalls down.

"Hey. Have you seen Lucy?"

He shakes his head. "No, but we haven't been back that long. Got in maybe half an hour ago? I'm just putting some hay out for the night before I head in, but everyone else has either already gone home or is at the big house."

"Okay, thanks."

I'm about to step outside when we're suddenly plunged into darkness.

"Fuck!" I hear behind me. "There goes the power. I'd better go check on Mom."

It doesn't really surprise me, it's not uncommon for the power to get knocked out during a storm. It's why we have a massive generator in the garage next to the house so we can keep some key electrical components running.

"I'll fire up the generator," I call back.

In this weather, chances are crews won't get to it until after it's cleared, which isn't supposed to be until sometime tomorrow morning. We have valuable stud sperm in the freezer in the breeding barn we don't want to go to waste.

I hear the squeal of the storm door on the side of the house off the laundry room as I round the corner and see Jonas coming down the steps. Probably heading for the generator as well.

"You got back just in time."

He spots me and grins. "No shit. Don't wanna be out in this."

I follow him into the garage.

"Nope and to illustrate that, there's a damn semi blocking the base of the driveway. Has got his trailer hanging in the culvert. Libby PD is down there, but warning it might be a while before it's cleared."

"Damn," Jonas grumbles as he checks the gas gauge on the generator. "Must've happened in the last half hour or so. Alex just got in and didn't mention anything other than she white-knuckled it all the way home. Nothing about the drive being blocked."

"Yeah, the roads are pretty bad."

Jonas grabs a gas can and I remove the gas cap so he can top up the generator.

"I should probably offer Ludwig that last cabin beside yours for tonight. His assistant, or whatever the guy is, already left earlier for the Airbnb they rented in town but it wasn't coming down as hard as it is now. Doesn't look like Ludwig should even try. Anyway, it may be a full house here for a bit."

The generator kicks on, no problem, but it's so loud conversation is impossible. I lead the way out the door, which Jonas closes behind us. A few visible lights, which are on the emergency grid, are back on.

"Coming in to eat? We've got bacon and eggs going. Dad says Ama had an emergency and had to go, so we're winging it."

"Lucy in there?" I ask, starting to follow him up the steps.

"Haven't seen her. I think Dad mentioned she went back to the cabin."

"I'll be heading there then," I announce as I change direction, leaving a chuckling Jonas behind.

Walking around the front, to the other side of the house, I notice the light in the barn is back on too. Maybe Dan is still in there. I make my way to our cabin, where the dogs start barking inside as soon as I step onto the small porch.

They're pretty excited when I walk in the door, jumping up on me, which is a bit unusual.

"Easy, boys," I admonish them.

Then I look around but see no sign of Lucy. The light is on in the bedroom so I poke my head in, but she's not there either. There's a pile of dirty clothes on the floor next to her duffel and the bed looks rumpled, but that could be from the dogs. The bathroom is empty too.

Her boots are gone, as is her coat.

A knot forms in my stomach as I'm trying to find a logical explanation before assuming the worst. I guess I could've just missed her at the house. Maybe she went to visit Pippa and the baby, or even Gemma.

By process of elimination, I stop by Sully and Pippa's place first where Sully opens up.

"Have you seen Lucy?"

"No, but about what you asked me the other day. I actually—"

"Can it wait? I wanna find Lucy first."

"Need some help?" he offers right away.

"If you wouldn't mind checking the barn?"

Maybe it wasn't Dan, but Lucy in there. I could see her wanting to check on the goats.

"Yeah, sure."

I'm already on my way to the next cabin where Dan answers my knock. I repeat my question and that knot in my gut gets a little tighter when he shakes his head.

"Lucy? No, I haven't seen her at all since we got back with the herd. Have you check—"

"*Lucy?*" I hear from inside the house.

Dan steps to the side and his mother appears.

"She was here earlier. I'd cut myself and she bandaged me up."

"How long ago was that?"

"Oh, I don't know. Probably around six, I was cooking."

That worst-case scenario looms closer as options are dwindling.

"Thanks, I'll check the main house."

I'm about to step off the porch when she calls me back.

"I did see her shortly after. Just a glimpse out the kitchen window."

That window would be at the back of the cabins, which face toward the east side of the property bordered by the river.

"I thought maybe she was going to check on those young horses in the field back there at first. It's funny, because I thought that was you going after her when I looked outside maybe ten minutes or so later. Although it was hard to tell with the snow coming down like that."

"Not me," I manage, tasting bile in the back of my throat as that twist in my gut gets tighter.

Then I start running toward the main house.

~

Lucy

I'll be lucky to have any toes left after this.

I dramatically underestimated the time it would take me to get from the creek to the shelter. This storm is throwing off my sense of direction, and I've somehow looped back around to the creek twice already by the time I almost trip over one of the exhaust vents.

There are vents on either side of the underground cylinder. Basically just a pipe sticking a couple of feet above the ground, topped with a small vent cap. Normally not hard to find if you know where to look. Only problem now is the almost foot of fresh snow, on top of what was already there, leaving much less of the vents exposed. Add to that near zero visibility and the dark night, and I'm going to have a hard time finding the one on the other side where the access door is.

I'm getting a little worried because at this point, I'm seriously in danger of frostbite if I don't start warming up my feet soon. That's why, when I finally locate the second vent, I'm on my knees digging around for the access door, which is a rectangular hatch in the ground and protrudes only a few inches. The blanket of snow almost eliminates that difference but once I find the straight edge of the frame, I'm quickly able to clear it enough to loop my finger in the latch and pull it open.

One of the benefits of an underground shelter is the climate is pretty constant. Only minor fluctuations in temperature between winter and summer. As I climb down the ladder, I'm greeted by warm air. At least it feels warm in comparison to the frigid temperature outside.

At the base of the stairs, I find the light switch operating a handful of LED lights spread out through the shelter. Enough light to get me to the far end where the generator room is. My plan is to run the generator during the night when you can't see the exhaust smoke unless you're on top of the vent on that end. I wouldn't risk it during the day, but if for whatever reason I end up staying here a bit longer, I could run a few light bulbs off the batteries so I'm not sitting here in the pitch-black.

Once I have the generator running, I find my way to the one room with furniture; a table, two kitchen chairs, and a couch left behind after the federal agents went through this place. Underneath the table I've stored a few water bottles, some food items including a box of granola bars, my emergency pack, and a sleeping bag.

I toss the sleeping bag, a granola bar, and a bottle on the couch, and hold on to one of the chairs to remove my sopping wet boots. My socks are next and then I strip off my pants and hang those over the back of a chair to dry. Finally, I unroll the sleeping bag on the couch and crawl inside.

I'm functioning on autopilot, afraid to let myself think about why I'm here. I'd be tempted to head back and face whatever is waiting for me, but I'm scared others will pay the price. I can't risk it, so I can't allow myself to fall apart. I need to be strong, I have to be, or they'll win.

I take a few bites of the granola bar, have a couple of sips of water, and pull the sleeping bag up to my chin, closing my eyes firmly. It'll take a while for my clothes to dry, and I need to replenish the energy I expended, I may as well try to get some sleep.

~

I'm not sure what woke me up but when I open my eyes it's pitch-black.

Instantly alarmed, I shoot upright, all my other senses in hyperdrive. I feel my heart beating in my throat and I can hear myself hyperventilate. Tucked like a sardine in my sleeping bag, I scramble to find the tab on the zipper with shaking hands. The sound seems so loud in the dark silence.

Wait a minute...

I can't hear the generator.

Struggling to clear the cobwebs from my mind, I try to remember if I checked the fuel level when I fired it up. I don't think I did. In fact, I'm pretty sure I didn't. It's not unusual for fuel to evaporate over time, especially if the cap wasn't sealed properly, and I'm pretty sure I haven't been down here since the beginning of spring.

I blow out a sigh of relief and kick the sleeping bag off my feet. Then I get off the couch and with my hands out in front, shuffle in the approximate direction of the table. I'm trying to get to my backpack. I have a flashlight tucked in one of the side pockets. The first thing my fingers encounter is the pay-as-you-go burner phone I tucked in here. If I'd been thinking straight earlier, I would've had that and the flashlight on me before I went to sleep.

I manage to power it on, grateful when the screen lights up. I have no reception down here but the display tells me it's only midnight. I'm able to use the meager light to locate my flashlight, which turns out to be in the other pocket.

I feel a lot better when I feel the weight of the torch in my hand. Grateful for the steady beam, I quickly scan the room I'm in. It's empty. I'm sure the gas in the generator ran out but it doesn't hurt to be cautious.

My bare feet are almost soundless on the concrete floor and I inch my way to the door. Once there, I shine the beam first toward the stairs, before I swing it around to the other side of the hallway.

Nothing.

A little more confident, I head toward the generator room at the far end. Pushing the door open, I shine the flashlight around the room before stepping inside. Then I focus on the generator.

That's weird. This generator has an electric start system, which basically means it should hold enough of a charge to start up as well as operate the LED display indicating the fuel levels, even if it runs out of gas.

The display is dark.

Suddenly every nerve in my body goes on high alert. The only way the display would be dark is if someone manually turned the unit off.

I feel him before I hear him.

"Fear is still my favorite smell on you, *Maggie*."

Twenty-Six

Bo

"What the fuck do you mean, she's missing?"

"Missing. Gone. Fucking nowhere to be found. What do you think I mean?" I yell back.

"*Easy, Brother,*" Jonas whispers behind me, a heavy hand on my shoulder.

"From the start. Highlights only," Reggie says on the other end.

I already explained, in as few sentences as I could manage, enough about Lucy's background to get everyone to understand the gravity and danger of the situation. All this talking won't bring her back.

Jonas was the one who suggested I call Williams. After I checked the house and Sully came back from the barn empty-handed, I was ready to grab Blue from the stable and go hunting. Jonas held me back, like he's holding me back now.

I close my eyes and force myself to take a deep breath.

Then I take Reggie through everything I know as quickly as I can.

"Timeline?" he snaps.

"Last time someone had eyes on her was around six."

"Jesus. That's over three fucking hours ago."

"I know that, asshole. If you remember I was with you twiddling my fucking thumbs while some sick bastard took Lucy!"

Jonas's fingers dig in my shoulder.

We're standing in the hallway of the main house but I can hear sniffling and the occasional low mumbling coming from the kitchen in the back where every-*fucking*-one else is congregated, except for my Lucy.

"Brother, we don't know that yet."

"Sure we fucking do. Our tenant saw the guy go after her," I repeat what I'd already told him.

"Who? Surely if some random stranger was walking around the ranch someone would've noticed. Is anyone missing right now who was there earlier? Is everyone accounted for?"

Before he's even finished speaking, Jonas lets go of my shoulder and marches past me into the kitchen. I automatically follow to find him standing in front of Ludwig.

"Your guy, what's his name? Your assistant? He went back to your rental place. Didn't he leave around that time? Sixish? He's the only one not accounted for. Call him."

Ludwig looks shocked and then annoyed, but he pulls his phone from his pocket.

"Hey, what the hell is going on there?" Reggie asks on the other end of the line.

"Hang on a second."

Ludwig listens as every eye in the room is focused on him. Then he pulls the phone away from his ear.

"I can't get hold of him."

"Bo, for fuck's sake," Reggie complains.

"We may be missing someone," I inform him.

Ludwig turns his head to look at me, his expression almost apologetic.

"I'm sure my assistant simply turned his phone off before he turned in or forgot to charge it. I'm so sorry the girl—"

"Her name is Lucy," I snap, interrupting him.

"Of course, Lucy. I'm sorry she's missing, but I think it's highly unlikely Marco had anything to do with that. We're from Kentucky, he doesn't know anyone here. Besides, he's worked for me for close to ten years and I've never had any issues with him."

"Did he say Marco?" Reggie hisses in my ear.

"Yes."

"*Fuck.* I'm coming up. Give me five minutes and nobody fucking better move," he orders before the line goes dead.

~

"I can't believe it."

It's probably the third time Ludwig repeats that and I'm about ready to plant a fist in his goddamn face.

"That's it," I announce. "I'm not waiting here with my finger up my fucking ass listening to you argue about whether this is the same guy or not for one second longer. Fucking wasting my time while I should be out there looking for her. Whoever the hell it is, he's got her. I'm heading out."

Williams came barging in ten minutes ago with the information the one who reported this Margaret White missing was her husband, Marco White. Same fucking first and last name as this pompous bastard's *assistant* who happened to disappear at the same time Lucy does.

"You won't be able to see a hand in front of your face," James argues.

"Well, I sure as hell can't see anything from in here," I fire back, shrugging into my coat. "And you don't have to come."

"Can't fucking let you go alone," he counters.

The front door flies open and Dan storms in. I hadn't even noticed he went out. He looks straight at me.

"I've got the horses saddled."

"Fuckin' A, Rookie." James claps him on the back, but he's looking at me. "Let's go."

"I'm coming with you," Ludwig announces.

My reaction is instant. "No fucking way. You'll just slow us down."

"That's preposterous. I assure you I can handle myself on horseback and it seems to me you'll need every eye you can get out there. I can help," he insists.

I'm ready to dismiss him when Jonas jumps in.

"Let him come. He's right, in this case there may be strength in numbers. Besides, if we need to split off in two groups, I'd rather have more bodies than less."

I don't like Ludwig, I don't like the patronizing tone he uses with me, but I hear Jonas's point and we're still wasting too much time talking about shit.

"Fine."

"Good thing I saddled Hazel, just in case," Dan shares with a smirk.

"Perfect choice for you, Darrin," Alex—who's been very quiet—suddenly tells the trainer.

Any other day, I would've laughed out loud. Hazel isn't

a horse, she's our very loyal and sedate pack mule. We use her to transport equipment or sometimes people we rescue.

Reggie is calling in the feds, even though the likelihood they'll make it here from Kalispell before this storm is over is highly unlikely. He reluctantly decides to stay behind, but only after Jonas reminds him we are trained for this kind of work. He'll stay here with Sully as a command post, in case we need to split up, and can offer radio support with the help of satellite images. Sully is going to monitor the weather so that as soon as there is any sign of clearing, he can send up his bird, a Matrice 210 RTK drone. It's outfitted with night vision as well as thermal imaging. If there's a mouse out there, this thing can pick it up.

It'll be James, Jonas, Ludwig, Dan, and I out on horseback. Sully called Fletch who doesn't live too far and is heading this way on his snowmobile and will probably meet us somewhere in the field.

I can tell Alex is struggling when we pass her on our way outside and I grab her for a quick hug.

"I'll find her," I promise her.

"I know you will. I just hope you find her in time."

"This is ridiculous," Ludwig protests when he sees Hazel. "I can't ride that."

"Take it or leave it," James comments as he swings on his mount, Pecos. "Aside from our horses, she's the only one trained for rough terrain."

"What about Sully's horse?" the asshole wants to know, but it seems Jonas has had enough.

"Not gonna happen. Like James says, Hazel or nothing. We're riding out now."

With that he gives Sugar his heels and heads out, the rest of us filing behind him. I briefly look back when I hear Ludwig curse loudly to see Hazel isn't waiting around for the man either. She is following us, while the idiot is still trying to get in the saddle.

Then I focus forward and send a silent message to Lucy.

Hang in there, Gorgeous. I'm on my way.

~

Lucy

Faced with my worst nightmare, I'm suddenly surprisingly calm.

I'm not sure if it's because I'm older, maybe hardened, but the man standing in front of me is just a man and no longer the monster of my memories.

I remember wondering how it was possible someone so handsome could be so evil.

Except time hasn't been kind to him. Without his hat, I can see every deep groove in his face and his dramatically receded hairline. Now forty-seven, he looks exactly like his father did all those years ago.

The gun is new. Back then he had other ways of controlling me, but I guess he's not taking any chances now. I find myself surprisingly unaffected by the sight of the barrel pointed at me. Hell, there are worse things than dying. I've lived through some of them at the hands of this man.

The only thing that remains unchanged is the cold stare from those soulless, gray eyes. They still cause a shiver to run down my spine.

To cover my discomfort—I don't want to give him the satisfaction—I swing around and reach for the starter switch on the generator, firing it back up. It takes a moment for the lights to flicker on and turn off the flashlight still in my hand.

Then I turn back to face him. His head is tilted slightly and he's looking at me like he can't quite figure me out.

"I have to admit you surprise me, Maggie. You're tougher than I remember, I didn't think you had it in you."

"I stopped caring what you think a long time ago, Marco."

Maybe it's not wise to rankle him but if I have any chance at getting out of here, it's by keeping him off-balance. I can't fall back into the old pattern where I would be terrified all the time and he would feed on that. It's what he wants and I refuse to give him that.

Let him guess at my reactions, let him wonder how I'm going to respond. All I need is one hesitation, one mistake on his part, and I may be able to capitalize on that moment.

I'm no longer that little girl he was able to terrorize for so long.

"Is that so?" he sneers. "Seems to me you cared plenty when that old hag of a horse of yours got sick. Granted, I was a little disappointed it didn't kill her, but you have to admit the yew in the feed was inspired."

I react before I can check myself.

"That was you?"

His smug grin confirms it.

"I told you, I missed the scent of your fear and I so love messing with your head. It felt powerful, watching you and knowing you had no idea I was there. Even when I followed you around in the grocery store, you had no fucking idea."

His laugh is high-pitched and manic, and I struggle not to show him it's creeping me out.

"That old guy ramming his cart into you; priceless. An opportunity I couldn't pass up on. He was still wearing the surprised look on his face after I shoved your pitchfork through his throat. Your run-in with him at the store, as well as the powdered yew I planted on the old guy, gave you plenty of motive."

I'm sick to my stomach. I did not like Lester Franklin one bit—the man shot me, for crying out loud—but I would never have even contemplated killing him so brutally. I want to yell at Marco to shut up, to stop talking, but I won't give him the satisfaction.

Instead, I ask as impassively as I can muster, "Why bother?"

Then I turn toward the door and start walking.

He is gagging to tell the story, I know it, and as long as he's talking, he's not doing other things. I want to keep him talking while I try to lure him to the room with my backpack and the Helle four-inch blade hunting knife tucked inside.

"I wanted them to arrest you, take your prints, and discover your real name was Maggie White, and you had a loving husband who'd been looking for you for *fourteen goddamn years!*"

I almost stumble over my own two feet when he starts yelling. We're in the hallway right outside the room when he grabs my shoulder and yanks me around to face him. His face is contorted and his eyes are crazy.

"I was going to walk into the police station and see the fear in your eyes when you realized who was in complete control. But the idiot cops took too fucking long."

The moment he removes his hand from my arm, I turn my back and continue into the room, even though I'm shaking inside. I need to get to that knife.

"Then I saw you with that guy."

I instantly know he's talking about Bo. The White family are bigots of the highest order.

Suddenly I'm being shoved violently with a hand in the middle of my back. I stumble forward, exaggerating slightly so I bump into the table, grabbing onto the edge.

"The damn goat was to teach you a lesson. I was gonna kill those little ones you'd been fawning over but the big one got in the way. Fucking a black cowboy, Maggie? You're my wife."

That's a joke. I was forced into marrying him when I turned eighteen, it's not like I had any choice. A quick fifteen minutes in the courthouse with only his brother and father in attendance does not make for a marriage. Not in my books anyway.

But Marco isn't done ranting yet.

"Is that what you need to get your jollies off these days? You must've missed me badly."

I want to laugh at the suggestion he had anything to do with what I have with Bo. The thought of him chokes me up, but I won't show Marco emotion. I don't want him to know the depth of my feelings for Bo, in case I don't get out of here. I don't want him to get hurt.

I need to get to my knife. I know I'm risking a lot, but I want to make use of his sexual reference to provoke him into hitting me.

"Is that a joke? Miss you? At least that man has all the proper equipment and the knowledge to *get my jollies off,* something you never did."

The taunt has success because his face contorts into an ugly mask a second before he launches himself at me. He knocks me to the ground and lands on top, pinning me down.

I grunt with the impact, a sharp flash of pain as my head

hits the concrete. One of his hands closes around my throat as he starts to tear roughly at my clothes with the other.

"We'll see how my equipment measures up when it's shoved down your throat, you fucking cunt! Clearly you need a refresher."

I fight through my panic as my fingers frantically search for my backpack. Both his hands occupied means he's no longer holding the gun. He thinks he can overpower me without it, but that's a mistake.

I try not to freeze when he frees a breast and claws at it so roughly, I know he'll leave marks. When my fingers encounter the strap of my pack, I block everything else out. The rest of me simply doesn't exist, only my hand as I find the zipper, manage to pull it open just enough to reach inside, and curl around the solid hilt.

Then, over the grunting and heavy breathing, I hear the faint squeal of metal hinges. Marco freezes above me.

He heard it too.

Twenty-Seven

Bo

"Hold up."

Jonas lifts his hand, bringing all of us to a halt.

I am beyond frustrated. So far, we've had to go mostly on guesswork since we had to leave Max at home—the snow is too deep for him to work effectively—and other than a broken branch about two hundred feet back from the tree line behind the house, there hasn't been a distinguishable track.

Sully and Williams haven't been able to provide much either. Although Sully said they were following a few leads online. I wondered if those leads have anything to do with what he was about to tell me when I arrived at the ranch, but at this point it doesn't matter much, does it? Lucy is still out there somewhere with someone who wants to do her harm.

Let them worry about the who and the why, I want to focus on the where.

Right now, it's all coming down to logic.

If I were Lucy and I was running, I'd head for the river. It provides both a way to the main road, and a means to throw off pursuers. It hasn't been cold enough to freeze over, you can't see tracks under water, and it's hard for dogs to follow a scent.

The same goes if the guy caught up with her. It would make sense the first thing he'd want to do is take her as far away as possible, which means he'd need wheels, which means the road.

Our focus so far has been the old logging road that runs parallel to the river and starts at Highway 2. Footprints are harder to detect by the time there's six or eight inches of snow covering them. At best, it leaves a divot that unfortunately looks like it could've been made by anything. Tire tracks, especially in the snow and even after a subsequent dumping, are much easier to recognize. The snow fills in the tracks from the sides until there's only a shallow indentation left, but the length stays about the same.

After spending too much time scouring the logging road toward the highway, we're back at the bank of the river where we first came out of the woods.

"We're splitting up," Jonas announces. "He may have caught up with her, but it's doubtful he got her away from here. No sign of any kind of vehicle. Which means they are out here somewhere, and on foot."

"Even at these temperatures, the length of exposure would be affecting them," James contributes, not making me feel any fucking better.

"They'd need shelter," Jonas agrees. "Anything that provides cover and shields them from the wind. Any kind of structure, a cave, even a felled tree or hollow tree trunk. Let's set out a grid."

A few minutes later, James and Jonas head south, and

Dan and I take the section immediately north along the river. I'm not thrilled when Ludwig announces he wants to come with us. Still, I have to admit the guy's trying to be helpful, pointing out possible tracks, he's made a couple of suggestions, none of which panned out, but at least he's making an effort.

This is tedious work and with every minute that passes I feel my anxiety ramp up.

"What about the old bomb shelter?" Dan suggests when we hit the mouth of Swamp Creek, which is the northern border of the grid we're searching.

"What bomb shelter?" Ludwig wants to know.

"It's an underground shelter at the back of a neighboring property," Dan explains as he points west.

Ludwig twists in his saddle and follows the direction of Dan's finger.

"How would Marco know it's there though? He's never been here before."

"He wouldn't," I answer his question, already directing Blue up the creek. "But Lucy would. We were up there not long ago. If she was able to stay ahead of him, she could've made it up there."

It would've been a hell of a hike, especially in this kind of weather, but Lucy is tough.

A warm ray of hope is starting to break through the icy cold that settled around my heart these past hours. I reach for my radio and raise Jonas, explaining we'll be going off-grid to check out the bunker.

"I'll call Fletch, see how far he is, maybe he can meet you there."

"Ten-four."

When Dan pulls up alongside me, I glance over. The kid's looking pleased as punch. He should be. He's thinking on his feet when the rest of us were spinning in circles. He made a good call.

"Good thinking, Brother. Too far up in my own head for me to have thought of it," I admit in a low voice intended only for him. "Gonna make a great tracker, an even better teammate, and I'm proud to have you at my side."

"Appreciate it," he mumbles before adding, "I just hope I'm right, and she's okay."

"Me too, man. Me too."

Even though it's still snowing and coming down steady, the winds have died down significantly, making for much better visibility up here. That's why it doesn't take much to recognize—even from a distance—the access hatch to the shelter below has been cleared.

I immediately bring Blue to a halt and hold up my hand, signaling for silence and motioning for everyone to dismount.

"Hey, is that a door?"

I swing around and give fucking Ludwig a death stare. The idiot. I pretend to slice my fingers across my throat, hoping he's not too dumb to get that message. He isn't, although he does mumble an audible, "Sorry," as he gets down from Hazel.

I don't need that guy potentially endangering Lucy or any of us. I'd rather go in with only Dan as backup, and I'm definitely not waiting for Fletch. It's possible White hasn't found her but I'm going to work on the assumption he has, and therefore I'm going in there ASAP.

I walk up to Ludwig and hand over Blue's reins, indicating for Dan to do the same. Then I lean in.

"Stay here and watch the horses."

He's obviously not pleased being sidelined, but I don't give a good fuck.

Snow will muffle most of the sound but I'm still careful where I put my feet, noticing Dan doing the same. When we get to the hatch, I point at myself and motion down before indicating for Dan to wait and listen.

Then I grab the handle on the door and ease it open, wincing at the squeal of the hinges. Whoever is down there is now forewarned. I slip my gun from the holster on my waistband and take the safety off. I catch Dan palming his own weapon and give him a nod.

With the element of surprise already blown, speed is my next best friend so I rush down the metal stairs two steps at a time.

Lucy's voice has my blood turn to ice.

"Bo! Watch out!"

~

Lucy

His hand tightens in my hair as he drags me back with him.

I hope he's so focused on the door he doesn't notice the knife I'm trying to keep hidden pressed between my forearm and my thigh.

"You stupid cunt," he hisses.

Marco had been on his feet so fast there wasn't time for me to slip it in a pocket or anything. He scrambled for his gun, giving me barely enough time to sit up before he moved behind me and grabbed my hair in one hand. Then with the other he pressed the barrel of the gun behind my ear.

I knew it was Bo when I heard heavy boots racing down those stairs and had to warn him. I couldn't let him race in here and walk straight into a bullet.

"Marco White, this is Bo Rivera! Looks like we've got ourselves a little dilemma here!"

Something inside me relaxes when I hear how calm Bo's voice sounds. However dire the situation I'm in, he seems controlled and confident.

"Fuck off!" Marco yells back.

"See? That right there is the dilemma, my friend. I'd love to fuck off but I can't...unless you let her come with me."

"Like hell I will! She's my fucking wife!"

"Ah yes, and I bet you've got a piece of paper to prove that, but it sure doesn't seem like she wants to be married to you."

The more agitated Marco gets, the more calm Bo sounds. He's not even raising his voice anymore, and I get the feeling he's right on the other side of that doorpost.

While he is keeping Marco focused on him, I ease the blade of the knife under my leg with my hand wrapped around the hilt, covering most of it. This way I don't have to change my grip first before I can use it. All I need is one opportunity. I'm ready.

"What the fuck do you care?" he yells at Bo.

"I actually care a great deal. In fact, I love Lucy. So you see, the likelihood that I'm gonna just walk away is zero. Not gonna happen. And there's only one way out for—"

I'm having a hard time processing what I just heard Bo say when all of a sudden, I hear a third voice interrupt Bo.

"Drop your weapon, Romeo."

The same Kentucky twang. This just went from bad to worse and I grab my knife tighter.

"Fucking shoot him," Marco yells at his older brother.

I hold my breath, hoping for a miracle, when I see Bo stepping into the door opening, Darrin right behind him with a gun aimed at his head.

My eyes lock on Bo's.

"Why don't you do the honors?" Darrin returns. "I nailed the other guy she shacked up with back in Kentucky. You can do this one."

Over my dead body will I let anyone kill another person I've taken into my heart. I try to convey my message with my eyes, hoping and praying Bo receives it, when I notice movement behind them in the hallway.

I recognize Fletch who has one finger pressed against his lips as he approaches Darrin from behind.

The moment I feel Marco shift the barrel away from my head, I twist my body, ripping my hair from his fist, as I swing my arm around and blindly plunge the knife into his body.

His screams don't sound human as he collapses to the ground. I scramble away from him, but I can't take my eyes off the amount of blood streaming from under the hands he has pressed against his groin.

A hand covers my eyes as I'm pulled back against a hard chest.

"Don't look, Gorgeous."

Twenty-Eight

Bo

"She did what?"

I rub a hand over my face. I still fucking see Lucy sitting on the floor in just her panties, her hair fisted in that bastard's hand, pulling her head back. The sick fuck had ripped her top exposing her breasts and I wanted to tear his fucking head off, but that cold steel pressed right against the tender skin behind her ear held me back.

There was strength in those blue eyes she fixed on me though. A silent power despite her precarious situation. She spotted movement behind me at the same time I heard it and the slight tensing of her body warned me she was about to make her move.

I went down the instant I saw her rip her hair from the guy's hold and saw the glint of a blade in her hand as she swung around. Behind me I heard a wet thud—the sound of a high impact hit to the head—followed by a body falling.

Then White started to scream.

Thomas is still waiting for an answer when Fletch does the honors.

"She stabbed him in the junk with a good-sized hunting knife. Fucking blood everywhere. He probably lost a couple of his jewels, which is gonna work well for him in the slammer."

"Mind the company, Fletch," Jonas mumbles tilting his head to the other side of the hospital waiting room, where an older couple is staring wide-eyed in our direction.

She actually did do some serious damage. I would have been prepared to let him bleed out—wouldn't have lost a single night's sleep over it—but Lucy turned those baby blues my way and asked me to help him. I couldn't refuse her, she carries enough trauma on her narrow shoulders, she doesn't need the added weight of having taken someone's life. No matter how much he deserved it.

As it is, he's going to have to learn to live with one nut and a stubby. Half his dick landed on the floor when I ripped down his pants to get to the bleeding. I may have accidentally pulverized it under the heel of my boot and, unfortunately for him, there wasn't a whole lot left to attempt to reattach.

It had been Fletch—arriving on the scene to find Dan knocked out cold next to the hatch—who took down fucking Darrin Ludwig. Never trusted the guy farther than I could throw him, but I never saw this coming. Those two were fucking brothers. How the older one ended up with the name Ludwig isn't clear yet, but I'm sure the full story will come out eventually.

Right now, the only thing I care about is Lucy, who is being checked out behind those doors. They wouldn't let me in, claiming they didn't have room in the ER to move as it was. Probably true. This is a small regional hospital and we just brought in four patients.

Dan got hit over the head and likely has a concussion, but he should be okay. Lucy has a tear in her scalp right along her hairline. That probably happened when she freed herself from that bastard's hold. A few stitches will fix that, but those bruises he left on her chest may go farther than skin deep. Only time will tell.

Of the two brothers, it's a tossup who's worse off. Ludwig is lucky he's still breathing. The fire extinguisher Fletch whaled him over the head with left a good dent in the guy's skull. He was still out when we got here. White will live, but it won't be much of a life. Both of them deserve everything coming to them.

Reggie walks in through the sliding doors, carrying a large tray of coffees.

"Fuck yeah," Fletch mumbles, reaching for a cup.

We've been waiting for the coffeeshop next door to open this morning. No one had a wink of sleep last night.

The storm had subsided but it would still be pretty much impossible for first responders to get to us. We had no choice but to get ourselves back to the ranch. Not an easy feat with more people—some injured—than horses. It took time. Then, instead of waiting until ambulances could get to the house, we loaded everyone in a couple of trucks and drove to the hospital ourselves. Reggie drove himself and had Thomas tagging along.

We've been here since close to five this morning, and this is the third time I watch Jonas pull his phone from his pocket. He walks away from the group, probably trying to talk to Alex again, who'd been livid with him when she found out about Ludwig's involvement. She had misgivings about this business venture of Jonas's from the start. Looks like she was right and I'm afraid the boss has some serious groveling to do, which so far doesn't seem to be getting him very far.

Reggie walks over and hands me a coffee before sitting down next to me.

"Ewing is still tied up with the mess on the roads, but the feds should be rolling into town shortly. Special Agent Wolff is in charge, he's a good guy."

"I know Wolff. He's okay."

We've dealt with the agent a few times before and Williams is right, he *is* a decent guy. Better than some others we've encountered.

"Both he and Ewing will likely want to talk to Lucy as well. It's probably easiest to head to the sheriff's office to meet up with them after we're done here. Get it over with."

It's on my lips to blow him off, but it occurs to me Lucy might actually want to get this part done.

"That'll be her call. But if she's had enough, I'm not letting you guys near her. You'll have to wait, it's not like you don't already have the guys in custody."

Reggie shrugs, smiling.

"Glad for you, brother, and I hear you. If that's the case I have something else to keep Agent Wolff busy."

"Oh?"

"Dwight Burns. Tax evasion is a federal crime, and I know for a fact that Panama account of his is not registered with the IRS, thanks to your buddy, Sully. He'd been looking into Burns's account a bit deeper, discovered two signatures are required for withdrawals larger than five grand. I have a strong suspicion Samantha is the second signatory and it's possible she's not with him voluntarily. Lucy may have been right, and we may be adding kidnapping or abduction to Burns's list of offenses."

"He never said anything."

"He said he was going to but you were a little busy trying to locate your woman."

I vaguely recall him starting to tell me something last night, but I brushed it off. I hope Burns gets his ass handed to him.

Reggie elbows me. "Talking about your woman..."

My eyes dart to the doors.

There she is, looking right back at me.

Fuck, I love her.

⁓

Lucy

"I could sleep forever."

Bo has his eyes peeled on the messy road, but reaches out to give my knee a squeeze.

"Then why don't I drop you off at home first, like I suggested?"

I hate it when people are reasonable before I've had coffee. Real coffee. It should be illegal to misrepresent that motor oil they serve at the sheriff's station as coffee. It's false advertising and it also makes me cranky.

"Because I want my animals," I insist stubbornly and near tears. "I've had a hell of a night—which included maiming someone and almost getting scalped myself— enjoyed an early-morning visit to the emergency room to get my head stitched back together, and finally sat through a fun-filled couple of hours of grilling by not one, not two, but three different departments of law enforcement, asking me to rip open my soul and bleed all over the damn table, holding my tiny cup of black tar they promised was coffee. I need my animals. I just want them home. Also, I need doggie snuggles."

I feel petty and childish and demanding, but I don't care. I need something loving and cuddly to help hold me together or I am going to lose it.

"How about this—"

I make a frustrated sound, cutting him off.

"Hear me out," he insists. "Let me call Alex, see if she or one of the guys can round up the animals and drive them over to the rescue. I'm gonna take you straight there now, put you in your own bed, and I'll be happy to snuggle with you until the dogs get there."

That sounds even better.

I hate crying but that doesn't stop the sudden tears from rolling.

Worse, Bo notices and reaches out, stroking my hair.

"You're being nice to me," I snap, and his hand freezes mid-air.

"Shouldn't I be?"

"No! It only makes me cry more."

I can feel him holding back a laugh and I know I'm being unreasonable, but I can't seem to help myself.

"Then I'll stop right away." Bo tries to sound serious but fails miserably.

"Not funny," I mumble.

"Sorry."

"Okay, you can call Alex."

I could call her myself but my phone is at the bottom of Fisher River and I'm afraid she's going to be nice to me too.

While Bo talks to Alex, I tune them out and let my mind drift off. I'm still trying to process the events of the past sixteen or so hours. I have trouble wrapping my head around the fact this trainer, Ludwig, I'd heard mention a time or two, was in fact Darrin White. Older brother to Marco, who'd apparently been keeping him up to date while chasing me.

Detective Williams told us he'd legally changed his last name to Ludwig—his mother's maiden name—right around the time his father was arrested for forging Certificates of Registration for some of his horses. Probably to distance himself, since Darrin was trying to get a foothold in the racing world on his own. All of it happened after I left and I hadn't exactly made an effort to stay up to date. I guess that's when Marco went to work for his brother too.

"What I can't wrap my head around is how they figured out I was here," I muse out loud. "Let alone my connection to the ranch. It doesn't make sense."

"Actually, it does to me. First time I met Ludwig, you were at the ranch dropping something off. I caught him staring when you left, mumbling something, so I asked if he knew you. He said he didn't know anyone named Lucy, but that you reminded him of a person who'd been gone a long time."

I shake my head. What are the odds of that happening?

"Weird coincidence."

"Maybe not. Maybe this was meant to happen," Bo suggests, taking my hand in his.

Maybe it was. I glance down at our joined hands, noticing how perfectly mine fits and feels in his. When I look up again, the sun is starting to peek out from behind the clouds, just as the rescue comes into view.

"Hey...who plowed the driveway?"

I hadn't even thought of that. Normally I do it myself

with a blade on the front of my pickup, but I haven't had a chance to put it on yet.

"Maybe James, or Sully. One of the guys at High Meadow anyway. It's what family does."

I don't have anything to say to that. Not that I'd have been able to say a whole lot with that lump steadily growing in my throat anyway.

A bottle of Kim Crawford Sauvignon Blanc—my favorite wine—was left on the kitchen counter along with a foil dish of cinnamon rolls. It has Alex all over it. She's the only other person I know who stocks Kim Crawford and the rolls look like Ama had at least a significant part in the making of them. She's the queen of dessert while Alex isn't really all that comfortable in the kitchen at all.

"Did she tell you she'd been by?"

"Nope, she didn't. She did say she'd load up your critters and bring them over along with our bags."

He helps me out of my coat as I kick my boots off. The damn things are still wet inside from my trek through the river. I peel my socks off and walk barefoot through the kitchen and into the laundry room where I strip out of my damp jeans, shoving it all in the washer. My ripped shirt and the bra I'd been wearing were tossed in a garbage bin in the ER. The only thing I'm not ready to strip off is the flannel shirt Bo covered me with in the bunker. It feels good.

"You gonna sleep in that?" he asks when I walk into the kitchen wearing only his flannel.

"Yes. Unless you want it back?"

He smiles, his eyes sparkling and his whole face crinkling up.

"It's yours. Come," he says, grabbing my hand again. "Let's get you to bed."

For a bulky, somewhat scary-looking man, he is incredibly tender as he tucks me under the covers. Then he tosses his phone on the nightstand before stretching out on top of the bedding beside me. Then he reaches for me and rolls me against his side.

"Is that okay?"

I'm lying with my head on his shoulder, resting my hand in the middle of his chest.

"Perfect."

I feel him take in a deep breath before exhaling slowly.

"He hurt you. Your bruises..."

"Mean nothing..." I finish, raising my head and lifting my hand to his face. I hadn't realized how much this affected him, although I should probably have guessed. "He doesn't have that power anymore. Neither of them do. I won't give it to them."

"You risked your life for me. I would never have forg—"

I cover his mouth with my hand.

"I couldn't sit by and let him shoot you. Especially since you were down there in the first place risking your life for me," I point out firmly.

I stare him down with a challenging eyebrow raised until he finally concedes with a grin.

"Guess that makes us both pretty badass."

I grin right back.

"You know it."

I've barely put my head back down on his shoulder when his phone rings.

"Sorry, forgot to turn off the ringer."

He rolls away from me and grabs it from the nightstand, putting it to his ear.

"Jesus, Williams. We're just trying to catch some sleep. What now?"

A moment later he abruptly sits up, his broad back toward me.

"You shitting me?"

Worried when he rubs his free hand over his head, I sit up and I lean forward against his back.

"Yeah, I'll tell her."

Next he drops his phone on the nightstand before he twists and rolls, taking me down with him.

He hovers over me and I try to read his eyes.

"Tell me what?" I prompt him impatiently.

His eyes drop down to my lips and he kisses me sweetly before taking my face in his hands, a serious look on his face.

"Ludwig didn't make it."

It takes a moment to sink in and then I take another moment to decide how I feel about this.

"Well...I guess I'll sleep even better."

Twenty-Nine

LUCY

"So you were a jockey?"

Alex hands me the next piece of plywood and I lift it in place. Then I take a nail from between my lips, and with a few solid whacks, hammer one side of it to the porch column.

"Was training to be one."

I smile, remembering how excited I was the first time I entered the starting gate and felt the adrenaline of the horse ramp up alongside mine. The moment that gate opens and a thousand pounds of lean, powerful muscle explodes underneath you. It's a thrill like no other and you can do little more than hang on for the ride.

"I could so see you doing that," Alex observes. "It certainly explains your confidence in the saddle."

Bo told me he had to give people a bit of my background story when everyone was looking for me, but I shared a little more detail with Alex. I know she was upset she had to hear it from Bo, so I wanted to make sure I was the one to provide some more detail before they come to light through other means.

I apologized for lying to her for so many years, she assured me she understood. She cried. So did I. We hugged, and then we got out the power tools.

Bo left with the High Mountain Tracker team for Eureka two days ago, to search for a couple of hikers who got lost hiking the Continental Divide Trail. He'd been reluctant to go and I know he worried about leaving me, despite my assurances. He's been staying here every night for the past week and although I'm grateful for that, it's probably not a bad idea for me to be on my own for a bit. Get my feet back under me and find my new balance.

After hiding my past for so long, it still feels a little weird to be this exposed.

I only lasted a day after Bo left before I got restless enough to call Alex. She was here half an hour later and came hauling the table saw I asked her to bring, so we could build a proper new shelter for Midnight and Mocha next to the back porch.

I couldn't bring myself to put them back in that pen by the barn and want to keep them closer to home. When I mentioned something to Bo, he immediately said he'd get one of the guys to help him put one up. Then the morning he kissed me goodbye, he promised he'd take care of it when they get back.

But then I got to thinking; why wait for him? Two months ago, I would've just tackled a project like that myself. Hell, for many years Alex and I didn't have a man in our lives, except of course Alex's son, Jackson, but he hasn't lived at home since he left for college. We did everything ourselves.

These days we're both immersed in testosterone and

don't get a chance to do any heavy lifting, so to speak. The helping hand is nice, don't get me wrong, but after many years of being independent, I don't want to risk falling into a traditional pattern where any time power tools or heavy equipment are involved, Bo automatically takes the lead and I'm left with laundry and dinner. I know that will start eating at me over time.

So the past day and a half we've been building a new goat pen while talking. Mostly Alex asking questions and me finally answering them honestly.

"What about your name?"

"What about it?" I lob back.

"Are you keeping Lucy or going back to Margaret or Maggie?"

I've thought about that and brought it up with Reggie Williams when he dropped by a few days ago. I paid five thousand hard-earned dollars for my Lucy Lenoir birth certificate, but it's fake. Reggie assured me no one had any interest in bringing any charges against me, but suggested a lawyer friend of his who could not only help me get a quickie divorce, but legalize whatever name I decide to go with as well.

"I don't even know the people who gave me the name Margaret, and the years I lived as Maggie don't identify who I am now. But Lucy, I chose myself, as well as the life I built as her."

Alex drops the board she had in her hands and reaches for me, pulling me into a hug.

"I love Lucy," she mumbles, sniffling.

"I love her too," I echo, patting my friend's back a little awkwardly. "I'm ready to warm up a little. Shall I put on some coffee?"

I've never been good with shows of affection but, under

Bo's influence, I'm trying. Although I have to say this past week, since the incident in the shelter, touching seems to be limited to handholding and chaste kisses, maybe a chaste cuddle in bed.

Alex follows me into the kitchen where it's nice and warm. I shrug out of my heavy coat, leave my boots by the back door, and head for the coffeepot. Just like my inexperience with public shows of affection, I'm not much better off when it comes to discussing things of a personal nature, but with my back turned it's easier to broach the subject.

"I think Bo may be starting to regret getting involved with me."

"Why would you say that?" Alex instantly responds.

"I don't know, he's...a bit more distant."

"Physically? Because I think that's to be expected. You were hurt." She walks up and leans a hip against the counter beside me. "That bastard left marks on you, that's probably messing with Bo's head. Guys don't handle it well when their women get hurt. It may be hard for him to let that go."

"Bo told Marco he loved me, back in the shelter," I share, glancing sideways at Alex.

"He did?"

I shrug off her excited response. "Yeah, but he was just trying to provoke Marco."

"Lucy...seriously?" She puts a hand on my shoulder and turns me to face her. "That's bullshit and you know it. Of course that man loves you."

"Well, he hasn't mentioned it since," I insist.

Alex rolls her eyes at me. "Have you brought it up? Have you told him how you feel about him? And for that matter, have you told him he doesn't need to hold back for you? Communication, my friend, that's what all good relationships are built on."

Of course she's right—I just need to ease into this relationship stuff with baby steps—but I'm not going to tell her that. Instead, I put her on the spot because...what is it they say? Doctor, heal thyself?

I grab a couple of mugs and pour coffee, handing one to Alex.

"While we're on the topic, how *are* things with Jonas? Have you *communicated* with him lately?"

She narrows her eyes to slits as her hand closes around the cup.

"Low blow, Lucy. Besides, it's not the same. Jonas knows I'm pissed at him and he knows exactly why too."

We all know why Alex is pissed. Her favorite colt, High Meadow, is somewhere in Kentucky facing God knows what kind of future now that Ludwig is dead and the training program disintegrated. She'd had a bad feeling about Jonas's business association with the man from the start.

"Right, but how long are you gonna punish him for something he has no way of rectifying now? And you have to admit, the concept for the program was a good idea, even though the source left much to be desired."

She makes a huffing sound but before she has a chance to come with a rebuttal, the dogs start barking. A moment later someone starts banging on the door, accompanied by angry yelling and some choice names for me.

"Wait," Alex says, trying to hold me back. "You shouldn't go out there."

But I'm done with people trying to fuck with my life. I'm done with men who think anger and violence will get them what they want.

I'm just done.

Already bracing myself, I yank open the door, startling

the man on the other side. Not giving him a chance to recover, I haul out with a clenched fist, clocking him right in the nose.

~

Bo

I wasn't expecting that.

Pulling up to the house, I catch Lucy taking a swing at fucking Dwight Burns on her porch, knocking him to his ass. I jam my truck in park and jump out, only now noticing Lucas Wolff racing up the steps toward them.

"What the fuck is going on?" I bark when I reach the top of the steps.

The agent already has Burns facedown on the floor, a knee in his back to keep him down as he slaps a pair of cuffs on him. Then my eyes find Lucy, who stands with her legs slightly spread a few feet away, looking pissed as all get out as she flexes her right hand.

"Fucker made a slip for it at the airport. I guessed he might come here looking for Samantha." Wolff fists a hand in the guy's hair and pulls his head up before leaning down and adding, "Who is in federal protective custody, you moron."

I notice Lucy's fist has done a good number on the man's nose, which is spraying blood like a geyser. Alex steps around Lucy with a wadded-up kitchen towel she hands to Wolff.

"Here, cover his face, would you? He's making a mess of the deck."

Wolff shakes his head as he does as she asks, before hauling Burns to his feet. The guy is swearing up a muffled storm behind the towel.

"Need a hand?"

The agent glances at me and grins.

"Nah, I doubt I was even needed for this. The ladies seem to have it under control."

I follow his gaze to where Alex has stepped back to stand next to Lucy.

"So it would appear."

"You need to tuck the tips of your fingers underneath when you make a fist, or else you're gonna break your hand one of these days."

Wolff didn't stick around but promised he'd be in touch later, and Alex went home to see Jonas.

I'm in the kitchen putting together yet another icepack for Lucy's fist, except this time my chin wasn't at the receiving end of it. Burns's nose was, and from the condition that it was in, it looks like she probably broke it.

"I'm sick of bullies," she grumbles.

She's still plenty annoyed, despite my sound kiss hello after I planted her ass on the counter.

"I can tell. Knocked that man right on his ass, Luce. Maybe I should start calling you Slugger."

Suddenly she's grinning.

"That's a pretty badass name. Almost as badass as the goat pen I'm building with Alex."

"You're what?"

I leave her sitting on the counter, open the door, and step out on the back porch in my socks, braving the cold.

Sure enough, they built a pretty solid-looking structure on the side of the porch. It appears to be anchored into the back wall of the house and already has two walls up.

"Not bad, eh?"

Lucy got herself down from the counter and is standing in the door, a smug grin on her face.

"I thought I was gonna do this when I got back?"

"I didn't want to wait," she states with a shrug as she backs up into the kitchen.

I follow her inside and shut the door against the cold.

"I realized I didn't have to wait. Alex and I used to do stuff like this ourselves all the time."

I'm tempted to tell her it's my job, but wisely keep my trap shut. There's a deeper meaning here I'm not entirely blind to.

"Fair enough," I choose to tell her instead. "Maybe next time we have a project, we can try tackling it together."

From the expression on her face, I gather that's a concept she hadn't considered yet. To be honest, neither had I, before now.

Then she puts a hand on my chest.

"I think I'd like that."

"Yeah, me too," I agree.

"Bo?"

Instead of looking at me, her eyes are focused on my shirt where her fingers are fiddling with one of the buttons. It's clear she's got more on her mind.

"Right here, Gorgeous."

"Down in the shelter...you said something to Marco."

Shit. I know what she's referring to and I have to admit, it wasn't one of my finer moments. Nothing like having a first declaration of love be forever associated with that sick psycho. Not how I'd planned to share that information with her, but I was flying by the seat of my pants in that moment.

I'd hoped maybe she'd missed it given the situation, and I'd have a second chance to do it right, but it appears she didn't miss a thing.

"I did and I meant it, but the timing was all wrong."

She tilts her head back and looks up at me.

"Yeah?"

I nod, reaching out to tuck a strand of hair behind her ear. Her eyes sparkle when I bend my head.

"How's the timing now?" she asks before I have a chance to steal a kiss.

I rest my forehead against hers, our noses almost touching and her eyes so close, I can see all the beautiful shades of blue.

"It's perfect. I love you, Lucy Lenoir."

Thirty

Bo

"Luce..."

I stop the progress of her hand down my waistband, but she's already stroking the crown of my dick with the tips of her fingers. Pressing her soft curves against my side, she brushes her lips against my ear.

"Please?"

Jesus, she tempts me.

It took me a few weeks and mounting pressure by Lucy herself to break my self-imposed abstinence. At first, it was because I didn't want to risk triggering her after the latest assault, but she was quick to assure me that wouldn't be the case. But then I also didn't want sex between us to be an itch to scratch, as it had been for me in the past, or a means to control or be controlled as had been Lucy's experience.

It's Lucy herself who pointed out the importance of being equal in everything we do. To me that means sex as well. I'm easy enough, I want her all day, every day. All I have to do is think of her and, boom, I'm ready. But for Lucy, sex has been more of a conditioned or even calculated response and not necessarily based on her own needs or wants.

It wasn't easy to hold back, especially on the nights I spent here, which is why I didn't stay over all the time.

Last week, we were discussing plans for Christmas. Lucy mentioned she didn't really have any traditions and was happy just having dinner at the ranch as in previous years. When I asked her if she had any wishes for Christmas, she burst into tears and then proceeded to get pissed because I'd made her cry.

"I want you to stop rejecting me, you big idiot."

I picked her up, tossed her over my shoulder, and carried her straight to the bedroom, where I demonstrated, rather than explained, rejection wasn't even on my radar. It turned out to be rather an explosive demonstration.

I've only been back to my place to pick up clean clothes since then.

Lucy has a healthy appetite and I already knew she could be a force in the sack, so the past days have not exactly been boring. But believe it or not, my damn dick needs a rest.

I fish her hand from my pants and kiss the inside of her wrist before lifting her on my lap.

"I've gotta go get Momma," I remind her.

It's Christmas Eve and my mother is coming for dinner and staying the night, which had been Lucy's idea. After dinner, she wants to trim the tree we went and cut down earlier today. Then, tomorrow morning, the three of us are supposed to go around dropping off tins of the Christmas baking she's been torturing me with for weeks now, and afterward we'll all head to High Meadow.

"Okay, but I need to give you one of my gifts first."

"Aren't we supposed to do gifts tomorrow morning?"

My own gift for her is planned for tonight, but I'm not going to tell her. I'll need Momma's help to pull that off anyway.

She hops off my lap with a grin.

"Yeah, but this one is for your eyes only."

I groan as she darts off to the bedroom. If she bought lingerie she's going to model for me, there's no way my cock's getting any rest today. But she surprises me when she comes back with a large, gift-wrapped package.

"Heavy," I comment, when she sets it on my lap.

Then she perches herself on the edge of the coffee table, her elbows on her knees and hands supporting her chin.

"Well? Open it."

I rip the paper off, uncovering an empty drawer. One that looks suspiciously like it fits the dresser in Lucy's bedroom.

"What's this?"

Lucy rolls her eyes. "It's symbolic."

"You're giving me a symbolic drawer from your dresser?"

"Yesss," she hisses, clearly annoyed as she gets to her feet. "I'm offering you half the dresser, and half the closet, and your favorite spot on the couch, and half the shelf in the bathroom, and—"

I surge off the couch, hook her with an arm around her waist, and pull her flush against me as I kiss her hard.

"Yes," I mumble against her lips. "Yes, to all of those and anything else you're offering. I fucking love you, Gorgeous."

"Yeah?" she asks, her eyes smiling.

"Yeah. I want it all with you."

Instantly her expression darkens.

"But what about kids?"

"What about them? I figure there's plenty of kids out there needing a home, if that's what you want. Or maybe you want to work with more kids like Amelia, who may not need a home but they need your guidance. I'm good with that too."

I watched Lucy with Amelia a few times these past weeks. She's good with her. I have no doubt she'd make a fantastic mother as well.

Lucy lifts up on tiptoes and cups my face in her hands, pulling me down for a sweet kiss.

"Yeah, you're a good man, Bo. The best. I love you madly. I think I have for a while."

Best fucking Christmas gift.

～

Lucy

I can't stop smiling.

Last night when Bo picked up his mother, she asked me to show her around the rescue. I appreciated her interest and with her arm firmly hooked in mine, so she wouldn't go sliding on the packed snow, I took her to meet some of the animals. She'd already bonded with the dogs, no problem, even though she'd never owned a dog in her life. She also loved Daisy, was a little more cautious with the horses, but absolutely adored Floyd, Hope's colt.

I kept the goats for last, since they're undoubtedly the cutest of our critters. I think she enjoyed playing with them.

Then, at some point, Bo stuck his head out the door and asked if we were done freezing our asses off.

It was all a ruse to keep me out of the house for half an hour while Bo and Reggie Williams, in record time, installed a brand-new, top-of-the-line, massive dual-oven, seven-burner, shiny stainless-steel range in my kitchen.

I cried. Again.

Not ever, in my whole life, have I been given such an amazing gift. Never.

Of course I protested—hell, I know what those things cost—but it's not like I was really going to make him return it. Instead, I preheated one of the ovens and pulled the scalloped potatoes I'd prepped earlier from the fridge.

I have the oven on again, this time for the fresh muffins I started throwing together at five this morning because I could no longer sleep.

The tree looks fantastic, the lights are on, and Bo's fat candle, the one he bought to impress me, is burning on the kitchen table.

My damn heart feels so full it's making me leak. I rip a paper towel off the roll and bury my face in it.

"Why are you crying?"

Bo's deep rumble sounds right behind me as his arm slips around me from behind.

"Because your fat candle is sitting on my kitchen table."

It's quiet for a beat, and then he says. "Oh-kay..."

"Never mind." I turn and pat his chest. "It's all good."

"What's for breakfast?"

Zuri shuffles into the kitchen, wearing a blindingly bright housecoat covered with colorful parrots and a pair of fuzzy slippers on her feet.

"I'm baking muffins."

"Please don't tell me they're bran muffins with prunes. They give them to old people with constipation. My neighbor Tonya tries to feed me those."

I snicker at her antics. She had me in stitches last night as well, sharing a few funny stories of Bo growing up.

"Banana, chocolate chip, walnut," I tell her.

"Thank the Lord. Now where is my coffee?"

Bo chuckles behind me as he lifts my braid out of the way and presses his lips to the sensitive patch of skin behind my ear.

"You go sit down, Gorgeous. I've got this."

"Merry Christmas!"

Alex has the door open and steps out on the porch before we reach the steps.

My "And Merry Christmas to you," is followed by a couple more greetings as Jonas and his father step out on the porch behind her. Hugs are exchanged, something I would've bristled at last year but take part in now.

"You're the first ones here," Alex announces.

"I thought you said to come half an hour earlier than originally planned?"

She sent me the text this morning at seven thirty, right after I opened another gift from Bo, this one a pair of boxing gloves and a punching bag. It took a little explaining to clue his mortified mother in on the joke.

"I did. Hold on a sec."

Thomas is already leading Zuri inside the house when Alex ducks in after them. Only to reappear a few moments later with her feet in snow boots and shrugging on a winter coat. Pippa is right on her tail, which leads to more hugs and happy Christmas wishes.

"Shall we?" Pippa says, heading down the steps.

Bo takes my hand in his and starts following her. When I check behind me, Alex is grinning wide and has hooked her arm through Jonas's as they stick right behind us.

"What's happening? Where are we going?"

"It's a surprise," Bo says beside me.

When we catch up with Pippa, she's entering a code on a panel on the side of the garage door and it slowly starts to open.

"Merry Christmas, Lucy," Pippa says grinning widely. "I would've had it ready but Alex suggested this last modification."

She points at the cool older Gator utility vehicle right inside the garage. It has a yellow snowblade mounted on the front and a small trailer hitched in the back. I look at Alex and Jonas, wondering if this is some kind of joke.

"It's yours," Jonas rumbles, tilting his head toward the signature green and yellow John Deere.

"It's from all of us, Luce," Bo explains. "Well, technically the only thing I contributed was the initial idea, Jonas provided the old Gator, Pippa worked her butt off to get it running, and Alex found a snow blade just the right size."

"That's...that's too much. You guys are doing too much."

"Are you kidding me?" Alex blurts out. "You deserve this and much more. But now I need you to come with me. There's something else you've gotta see."

She walks up to me and pulls me from Bo's hold.

"You guys go on in, we'll be right there," she tells the others before linking her arm in mine and tugging me toward the barn.

I'm still reeling from that awesome gift. I'm going to have to properly thank everyone later.

"I wanna show you what Jonas gave me for Christmas."

Alex slides the large barn door open and flicks on the light. A familiar head pops over the stall to my immediate left. The white star and stripe markings against the black face immediately recognizable.

"Oh, my God. Look at that."

I walk over and rub his soft muzzle with both hands.

"High Meadow is home," Alex clarifies unnecessarily.

"I see that. How did that happen?"

"He won't tell me, but he dragged me out here this morning at the butt crack of dawn and my boy was right here. Mine to keep."

"That's awesome."

I look at my best friend in the world and notice the soft tilt of her mouth and the light in her eyes. A lot has changed since we landed here in Libby, Montana.

"Are you happy?"

She aims that smile at me and nods.

"I am, are you?"

The colt demands more of my attention by nudging my shoulder with his head, so I rub his face again as I answer Alex.

"Yeah. Me too."

She steps up beside me and puts a hand on the horse's neck while bumping me with her hip.

"Glad you decided to move here with me?" she asks.

I grin at her. If she'd asked me a couple of months ago, I would've simply answered with yes, but that's no longer enough.

"Best decision I ever made."

I hear footsteps behind us but before I can turn around, I have a hand on my hip and Bo's voice in my ear.

"Damn right it was."

THE END

Also by Freya Barker

High Mountain Trackers:

HIGH MEADOW

HIGH STAKES

HIGH GROUND

HIGH IMPACT

Arrow's Edge MC Series:

EDGE OF REASON

EDGE OF DARKNESS

EDGE OF TOMORROW

EDGE OF FEAR

EDGE OF REALITY

PASS Series:

HIT & RUN

LIFE & LIMB

LOCK & LOAD

LOST & FOUND

On Call Series:

BURNING FOR AUTUMN

COVERING OLLIE

TRACKING TAHLULA

ABSOLVING BLUE

REVEALING ANNIE

DISSECTING MEREDITH

WATCHING TRIN

Rock Point Series:

KEEPING 6

CABIN 12

HWY 550

10-CODE

Northern Lights Collection:

A CHANGE OF TIDE

A CHANGE OF VIEW

A CHANGE OF PACE

SnapShot Series:

SHUTTER SPEED

FREEZE FRAME

IDEAL IMAGE

Portland, ME, Series:

FROM DUST

CRUEL WATER

THROUGH FIRE

STILL AIR

LuLLaY (a Christmas novella)

Cedar Tree Series:

SLIM TO NONE

HUNDRED TO ONE

AGAINST ME

CLEAN LINES

UPPER HAND

LIKE ARROWS

HEAD START

Standalones:

WHEN HOPE ENDS

VICTIM OF CIRCUMSTANCE

BONUS KISSES

SECONDS

About the Author

USA Today bestselling author Freya Barker loves writing about ordinary people with extraordinary stories.

Driven to make her books about 'real' people; she creates characters who are perhaps less than perfect, each struggling to find their own slice of happy, but just as deserving of romance, thrills and chills in their lives.

Recipient of the ReadFREE.ly 2019 Best Book We've Read All Year Award for "Covering Ollie, the 2015 RomCon "Reader's Choice" Award for Best First Book, "Slim To None", Finalist for the 2017 Kindle Book Award with "From Dust", and Finalist for the 2020 Kindle Book Award with "When Hope Ends", Freya spins story after story with an endless supply of bruised and dented characters, vying for attention!

www.freyabarker.com